HOMEKEEPERS
At
The Last Gate

A Wounded Sky • A Secret Exodus • The Choice That Saved the World.

By Dave Barnabas

ISBN: 979-8-9904038-6-4

Published by Kaku Publishing LLC in the United States of America

Care is the quiet courage of staying

Contents

CHAPTER 1 — Aurora in Kansas

The first time Mara Keene saw the northern lights in Kansas, she thought someone had set the sky on fire and was doing it politely, quietly, in soft colors, like a secret the atmosphere wasn't supposed to know how to keep.

She stood barefoot on the back porch, her coffee cooling in her hand, the December air biting at her ankles. It wasn't late, not really, just after seven, and the horizon still held the last bruise of dusk. Her little rental house sat on the edge of town where the streetlights thinned, and the fields began, where the wind had room to build up speed and throw itself around.

Above the wheat stubble and the skeletal cottonwoods, the sky glowed. Not from lightning, or a plane's blinking confession.

Green and orange, mostly, a pale ribbon wavering like breath on glass. And then, so faint, she almost missed it, an edge of violet, a subtle bruise of color that made her heart do something foolish and young.

"Mara," she whispered to nobody. "You're not in Alaska."

From inside the house, her laptop chimed, a bright little sound that didn't belong to the moment. Another email. Another automated alert from one of her sensors. Another reminder that wonders, in her life, usually came tethered to numbers.

She stayed a moment longer and watched the sky move. The ribbons didn't dance like the photos. They *hesitated.* They gathered and thinned and gathered again, as if the air itself couldn't decide what shape to be. A pulse ran through the green, a slow shiver, and then the whole curtain shifted west in a blaze of orange, sliding across the stars like a hand pulling a veil.

A chill ran up Mara's back, but it wasn't from the cold.

Behind her, the porch light flickered once, just a hiccup, and steadied. The neighbors' Christmas lights across the street did the same, red and white blinking in a pattern that hadn't been programmed. Power fluctuation, she thought automatically. Solar activity can mess with grids.

Except Kansas wasn't supposed to see auroras strong enough to make the power lines nervous. Not this far south. Not like this.

The car went by slowly. The driver leaned out the window, phone raised, face lit blue by his screen. He stopped at the corner and rolled down the window further.

"Hey!" he called. "You seein' this?"

Mara lifted her coffee like a toast. "Hard to miss."

"Is it... is it normal?" His voice carried that half-laugh people used when they didn't want to sound afraid.

"No," she said, honest by reflex. Then she softened it, because she was a scientist, not a disaster preacher. "It happens sometimes when the sun throws a tantrum."

"The sun's throwin' a tantrum now?"

Mara looked back up at the wavering green. "Looks like it." The man nodded, satisfied that the universe was just being dramatic, and drove on.

Mara stood there until her toes ached and her coffee was cold enough to taste like metal. She watched the sky as if it might speak in a language she could understand without instruments. Then her laptop chimed again, insistently. She went inside.

Her kitchen was small and warm and cluttered with the evidence of a life built around measurement: printouts on the table, cables coiled like sleeping snakes, a UV meter sitting beside a bowl of oranges. She'd moved here, back here, to central Kansas, after the university in Colorado decided it needed someone "more grant-active" in her position. That was the polite phrasing. What it meant was: the department wanted someone younger, someone who smiled more at donors, someone who didn't ask hard questions in faculty meetings.

Kansas had been an unplanned return, a retreat that still stung. But the sky didn't care about tenure politics. The sky did what it did.

Her laptop screen was a constellation of open tabs. Data feeds from NOAA stations. Her own makeshift array in the backyard: a homemade magnetometer setup, a UV-B sensor, and an ozone proxy she'd cobbled together because she couldn't stand not knowing.

The new alert blinked at the top of her inbox.

UV-B SPIKE: 32% ABOVE BASELINE (LOCAL) TIME: 19:04 DURATION: 00:07:12

Mara's stomach tightened.

"Okay," she murmured. "Okay, that's… not nothing."

A UV spike could occur due to changes in cloud cover, instrument errors, or certain atmospheric conditions. She clicked into the sensor log and pulled up the raw data. The curve rose sharply, like a breath held too long, then fell back.

She cross-checked against the nearby weather station feed. Cloud cover: minimal. Humidity: normal. Temperature: dropping.

Then she checked the magnetometer.

The line looked like a heartbeat in a panic.

Mara hated the tug of narrative. Humans saw a rare aurora and wanted it to mean something. A sign. An omen. A divine Instagram post.

She did not believe in omens. She believed in systems. But systems, she also knew, could fail.

Her phone buzzed on the table—unknown number. She almost ignored it. Almost. Something in her, call it intuition, or call it pattern recognition built from years of watching storms form from small signals, made her pick it up.

"Hello?"

Silence. Then a voice, low and rough as gravel. "Dr. Keene."

Mara straightened. "Who is this?"

"You don't know me," the voice said. "But you know what you're looking at. And you know this isn't normal."

She glanced at the laptop screen, the ugly curves, the neat numbers, trying to pretend they were safe. "I'm looking at an aurora and a UV spike."

"No. You're looking at a symptom."

Mara's pulse kicked. "How did you get this number?"

A pause. A faint crackle like static. "You published a paper on ozone depletion patterns after geomagnetic events in 2019." It wasn't a question. It was a test.

"So did a lot of people."

"Your model was dismissed because it suggested the wrong kind of vulnerability."

Mara's throat went dry. "Vulnerability to what?"

Another pause, longer. The voice got quieter, as if the person had turned away from something, or was speaking from a place where walls had ears. "Not flares," he said. "Not storms. Something else."

Mara's grip tightened on the phone. "How would you know?"

A breath. "Because I'm someone who's seen it."

"Seen what?"

The voice made a sound that sounded like a laugh but lacked humor. "The sky from above."

Mara's mind threw up a dozen possibilities. Astronaut. Pilot. Satellite tech. A prankster with research skills. "Listen," she said, trying for calm. "If you're calling because you think the aurora means the end of the world, I'm not—"

"It does."

Mara's mouth snapped shut. Outside, the wind picked up, rattling the windows. "Don't say that," but it came out smaller than she wanted.

"I didn't call to scare you. I called because you're one of the few people who will understand without turning it into a religion or a stock opportunity."

Angry now, Mara demanded, "What do you want?"

"I'm sending you something. A file. You need to see it."

Her laptop chimed again—another alert. Mara glanced. This one was worse.

OZONE PROXY DROP: 4.8% (LOCAL) TIME: 19:11 RATE: ANOMALOUS

She stared at the screen until the numbers blurred. "That's impossible," she whispered.

"It's not," the voice said. "It's just… not public."

Mara's skin prickled. "Not public? What are you talking about?"

"There's a plan. A secret plan. Because the people with power decided the truth was too dangerous."

Mara's heart pounded against her ribs like it wanted out. "A plan for what?"

"To leave," the voice said. "To take a few and abandon the rest."

Mara's mind recoiled. She wanted to laugh. She wanted to throw the phone across the room. She wanted to demand proof and then burn it. "This cannot be real."

"It has a name," the voice continued, as if he hadn't heard her. "**ELXON.**" Mara blinked. **EE. Lex. On.** The word tugged at her memory. She had seen it on sponsor banners, maybe tucked into the fine print under a research headline. Not a product or a place. Just a name that showed up around money and initiatives, the kind of name people repeated as if it explained itself.

The syllables landed oddly, too clean, too branded. Mara frowned. "What is that supposed to mean?"

"It's a protocol. An ark with marketing."

Mara stared at the ozone drop again. Outside, the sky glowed green through the kitchen window like a ghost pressing its face against the glass. She forced her voice steady. "If you're real, if you're not messing with me, tell me something only someone who's seen it would know."

The line crackled. For a moment, she thought he'd hung up. Then, "The atmosphere doesn't look like air from up there," he said. "It looks like a lens. A thin blue curve that makes you realize how stupid all our arguments are. And now—" He stopped. She heard breathing, strained.

"And now what?" she pressed.

"And now there's a place where the blue is thinning. Not like weather. Like a wound."

Mara's throat tightened. "Where?"

"Over the Southern Hemisphere. Expanding. Not on the evening news. Not in your feeds. Not in your textbooks yet."

"Why call me?" she demanded, anger rising again, because anger was easier than fear. "Why not call the networks? Why not—"

"Because they already know," he said, and there it was: the note of exhaustion, the sound of someone who'd run into a wall too many times. "And because if you shout without proof, you'll disappear."

Mara's skin became cold. "That's not—"

He cut her off. "Do you have kids?"

Mara froze. The question wasn't a threat. It was worse. It was human. "My daughter is grown," she said carefully.

"Then you have something to lose. Be smart."

Mara's mouth went dry. "What's your name?"

Silence again. Then: "Jalen."

A first name felt like a concession. Like a handshake offered in a dark room. "Jalen, what?"

Another pause. "Royce."

Mara searched her memory. Astronaut rosters. Headlines. Training accidents. There was one, years ago. A capsule test. A "malfunction." One survivor, barely. Her stomach rolled. She began to speak but he cut her off.

"I'm alive." He cut in as if answering the thought. "That's all you need right now."

Her laptop pinged sharply, and a new window popped up **in** the corner: **INCOMING FILE REQUEST.** No email address. No recognizable server. Just an encrypted transfer prompt. Mara's pulse jumped.

On the phone, Jalen said, "Do you see it?"

"Yes," Mara whispered.

"Accept it. Then disconnect from your network. Unplug everything. You will understand."

Mara stared at the prompt. Her cursor hovered. "What is it?" she asked.

"The wound," he said. "The proof."

Mara's hands shook. She hated that they shook. She was Dr. Mara Keene, who had presented at conferences, who had faced down smug administrators, who had delivered lectures while her life fell apart quietly in the background. She did not shake at the files. She clicked **ACCEPT**. The download bar appeared, creeping agonizingly slowly across the screen. Ten percent. Twelve. Fifteen.

Outside, the porch light flickered again. This time, it stayed dim for a full second before it brightened. Mara listened to the faint hum of her refrigerator, the small domestic sounds that made the world feel stable. She felt, suddenly, that stability was a lie she'd been breathing her whole life.

The download hit fifty percent.

"Mara," Jalen's voice changed, tightening. "Someone is tracking this transfer."

Mara's blood turned to ice. "What?"

"I shouldn't have called," he muttered. "Damn it."

The laptop's fan whirred louder. The cursor stuttered. "Jalen—"

"Listen," he said quickly. "If anyone comes to your door, do not open it. If you see a black SUV, run. And don't answer another unknown call."

Mara's heart hammered. "This is insane."

"It's real. That matters more."

The download hit ninety percent. Mara's mouth felt numb. "Who are 'they'?"

"ELXON. The ones who believe survival should be purchased."

The download completed. A folder appeared on her desktop: **SKY_LENS.** Mara's fingers hovered above the trackpad. She wanted to open it at once, and also never open it at all.

"Mara," Jalen said, softer now. "When you see it, don't look away."

"I—" Mara began. But the line went dead. Mara stared at her phone. No signal bars. Just the little spinning wheel, searching like it could still find a world where this conversation hadn't happened. She set the phone down slowly.

Then she did what Jalen told her. She yanked the router plug from the wall. The Wi-Fi lights died. She unplugged the Ethernet cable. She shut her laptop's wireless off, her fingers moving on instinct. Only then did she click the folder.

Inside was one file: **ORBITAL_COMPOSITE_07B.png.**

Mara hesitated long enough to hear her own breathing. Then she opened it. At first, it looked ordinary: Earth's curve, the blue halo, the soft white of cloud systems. Beautiful. Fragile. Familiar.

Then her eyes adjusted to what the file had been designed to show. A distortion in the blue. Not weather. Not shadow. A thinning. A patch where the atmosphere's blue rim looked… torn. Like fabric pulled too hard. Like a seam unraveling.

And once she saw it, she couldn't pretend it was an artifact or a trick of contrast. Because near the bottom corner, there were tiny calibration marks and label numbers, indicating that someone had measured this precisely. There, in crisp black and white.

ATMOSPHERIC DENSITY ANOMALY: 18.6% BELOW EXPECTED EXPANSION RATE

ACCELERATING PROJECT: ELXON

Mara's hand flew to her mouth. "No," she whispered.

Outside, beyond her window, the aurora pulsed, green and orange lights sliding across Kansas like a slow wave of warning.

Mara stood very still in her kitchen with the proof on her screen, and she understood, in a single sickening instant, why people stayed ignorant when they could.

Ignorance wasn't stupidity. It was shelter. And someone had decided shelter was only for those who could afford it.

She stared at the torn blue edge of the Earth. And in the reflection of her laptop screen, her own face looked like someone else's; older, whiter, as if the truth had already stripped something essential away.

The porch light flickered again.

This time, it went out.

CHAPTER 2 — The Numbers Don't Lie

Mara didn't sleep.

She tried, she really did. She lay on her back in bed with the covers pulled up to her chin and told herself that exhaustion would win eventually, the way it always did. She counted breaths. She listened to the furnace kick on and off. She stared at the faint rectangle of moonlight on the ceiling like it might rearrange itself into a rational explanation.

But every time she closed her eyes, she saw the image again: the thin blue curve of Earth… and the place where it wasn't thin anymore. Where it was *missing*. At 2:13 a.m., she gave up and went back to the kitchen.

The porch light still didn't work. The bulb had either burned out or the power had done something strange. She didn't step outside to check. She didn't want to look at the sky again. She didn't want to see beauty and fear stitched together. Instead, she made fresh coffee and sat at the table with her laptop open and her router unplugged, the screen dimmer than usual, like the house itself had decided to whisper.

She didn't connect to the internet. She didn't dare. Jalen's warning was still lodged in her like a splinter: *Someone is tracking this transfer.*

Mara had lived her life in a world where data moved freely, maybe not *freely* (publishers and paywalls existed), but predictably. Click a link, load a paper, email a colleague, pull a public satellite feed. A civilized rhythm. Tonight, the rhythm felt broken as if the air between her and the rest of the world had become unreliable.

She opened the folder again.

ORBITAL_COMPOSITE_07B.png

She stared at it until her eyes began to invent movement in the pixels. The file held a picture that could also be taken as a confession. It had calibration marks and density labels, and it had something that chilled her more than the missing blue—

A project name. **ELXON.** A brand. A plan. A *decision*.

Mara checked the image metadata: timestamps, satellites, and any other clues to confirm its authenticity. The metadata was scrubbed.

Of course it was. She sat back, coffee untouched, and let the first truly ugly thought surface: *This could be fake.* A deepfake. A trap. A prank engineered by someone who'd googled her work and decided to see how far her paranoia could run.

But the thought didn't comfort her the way it should have, because the numbers on her own local sensors were still sitting on her hard drive like a second witness.

She opened her UV and ozone logs. The UV spikes were real. Her sensor wasn't fancy. It was homemade and cheap compared to university-grade equipment, but it was consistent. It had been consistent for months. The ozone proxy drop was real, too. And most damning of all: both anomalies had lined up with the aurora.

Mara zoomed in on the time stamps and cross-referenced them with the geomagnetic data her magnetometer had captured. Her breath caught. The jagged heartbeat on the magnetometer chart peaked at exactly the same time as the UV spike.

She pulled the old files, last month's quiet nights, last winter's normal fluctuations, and compared them.

Tonight's chart didn't look like Kansas. It looked like something that belonged closer to the pole. Something that belonged elsewhere. Where the sky knew how to crackle.

Mara rubbed her face hard enough to hurt. "Okay," she whispered. "Okay. I believe my own instruments. I believe the aurora. I believe—" She stopped herself before the next sentence could fully form. *I believe the Earth is dying.*

She wasn't allowed to believe that yet. Scientists didn't get to believe things just because the idea had claws. They had to *test.* They had to *verify.* And they had to prove a thing until it stopped being a fear and became a fact.

So, Mara did what she had trained herself to do for twenty years. She built a chain of confirmation.

Step one: external verification.

Without internet access, that was a problem. But she had one other thing—an old NOAA data dump saved on an external drive from a workshop she'd attended back when she still had grant money. It included archived solar flux indexes and historic geomagnetic storm logs.

She plugged the drive into her laptop and opened a spreadsheet, scrolling through columns until her eyes blurred. Solar activity has always been cyclical. Peaks and valleys, storms and lulls. People loved that word *'cycle,'* because it made the sun feel domesticated. Predictable. A big nuclear beast on a leash.

What was happening tonight, didn't look cyclical. It looked sharp like a knife.

Mara's phone lay on the table, face down. No signal. Searching and still searching. She picked it up and tried again, out of habit, out of stupidity, out of hope. Nothing. She set it down.

"Fine," she murmured. "Old-school." She reached for her landline, yes, she still had one, mostly for her mother's old habit of calling "the house" even though Mara had moved back alone. The dial tone was there. Good. Mara hesitated only a second before she punched in a number she knew by heart. It rang twice.

Then a sleepy voice, annoyed and familiar: "Keene? If this is about peer review at two in the morning, I'm quitting science."

Relief punched through her so fast she almost laughed. "Kofi," she said, and her voice cracked on his name. "I'm sorry. I know it's late."

Silence, then a shift, his brain turning on. "Mara? What's wrong?"

She swallowed. "I saw auroras. Here."

A pause. "Kansas?"

"Yes."

He didn't laugh. He didn't dismiss it. "How strong?"

"Strong enough to flicker my porch light. Strong enough to spike UV-B thirty-two percent above baseline for seven minutes. Strong enough to drop my ozone proxy almost five percent in minutes."

Kofi exhaled slowly. "Okay. Okay. That's… not nothing."

Mara closed her eyes briefly at the echo of her own thought. "I need you to check something," she said. "But I'm offline. My phone is—" She glanced at the dead screen. "It's not cooperating."

"Why are you offline?" Kofi asked.

Because someone is tracking me, she thought. Because the sky has a wound and people with power are running. Because a stranger called me by name and said the word ELXON as if it were a prayer. She didn't say any of that. "Because my internet's down," she lied, and felt the lie taste bitter even as she swallowed it. "Storm-related."

Kofi made a sound that was half skepticism, half acceptance. "What do you need?"

"Geomagnetic indices," she said. "Tonight's Kp, Dst, whatever you can get fast. And I need solar flare reports. Anything unusual."

Kofi was quiet for a beat. Mara pictured him in his apartment in Maryland, hair sticking up, glasses somewhere on a nightstand, his mind already reaching for data. "You're scared."

"I'm *working*," Mara corrected.

That got a small huff of laughter, then his tone turned serious again. "Give me ten minutes. Don't hang up. I'll put you on speaker and log in."

Mara listened to the faint sounds of him moving around, the click of a keyboard, and a kettle starting somewhere. Life continuing. It was strangely comforting. But the comfort didn't last.

"Okay," his voice now fully alert. "I'm pulling NOAA and ESA feeds. There was a moderate geomagnetic storm watch earlier, but hold on."

Mara's fingers curled around her coffee mug like it could anchor her.

"Here," Kofi said. "It's higher than forecast. Kp is climbing. And there are flare reports, multiple M-class over the past forty-eight hours."

"That alone isn't unusual," Mara said.

"No," Kofi agreed. "But the pattern is."

"How?" she pressed.

"It's not just the flares. It's what they're doing to the magnetosphere. There's compression that doesn't line up with the usual solar wind parameters. It's like—" He paused.

"Like what?" Mara demanded, a little too sharply.

Kofi lowered his voice. "Like the shield is already weakened."

Feeling her stomach drop, Mara asked, "Can you quantify that?" She needed numbers, needed something she could grip without bleeding.

"I can't from here," he admitted. "Not with confidence. But Mara, I've been watching this season's solar activity. I've been telling people in my department it's... off. Not apocalyptic. Not—" He stopped himself. "Just... off."

Mara stared at the laptop screen where her own graphs sat, neat and brutal. "Kofi, if atmospheric loss was accelerating, what would you expect people on the ground to see first?"

Kofi didn't answer right away. Then, slowly, "Auroras where they shouldn't be. Communications glitches. Power grid instability. Higher UV exposure. Changes in upper-atmosphere chemistry."

"My neighbor's kid got sunburned yesterday," she said quietly. "In December."

Kofi went still on the other end of the line. "That's... not normal."

"I know."

They sat in silence for a second, listening to the line hum. Listening to the universe breathe. "Mara," Kofi said carefully. "Why are you calling me at two in the morning?"

Mara looked at the dead phone on the table, then at the image file, and felt the weight of choice settle on her shoulders. She could tell him. He was a scientist. He was a friend, in the way scientists were friends, built on arguments, shared coffee, and a mutual refusal to let ignorance win.

But if Jalen was right, if someone *was* tracking her, then telling Kofi could put a target on his back too. Mara's throat tightened. "I need you to do something," she said instead.

"What?"

"Run your best model. Localized atmospheric loss. Eighteen percent below expected. Tell me how fast it could spread?"

Kofi inhaled sharply. "Eighteen percent?"

Mara's pulse jumped. "Run it."

"This isn't hypothetical," he said.

Mara closed her eyes. "Kofi."

He swore softly under his breath, not at her but at the universe. "Okay. I'll run it. But I need data. Real data. Where did you get eighteen percent?"

Mara stared at the folder. She could lie. She could say, "a rumor." She could say, "a colleague." She could say, "I don't know." But Kofi would smell a lie like smoke. Mara's voice came out thin. "I'll explain later."

Kofi was quiet for a moment. "All right. I hate this. But I'll run it. Mara?"

"Yes?"

"If this is real, you stop protecting me and tell me."

Mara swallowed hard. "Okay."

They hung up. The kitchen felt too quiet afterward, as if the phone call had been the only thing keeping the walls from leaning in. Mara stood and began to move, not from panic, but from a stubborn need to do something physical in a world that had suddenly turned abstract and terrifying.

She found a USB drive in a drawer and plugged it into her laptop.

She copied the file: **ORBITAL_COMPOSITE_07B.png.** Then she copied the entire folder. Then, because paranoia had become a roommate in her house, she copied her sensor logs as well.

She made two backups. She labeled one **SKY.** The other: **DON'T LOSE.** Ridiculous, but true.

She considered printing the image. Then she remembered: her printer connected through Wi-Fi. No. No more networks.

She unplugged the printer entirely, then dug around until she found an old USB cable she hadn't used in years. When she plugged it in, the printer beeped, as if it objected to the job. It printed slowly and loudly, as if it knew the job mattered.

The image slid out in glossy color. It looked even worse on paper. On screen, the wound had felt like a puzzle. On paper, it looked like damage. A bruise on a body you love. Mara held it by the corners, afraid to touch it too much, as if the ink could smear reality.

Her hands were shaking again. She set the printout on the table beside her coffee. And that's when she noticed something else.

The air in the kitchen had a sharpness to it she hadn't noticed before, a faint sting in the back of her throat like she'd been cleaning with bleach. She touched her face and rubbed under her eyes. Her eyes felt dry.

She checked the UV meter again, even though it was night. The reading was low. Normal. But the dryness lingered, and Mara suddenly remembered the line from one of her old lectures, something she'd said to undergrads who liked to pretend the atmosphere was an infinite resource. "It only takes a small change," she used to tell them, "For a big system to become hostile."

She sat back down and tried, for the tenth time, to call the number that had called her. Unknown. No history. No callback. Jalen had made sure of that. Mara's stomach churned. She glanced at the clock: 3:41 a.m.

She thought of her daughter, Wren, working occasional EMT shifts while finishing her nursing program, always tired, always half-laughing at the state of the world. Wren would hate this. She would hate the secrecy. She would hate the injustice of it.

Mara reached for her phone again and tried to text Wren, even though the signal was dead. Are you awake? The message didn't send. It just sat there with a hollow little arrow icon, a wish without wings. Mara put the phone down.

She stood and paced to the window. Outside, the aurora had faded, but the sky still carried a faint green haze near the horizon, like an afterimage. The fields beyond her yard were black and still. The road was empty. For a moment, everything looked normal.

Then the headlights appeared. A vehicle turned slowly onto her street. Mara's body went rigid. The car didn't speed.

It didn't creep, either. It rolled at a controlled, careful pace of someone looking for a specific address without wanting to look like they were looking.

It was dark-colored—maybe black or navy. Mara's heart hammered. It passed her house. Mara exhaled shakily.

Then, at the corner, it turned around. And came back. Mara's mouth went dry. The vehicle slowed in front of her house, idled for a moment, then continued past again. A simple pass. Probably nothing.

Except Mara had lived in this neighborhood long enough now to know who belonged. Old Mr. Henley with his red pickup. The Ramirez family with their minivan. The teenage boy who drove too fast and thought mufflers were optional. This car wasn't any of those.

Mara backed away from the window and switched off the kitchen light, letting darkness swallow her reflection. She stood in the dim with the printout in her hand.

The car came back a third time. This time, it stopped right in front of her house.

Mara couldn't see the driver through the tinted glass. She could only see the shape of the vehicle sitting there like a question that didn't need an answer. Her breath went shallow.

She thought, absurdly, of hiding the printout in the freezer. She thought of running to the bathroom and locking herself in. She thought of calling 911 and trying to explain that someone might be coming for her because she had an image of the Earth's atmosphere tearing open.

She didn't do any of those things. Instead, she forced herself to move like a person who still believed she had agency.

She folded the printout carefully, slipped it into a manila envelope, and put it in the microwave. Not because she planned to cook it. Because it was metal. Because it was shielding. Because it was the closest thing she had to a small, stupid safe. Then she grabbed the USB drives and shoved them into the pocket of her jeans.

She turned off her laptop. The kitchen went fully dark. Only the faint glow of the stove clock remained, blinking as if it couldn't decide what time it was anymore. Mara moved into the hallway and stood near the front door, listening.

Outside, the car's engine idled. Then it cut off. A door opened. Mara's pulse slammed. Footsteps on gravel. Slow. Purposeful. Not a neighbor. Not a lost delivery driver.

Mara's hands clenched into fists at her sides because she couldn't find anything else to hold. She didn't own a gun. She owned books. She owned sensors. She owned an overpriced coffee grinder and an old aluminum baseball bat in the closet she'd never used.

She backed into the living room and reached for the bat without turning on a light. Her fingers closed around it. Cold metal. Better than nothing.

The footsteps stopped on her porch. Silence. Then, softly, almost politely— A knock. Mara didn't move. The knock came again, a little firmer.

"Mara Keene," a voice called through the door. Not shouting and not threatening. Just… certain.

Her throat tightened. Whoever it was knew her name. She held the bat like a ridiculous talisman, her hands sweating on the grip.

The voice spoke again, calm as a business meeting. "Dr. Keene. We need to talk."

Struggling to breathe, Mara forced her voice out in spite. "Who am I speaking with?"

A pause. Then: "Federal liaison. Atmospheric security. This won't take long."

Atmospheric security? A cold wave of fear moved through Mara's body. That wasn't a real thing. Was it?

The voice continued, smooth as oil. "You've had some unusual equipment activity recently. We're here to help you understand what you're seeing."

Help you understand. Mara almost laughed. The sound died in her chest. She thought of Jalen's warning. *If anyone comes to your door, do not open it.* She thought of the wound in the sky. She thought of ELXON. Mara tightened her grip on the bat.

"No," her voice shaking despite her best efforts. "It's the middle of the night. Come back tomorrow."

Silence. Then the voice softened, as if offering kindness. "Dr. Keene… you don't want to make this harder than it has to be."

Mara's spine went stiff. Harder. There it was, beneath the politeness, the edge. She backed away from the door with bat raised slightly, and her mind raced through the house: back window, kitchen door, the narrow hallway, the small bathroom with no exit. She didn't have time.

The doorknob turned. Just once. Testing. It didn't open; she'd locked it earlier out of habit, never thinking that habit would become survival. The knob turned again, firmer. Mara's heart pounded so loud she thought it might give her away.

Then the voice, still calm, said, "All right." Footsteps moved away from the porch.

Mara held her breath so long her lungs burned.

A car door opened. Closed. The engine started. For a moment, she thought it was over. Then the porch light—dead all night—flared on. Bright. Blinding through the front window.

Mara froze. The light held steady, like someone had flipped it from the street. A second later, her laptop, off the table, powered itself on. The screen glowed in the dark kitchen like an eye.

Mara's mouth went dry. Because she hadn't turned it on. And she hadn't plugged the router back in. Yet the laptop's screen lit up anyway, and a single line of text appeared in the center as if someone had typed it just for her:

WE CAN DO THIS QUIETLY.

Mara stood in the dark with a bat in her hands and the USB drives burning against her thigh, and she understood something with stunning clarity:

They weren't here to *talk*.

They were here to erase the proof.

And if she didn't move, right now, she might get erased
too.

CHAPTER 3 — The Man in the Wheatfield

Mara moved before she could talk herself out of it.

She didn't run. Running made noise and she didn't want to draw attention or make mistakes. She slid backward from the hallway into the living room, keeping low, the bat still in her hands like a child's idea of protection. The laptop's glow spilled from the kitchen like a nightlight from hell.

WE CAN DO THIS QUIETLY.

The words were not just a threat. They were a promise: *We're already inside.* Mara's mind flashed through every possible entry point. The router was unplugged. The Wi-Fi was dead. But that didn't matter if someone had planted something weeks ago, something that didn't need her permission.

Her laptop fan whirred faintly, like it was breathing. Outside, the porch light stayed on, harsh and steady, as if the street had decided her house belonged to someone else now.

She forced herself to think in simple steps. Step one: leave. Step two: keep the proof. Step three: Don't die in Kansas with a bat and a microwave full of paper.

She eased toward the back of the house, moving through shadows. The kitchen window showed her the street without showing *her*—the car was still there, a dark shape at the curb, headlights off now, as though it wanted the night to hide it.

Mara didn't look long. Looking made you freeze. She slipped into the laundry room and quietly unlatched the back door. The cold hit her face like a slap.

She stepped out onto the back stoop and paused, listening. The neighborhood felt hushed in a way that wasn't peaceful, as if the world were holding its breath. No footsteps. No voices. No sirens. Just wind and the distant hum of a transformer.

Her yard backed onto a narrow stretch of scrub and then open fields, winter wheat cut low, the land rolling away into darkness like an ocean. She had moved here because it was quiet. Tonight, the quiet felt like cover.

Mara stepped off the stoop and kept low, moving along the side of the house where the fence met the shed. The shed was a small wooden box full of tools she never used and old paint cans that belonged to the earlier owner. She pressed her back against it and peeked around the corner.

The porch light on the front of the house still burned too brightly. The dark SUV sat at the curb like a patient animal. A figure stood near it, not at her door anymore, but by the driver's side window. He glanced at a device in his hand and tilted his head, listening to an earpiece. Another figure sat in the passenger seat, barely visible.

Mara's stomach turned cold. Two at least. And if the message was real, the number did not matter. She was a location on a map now, not a person.

She backed away from the shed and crept toward the field. Her shoes were by the back door, but she hadn't grabbed them.

Bare feet on frozen ground were a miserable choice, but a quiet one.

When she reached the edge of the property, she slid under the lowest strand of barbed wire, where a rabbit had already flattened the grass and made a gap. The metal caught her jacket and tugged. She held her breath, eased free, and crawled into the field like she was slipping out of her own life.

The wheat stubble scratched her palms. The earth smelled sharp and dead. Somewhere nearby, a coyote barked once, then fell silent again. Mara kept moving. She didn't aim for the road. Roads were obvious. She angled toward the tree line that cut across the field like a dark seam, a drainage ditch with cottonwoods that locals used as a windbreak.

The cold gnawed at her feet. After the first minute, she stopped feeling pain and started feeling numbness. She told herself she could lose toes tomorrow if she survived this night.

Behind her, the porch light flared even brighter. Then, so faint she almost missed it, she heard the front door open. A voice carried across the yard, muffled, calm. "The house is dark." Another voice answered, lower. "She's still here."

Mara's lungs seized. Still here. Not *was*. They weren't guessing. They were tracking.

She went faster, no longer careful about the wheat stubble snapping under her knees, no longer thinking about how ridiculous she looked crawling through a field in her jeans with two USB drives in her pocket and nothing else.

The ditch came closer. The cottonwoods rose like thin, black pillars. Then she heard it. A car door closing. An engine turning over. The SUV rolled. Not fast. Not frantic. Controlled and methodical, like a metronome. They were going to circle around.

Mara slid down into the ditch, grateful for the depression in the earth. The ditch smelled of wet soil and old leaves. Mud sucked at her hands as she crawled along the bottom, keeping the tree line between her and the street. Her teeth chattered, loud in her own ears. She stopped and pressed herself onto the side of the ditch, breathing hard, listening.

Headlights swept across the field above her, pale beams cutting through the wheat stubble. The SUV moved slowly along the edge of the road, then paused. Mara held her breath. The headlights shifted, angling toward the cottonwoods.

They were scanning for movement. For footprints. For panic. Mara stayed still enough to become part of the ditch. A spotlight snapped on. It was white, intense, and sweeping across the tree trunks.

Mara squeezed her eyes shut. Don't move. Don't flinch. Don't be a deer in the beam. The light passed over her hiding place, cutting through branches and weeds, but it didn't land directly on her. It slid on. Then the engine revved slightly, and the SUV continued, turning onto the road that led toward the edge of town.

Mara waited another full minute after the sound faded. Then she crawled out of the ditch, shaking, and ran, finally ran, toward town through back lots and alleyways, keeping to darkness, keeping off the main streets, her bare feet slapping frozen ground and not feeling it.

By the time she reached the first row of houses, her lungs burned, and her legs trembled. She ducked behind a dumpster near the closed hardware store and pressed a hand to her mouth to keep from making noise.

The town was asleep, unaware. Streetlights hummed. A dog barked once and then quieted. Christmas lights blinked on and off like tiny, indifferent stars.

Mara looked down at her hands. They were scraped and dirty, bleeding in thin lines where wheat stubble had cut her skin. She didn't care.

She reached into her pocket and touched the USB drives. Still there. She let out a shaky breath that was half sob, half laugh.

Then her phone buzzed. Mara froze. She stared at it like it might be a grenade. The screen lit with a single bar of service. One bar, but it was enough. A text came through, delayed, timestamped earlier.

Wren: *Mom? You texted. I'm up. What's wrong?*

Mara's throat tightened so hard it hurt. She typed with trembling fingers, keeping the message short because short was safer.

Mara: *I'm okay. I don't want you to come to my house. Go to the hospital. Stay there. Explain later.*

Her thumb hovered. She added one more line, because she couldn't not.

Mara: *I love you.*

The message sent. A second later, Wren called. Mara didn't answer. She couldn't risk sound. Couldn't risk someone tracing the call. Couldn't risk Wren hearing the fear in her voice and deciding to drive toward danger. Instead, she texted again.

Mara: *No calls. Please. Trust me.*

She shoved the phone back into her pocket and forced herself to move.

The town ended quickly. Kansas towns did. One moment you had a diner and a pharmacy and a grain elevator, and the next you had fields again. Mara didn't go to the diner. Too public. Too many windows. She went to the only place in town that stayed lit at night besides the gas station: the twenty-four-hour laundromat.

It smelled like detergent and damp fabric and the faint sourness of old socks. Two machines spun in the corner, churning clothes in endless circles. A man slept in a plastic chair, his hood up, his face turned away. A woman sat folding tiny shirts with a tired intensity that looked like prayer.

Mara slipped into the bathroom, locked the door, and sat on the closed toilet lid, shivering so hard her bones felt like they were rattling. She pulled out her phone and called Kofi.

It rang once. He answered quickly, like he'd been waiting with the phone in his hand.

"Mara," he said. "I was about to call you back. Are you…"

"I have to be quick," Mara whispered. Her voice sounded wrong—thin, scraped. "Someone came to my house."

A pause. "Someone like… who?"

"I don't know," she said. "They knew my name. They used the phrase 'atmospheric security.' They got into my laptop without my network."

Kofi's inhale was sharp. "What?"

"I ran. I'm not at my house anymore."

"Jesus, Mara." The words came out like pain. "Okay. Okay. Where are you?"

"In town," she said. "Inside. Safe for the moment."

Kofi went quiet, then his voice shifted into the tone he used when he was forcing his brain to build a ladder out of panic.

"I ran the model. The one you asked for."

Mara squeezed her eyes shut. "And?"

"It's… bad," Kofi said softly. "If you're right about the density anomaly, and if the magnetosphere is compromised, you could see runaway loss. Once it crosses a threshold—"

"How long?" Mara interrupted.

Kofi hesitated, and that hesitation told her everything before he spoke.

"In the worst case," he said, "months. In a more conservative case, maybe a year or two. But Mara… the acceleration curve, if it's real—it bends fast."

The world seemed to tilt around Mara. She pressed her forehead against the bathroom door. "Can you verify the anomaly from independent sources?"

"I tried. That's the problem. The public feeds have gaps. Delays. Missing segments. And some atmospheric datasets look trimmed. Like somebody cleaned the evidence."

Mara's blood went cold. "Trimmed?"

"Yes," Kofi said. "And Mara, someone accessed my university account ten minutes ago from an IP that isn't ours. They didn't get in. Two-factor stopped it. But they tried."

Mara's hand clamped over her mouth. "I'm sorry," she whispered.

"Don't apologize," Kofi snapped, then softened. "Just listen. Whatever you have, whatever you saw, you need to assume they'll come for it. And for you."

"I have it backed up. Two USB drives."

"Good. Now you need a person. Someone you trust who can hold one if you get caught."

Mara thought of Wren and felt sick. "I can't bring my daughter into this,"

"Then find someone else," Kofi insisted. "And Mara, if you can, get to a place with cameras. Not because cameras protect you, but because they make it harder to make you vanish quietly."

Mara thought then offered. "There's a hospital."

"Yes. Go there."

Mara hesitated, then forced herself to say the next thing. "Kofi… the file I got—" Her voice shook. "It had a name on it."

"What name?"

Mara stared at the chipped tile under her feet, as if she could anchor the words there instead of letting them live in the air. "ELXON."

Silence. Then, very quietly, "That's not a scientific acronym."

"No," Mara agreed. "It's a brand."

A long pause, filled only by the hum of the laundromat machines outside. "Mara," Kofi said. "I need you to promise me something."

"What?"

"If this turns out to be what it sounds like, you do not try to fight it alone."

Mara's laugh came out bitter. "I don't even know what 'it' is."

"You will and when you do, you call me again. We build a chain. We find people. We get it out in a way they can't erase."

Mara nodded even though he couldn't see her. "Okay."

Kofi exhaled. "One more thing. The auroras—"

"Yes?"

"They're being dismissed publicly as cycles. But my colleague at Goddard texted me something strange. She said there's chatter about a 'private sector continuity initiative.' She didn't name names, but—"

Mara's stomach tightened.

"—but she said the phrase 'ticketed access.'" Kofi's voice turned grim. "Like someone is selling a seat."

Mara's throat went dry.

Kofi continued, "Mara, get to the hospital. Now. And turn your phone off between check-ins."

Mara ended the call, hands shaking. She pocketed the phone and stared at her reflection in the bathroom mirror. She looked like a woman who'd crawled out of a ditch. Because she had. She splashed water on her face, dried her hands on paper towels, and stepped back into the laundromat.

The sleeping man in the chair hadn't moved. The woman folding clothes glanced up once, eyes sliding over Mara and away again. Everyone had their own survival.

Mara walked out into the cold. The hospital was six blocks away. Six blocks didn't sound like much until you were barefoot and trembling and felt like the whole world had turned predatory. She moved quickly, sticking to side streets, using parked cars as cover when headlights approached.

Halfway there, she heard it again. An engine. Slow. Controlled.

She ducked behind a hedge and watched as the same dark SUV rolled through the intersection ahead, turning without signaling, as if it didn't care about traffic laws because traffic laws were for people who believed in consequences. The SUV paused near the gas station, then continued. Searching.

Mara's heart hammered. She waited until it disappeared, then crossed the street and slipped behind a line of trees that bordered the hospital parking lot.

The hospital's lights glowed warm and steady, a beacon that promised help even when it couldn't guarantee safety. Ambulances sat like sleeping beasts near the ER entrance. A nurse in scrubs stepped outside for a cigarette and stared at the sky, frowning, as if she'd noticed the aurora earlier and couldn't stop thinking about it.

Mara's chest tightened with relief at the sight of her. Human. Ordinary. Real. Mara hurried toward the entrance. The automatic doors whooshed open, and the smell hit her: disinfectant and coffee and the faint metallic note of too many hours awake. The waiting room was quiet, a few people slumped in chairs, a toddler sleeping across his mother's lap, a man holding an ice pack to his cheek. Normal.

Mara walked to the front desk and forced her voice into something steady. "I need to report something."

The receptionist looked up, tired but polite. "Are you hurt?"

Mara lifted her hands, showing the scrapes, the dirt. "Not… badly. But I need to talk to security. And I need to call someone. My daughter might come here."

The receptionist's eyes sharpened at the word security. "Okay. Hold on."

Mara's phone buzzed again. Another text from Wren:

Wren: *Mom, WHAT? I'm at the ER entrance. Where are you?*

She typed fast.

Mara: *Stay inside. Do not go back outside. I'm inside already. I'm coming to you.*

She shoved the phone into her pocket and turned away from the desk. She scanned the ER entrance area, and then she saw her. Wren stood near the vending machines, hair pulled into a messy bun, wearing a hoodie under her jacket, her posture rigid with worry. She looked up, spotted Mara, and started forward, eyes wide.

"Mom—" Wren began.

Mara reached her and grabbed her hands, squeezing hard. "Don't," Mara whispered. "Not loud."

Wren's face tightened. "What is going on?"

Mara glanced toward the glass doors. Outside, the parking lot lights threw pale circles on the pavement. "I'll tell you. Just… trust me for five minutes."

Wren's jaw clenched. She looked angry, scared, and furious that those two emotions could coexist. "Did someone hurt you?" Wren demanded, voice low but sharp.

"Not yet," Mara regretted it instantly when Wren's eyes widened.

Wren stared at Mara's bare feet, the dirt, the blood. "My God, Mom. Your feet."

"I need you to listen carefully," Mara said, leaning in close. "I need you to take this." She slipped one of the USB drives into Wren's palm and closed Wren's fingers around it.

"What is it?" Wren whispered.

"Insurance. If something happens to me—"

"Don't say that."

Mara held Wren's gaze. "If something happens, you call Kofi Mensah. I'll text you his number. You give him the drive."

Wren's breathing went shallow. "Mom, you're scaring me."

"Good." Emotion rising sharp in her chest. "Be scared. But be smart."

Wren looked like she wanted to argue. Then she did something surprising, she nodded. "Okay," she whispered. "Okay. But you tell me what's going on."

Mara opened her mouth. And then the hospital TV, mounted in the corner of the waiting area, volume low—shifted to a glossy morning-news segment. A bright studio. Smiling anchors. A headline banner scrolled beneath them:

"BILLIONAIRE-BACKED 'EDGE OF SPACE' RIDES SELL OUT IN MINUTES"

Mara's blood ran cold. On the screen, an elegant woman with perfect hair laughed lightly, wearing a sleek white jumpsuit with a logo stitched over her heart, an X inside a circle. She waved at the camera as if she were greeting fans.

The anchor beamed. "And with us this morning is global icon Anika Sato, partnering with the ELXON Foundation to promote what they're calling 'Humanity's Next Horizon!'"

The camera cut to Anika's smile, warm, practiced, comforting.

"We're so excited," Anika said, voice soft and sincere. "These rides are about inspiration. About reminding people how precious our planet is. And yes, the proceeds support scientific innovation."

Mara felt the room tilt. Wren turned toward the screen, frowning. "ELXON?"

Mara couldn't speak. On the TV, the anchor continued cheerfully. "Tickets start at fifty million dollars, with VIP tiers available. But the demand is incredible. People are calling it the most exclusive view in human history."

Mara's ears rang. Fifty million dollars. A view. A hole in the sky—sold as inspiration.

Wren looked back at Mara, and in her eyes, Mara saw it: the moment the world stopped being normal for her, too. "That's…" Wren began.

Mara leaned close and whispered the truth as carefully as if it were glass. "That isn't charity," Mara said. "It's a filter."

Wren stared, lips parted. On screen, Anika smiled again. "When you see Earth from above," she said, "you realize we're all connected."

Mara's hands curled into fists. Because she knew, now, that somewhere behind that smile, behind that logo, behind that foundation—Someone was deciding who counted as "all."

And at that moment, through the glass doors of the ER entrance, Mara saw a dark SUV roll slowly into the hospital parking lot. It wasn't in a hurry, but it didn't hesitate either. It came straight toward the entrance, as if it already knew she was there.

Mara grabbed Wren's wrist.

"Come with me," she whispered.

Wren's voice shook. "Where?"

Mara's mind flashed to Jalen's warning, to Kofi's urgency, to the words on her laptop. She didn't have a plan. She had only one thing left that might count as a plan: A man who had called himself an astronaut and sent her proof. A man who had said he'd seen the wound.

Mara pulled her phone out and, with shaking fingers, opened the notes app where she'd copied the one thing Jalen had typed into the file folder, hidden in a plain text document like an afterthought. A location. A time. A message.

If they find you, go to the grain elevator on 14th. 4:15 a.m. Come alone.

Mara looked at the clock in the waiting room. 4:02 a.m. She looked at the SUV outside. Then she looked at her daughter, who was holding a USB drive as if it were suddenly the weight of the world.

Mara's voice came out steadily, even as her heart tried to rip itself free. "We're going to the grain elevator," she said.

And as the SUV stopped and its doors opened, Mara understood that the next fifteen minutes would decide whether the truth lived… or disappeared quietly.

CHAPTER 4 — The Grain Elevator

The SUV doors opened like the world had rehearsed it.

Two men stepped out, in dark coats, no visible insignia, posture too controlled for anyone who belonged in a hospital parking lot at four in the morning. They didn't rush. They didn't look around like they were lost. They walked with the quiet certainty of people who expected doors to unlock for them.

Mara's mouth went dry. Wren leaned closer, eyes wide. "Mom..."

"Don't stare," Mara whispered. "And don't run. Not yet." Wren's fingers tightened around the USB drive in her pocket like she could crush it into safety.

At the front desk, the receptionist was on the phone, nodding, looking toward the entrance with a confused frown. She didn't look frightened. Not yet. Because fear requires context.

Mara grabbed Wren's sleeve and guided her away from the waiting room windows, toward the corridor that led deeper into the ER. The hospital was a maze, bright halls, closed doors, fluorescent calm, but Mara had spent enough hours here, visiting patients when she worked community health programs years ago, to remember its logic.

There would be a back hallway. There would be a staff exit. There would be a way out that didn't involve walking straight into those men.

Wren hissed under her breath, "What have you gotten into?"

"I know," Mara whispered. "I didn't choose this."

"You never choose anything," Wren muttered, and the edge in her voice broke Mara's heart because it was fear wearing anger as armor.

Mara didn't answer. She couldn't afford to. They slipped into a hallway where the noise softened: a nurse pushing a cart, a doctor leaning against a wall, drinking coffee like it was medicine, a janitor humming softly as he mopped. Ordinary people in an extraordinary moment, unaware they were sharing oxygen with a secret.

Mara's bare feet were finally starting to hurt again, stinging, pins and needles, the delayed protest of nerves returning to life. She forced herself to keep moving normally. The worst thing you could do was behave like prey.

They passed a set of double doors marked **AUTHORIZED PERSONNEL ONLY**, and Mara kept going as if she belonged. Wren followed, close enough to grab, close enough to lose.

A nurse glanced up. "Ma'am?" the nurse called, polite but wary. "That door is—"

Mara didn't slow. She turned her head just enough to meet the nurse's eyes and put all her desperation into a whisper that sounded like certainty.

"My daughter's a student nurse," Mara said. "We got turned around back there"

The nurse hesitated, then shrugged, already too tired to police every wandering soul at dawn. "Okay, but stay near the ER side."

"Thank you," Mara said, and kept walking. The doors swung shut behind them with a soft click that felt like stepping behind a curtain. The hallway beyond was dimmer, utilitarian, full of carts and supply closets. A faint smell of bleach and stale coffee hung in the air. This was where the hospital's calm face ended, and its bones showed through.

Wren leaned close, voice shaking. "Where are we going?"

"Loading bay," Mara said. "There will be an ambulance exit."

"You know this, how?"

"Because hospitals always have one," Mara said, and pushed through another door. They entered a stairwell with concrete walls and a buzzing light overhead. The air was colder here. Wren's breath sounded loud.

Mara paused on the landing and listened.

Above them, faint footsteps. Below them, a door closing. Somewhere distant, a muffled voice on a radio. Then, so subtle it could have been imagination, a sound behind the ER-side door. A soft thud. A hand on metal. Testing.

Mara's stomach clenched. "They're inside."

Wren's eyes went wide. "How—?"

"Save that for later," Mara said and started down.

They descended two flights quickly, shoes or no shoes, and Mara pushed open the lower door. A long corridor stretched ahead, ending in a red EXIT sign. On the right, there was a row of lockers and a break room with a vending machine humming softly. On the left, a closed door labeled **SECURITY**.

Mara stopped. Security. Cameras. Kofi's voice echoed in her head: *Get somewhere with cameras. Make it harder to vanish quietly.* Mara grabbed the handle and tried the security door. Locked. Of course. She hesitated for only a second, then banged on it, once, hard. "Hello?" she called, keeping her voice steady. "Security?" Nothing.

She banged again. Inside, movement. A chair scrape. Then a voice, irritated. "What?" The door opened a crack, and a man's face appeared, mid-fifties, tired eyes, coffee breath.

Mara leaned in close and spoke fast. "Two men just came in. They're looking for me. They said they're federal, but I don't believe them."

The guard's eyes narrowed. "Ma'am—"

"They accessed my laptop remotely with my network unplugged," Mara said, and watched his expression shift from annoyance to confusion to unease. "They're in the building. Please, just look at the cameras. Dark SUV, parked by the ER entrance."

The guard opened the door wider. "And who are you?"

Mara didn't have time for truth. She had time for leverage. "Dr. Mara Keene, atmospheric research."

The guard blinked like that meant nothing, then looked at Wren—at her shaking hands, her hoodie, her face pale with fear. "Okay," he said slowly. "Okay. Come in."

They slipped into the small security room. Monitors lined one wall, each showing a different angle of the hospital: entrances, corridors, the ambulance bay, the parking lot. The guard tapped a keyboard, squinting.

"There," Mara said, pointing at the ER entrance feed. The two men were inside now, walking past the front desk. They weren't talking to anyone. They weren't checking in. They moved like they owned the hallway.

The receptionist, God bless her, stood, flustered, trying to intercept them. One of the men showed her something, a badge, a piece of paper, a screen, too fast for the camera to capture clearly. The receptionist's shoulders dropped. She stepped aside. They continued straight toward the hallway leading to the authorized personnel doors.

Mara's blood chilled. "They're coming this way," she whispered.

The guard swore softly. "That's restricted."

"Exactly," Mara said. "They don't care."

The guard grabbed a radio. "Hey, Lisa, front desk. Those two guys that just came through, did they sign in?"

The radio crackled. A tired woman's voice: "They said they were federal. Something about an atmospheric incident. They told me not to delay them."

The guard's jaw clenched. "Atmospheric incident," he repeated, glancing at Mara like she'd just confirmed the impossible.

Mara's throat went tight. "Please, can you stall them?"

The guard hesitated, then made a small but brave decision. He reached for the door lock panel. "There's a controlled access door between here and the supply corridor," he said. "I can lock it down. Keep them from coming through."

Mara nodded, relief and terror tangling. "Do it."

The guard hit a switch. On the monitor, a door further down the corridor clicked shut, its magnet lock engaging. The guard lifted his radio again. "Maintenance, lockdown Door C-12. Unauthorized personnel."

A crackle. "Copy."

Wren grabbed Mara's arm. "Mom, if you lock them in here, doesn't that—?"

"Buys us minutes," Mara whispered.

The guard looked at Mara, eyes hard. "Where are you trying to go?"

Mara's mind flashed: **grain elevator, 14th, 4:15 a.m.** She didn't want to say it out loud. But there wasn't time for secrecy now. There was only motion. "Out. Back exit. We need to leave now."

The guard nodded sharply. "Follow me." He opened the security room door and led them down the corridor to the red EXIT sign. He punched a code on the keypad and shoved the door open.

Cold air slapped Mara's face. They stepped into the ambulance bay. Ambulances sat lined up, quiet for the moment, their reflective stripes catching the overhead lights. A paramedic leaned against the wall, sipping from a Styrofoam cup, staring at the sky as if it had personally offended him.

The guard pointed. "That alley leads to 14th," he said. "Go. And don't stop."

Mara's heart jumped, 14th. He had unknowingly pointed them toward Jalen's location like fate had put its thumb on the scale. "Thank you," Mara whispered.

The guard didn't answer. He was already walking back inside, squaring his shoulders, ready to face whatever came next.

Mara grabbed Wren's wrist and pulled her into the alley. They moved fast, half-running, the cold slicing through them. Wren's shoes slapped pavement; Mara's bare feet bit into every pebble, every crack, but pain was a distant thing now.

Behind them, a siren chirped once, not an ambulance, but the sharp, brief warning tone of a security alarm. The hospital doors thudded open. A voice shouted, not panicked, but angry. "Ma'am! Stop!"

Mara didn't look back. "Keep going," she hissed. They cut between buildings, crossed a side street, and sprinted past a closed diner with a darkened neon OPEN sign. Their breath steamed in the air. The sky above still held a faint greenish stain, like the aurora had left a bruise.

Wren stumbled once, and Mara caught her. "I can't—" Wren gasped.

"Yes, you can," Mara said, voice fierce. "You're an EMT. You run toward blood. You can run toward this."

Wren swallowed hard and nodded, tears shining in her eyes. "I hate you."

Mara barked a laugh that was almost a sob. "Fair."

They reached 14th Street and slowed, pressing themselves into the shadow of a parked pickup. Ahead, the grain elevator rose out of the darkness like a concrete cathedral, tall, brutal, the kind of structure that made you feel small even when you weren't afraid of the end of the world. A single security light glowed near its base, casting a pale circle.

The clock on Mara's phone read **4:14 a.m.** One minute. Mara scanned the area. She couldn't detect anyone. No movement. Only the elevator's hulking silhouette and the whisper of wind slipping around it.

Wren's voice shook. "This is where we're meeting someone? Who?"

Mara didn't answer. She couldn't answer. Not until she saw him. Then, behind a stack of pallets near the elevator's loading dock, a figure stepped out. Mara's chest seized.

He was tall, wearing a dark jacket and a knit cap pulled low. His posture was wrong. He was too stiff, like he was carrying pain under his clothes. He moved like someone trained, but not at ease. He lifted a hand in a small signal.

Mara's breath hitched. "Jalen?"

The man nodded once. He stepped closer into the light, and Mara saw his face properly for the first time. Not a stranger's face. Not a heroic movie face. A face with bruises on the jawline. A cut on the eyebrow. Eyes that looked older than his years, alert and tired and angry at the right things. "You weren't supposed to bring anyone," he said. His voice was the same as the phone—rough, controlled—but softer now, as if he'd been forced to become careful with words.

Wren stiffened beside Mara. "I'm not going anywhere without my mom."

Jalen's gaze flicked to Wren, quick, assessing, then back to Mara. "They found you fast," he said.

Mara agreed. "They were at my door within an hour."

Jalen's jaw tightened. "Then the transfer lit you up. Damn it."

"I unplugged everything," Mara said, the words coming out sharp with frustration and fear. "It didn't matter."

"No," Jalen agreed. "It didn't."

He reached into his pocket and pulled out a small, black, palm-sized device with a single switch. He clicked it on. A faint hum filled the air.

Wren stared. "What is that?"

"Insurance," Jalen said, echoing Mara's earlier word like he'd used it himself before. "A signal jammer but with limited range."

Mara's pulse jumped. "You have—"

"I have what I can steal," Jalen cut in. His gaze snapped upward, scanning the street. "We don't have time. Give me the drive."

Mara hesitated, then realized what he meant. "I gave one to my daughter." Her voice broke on the word daughter like she couldn't believe she'd dragged Wren into this.

Wren's hand went to her pocket protectively. "I'm not handing it to anyone I don't know."

Jalen stared at her, then did something unexpected: he nodded, once, almost respectfully. "Good," he said. "Don't trust easily."

He turned back to Mara. "You have the other one?"

Mara pulled the USB drive from her jeans pocket and held it out. Jalen took it, quick and careful, like it was a live wire. "Okay," he said. "Now listen. They'll lock down this town in the next hour. Quietly. Road closures, power issues, a fake gas leak, something. You're going to disappear into paperwork and polite threats."

Mara's throat tightened. "Who are they?"

Jalen's eyes flashed. "Not the government. Not exactly. It's a coalition. A private continuity network that uses governments as a mask."

Mara felt sick. "ELXON."

He nodded.

"You said it started as a plan," Mara said. "To leave."

"It started as an idea," Jalen corrected. "Then it became a brand. Then it became a religion for people who think they're the only ones who matter."

Wren's voice came out small. "You're saying they're going to abandon everyone."

Jalen's gaze hardened. "They're already doing it. The ships are being built. The launch sites are active. The seats are being sold as 'inspiration rides' and 'scientific philanthropy.' But the real product is selection."

Mara's stomach twisted. She thought of Anika's smile on the hospital TV. "A filter," Mara whispered.

Jalen's expression softened a fraction. "Yeah. A filter."

Mara forced herself to stay in science. "The atmosphere, what exactly is happening?"

Jalen looked away toward the hulking elevator, then back, eyes sharp. "You know how thin it is from up there," he said quietly. "That blue curve everyone posts and forgets. It's not a metaphor. It's a measurement." He leaned closer, lowering his voice. "There's a region where the upper atmosphere is thinning too fast. A structural failure. And once it hits a threshold, the loss accelerates. Like a rip in fabric. It doesn't stop ripping because you want it to."

Mara's mouth went dry. "How long?"

Jalen didn't answer right away. Then, very softly, "Soon enough that they've stopped pretending it's hypothetical."

Wren made a small sound, half breath, half prayer. Mara's hands curled into fists. "Why tell me?" Mara said. "Why not go public?"

Jalen's face tightened with something like grief. "Because I tried," he said. "And I got 'accidented.' And everyone I talked to got warned. And the people who could broadcast it got bought." He lifted the USB drive slightly. "Proof is the only weapon you have. And even proof gets buried if you release it wrong."

Mara's voice trembled. "So, how do we make it happen?"

Jalen looked at her like the question hurt. "We build a chain. People in different places. Redundancy. You don't make one big leak. You make a thousand small ones, they can't catch. Scientists. Journalists. Pilots. Weather nerds. Amateur satellite trackers. You don't convince everyone. You convince enough."

Mara's mind raced. "Kofi—"

"Yes," Jalen said immediately. "Kofi Mensah. I know."

Mara stared. "You know him?"

"I know of him," Jalen corrected. "I've been watching who asks the right questions."

Wren's voice sharpened. "Who are you really?"

Jalen met her gaze. "Someone who saw what was happening and refused to stay quiet. Someone who's running out of places to run."

A low rumble sounded in the distance. Mara's head snapped toward the street. Headlights. Two sets now.

Approaching slowly, sweeping across buildings as they turned onto 14th.

Wren's breathing hitched. "Is that them?"

Jalen's jaw clenched. "Yes."

Mara's pulse spiked. "How can you tell?"

"They don't drive like locals and my jammer just started pulling interference." He clicked the device off. The hum died. "Stay behind me," he said, as his hand moved under his jacket.

Wren's eyes widened. "Do you have a gun?"

Jalen didn't answer. Mara grabbed his arm, fierce. "No. No shooting. This isn't—"

Jalen looked at her, eyes hard. "This is exactly that."

The headlights grew brighter. One vehicle. Then another behind it. SUV silhouettes. Mara felt the world narrow to choices.

Jalen grabbed Mara's elbow. "There's a service ladder," he said, nodding toward the elevator. "We go up. Now."

Wren shook her head. "Up? That's—"

"High ground," Jalen snapped. "And cameras. The elevator has cameras."

Mara stared up at the towering structure, the concrete rising into darkness. Her fear screamed *no*. Her brain screamed. She grabbed Wren's hand and ran with Jalen toward the base of the elevator, toward the shadow where the ladder clung to the concrete like a thin, vertical promise.

Behind them, one of the SUVs slowed, tires crunching gravel. A voice boomed through a speaker, calm and amplified, like a public announcement. "Dr. Keene," it said. "You don't need to do this."

Mara's blood went cold. They weren't yelling. They weren't threatening. They were offering her a choice as if it were polite. As if it were reasonable.

Jalen hissed, "Climb."

Wren's hands shook as she grabbed the ladder. Mara went behind her, pushing her upward. The metal was icy. It bit into Mara's palms.

The SUV's headlights swung, catching the ladder, catching them, washing them in bright white light. The speaker's voice continued, even and practiced. "We can still do this quietly."

Mara climbed faster, panicking. Below, Jalen started up after them. Then a sound cracked the air. Not thunder or a car backfiring. A gunshot. The ladder shuddered as something struck metal near Mara's foot, sparking.

Wren screamed. Mara's heart slammed into her ribs as she hauled herself upward, dragging her fear like a weight. Below them, Jalen swore, a low, vicious sound, and climbed one-handed, the other hand raised as if ready to fire back.

Mara didn't look down. She couldn't. She just climbed. And as they rose into the cold Kansas air, the grain elevator turning from a shelter into a trap beneath them, Mara realized with terrifying clarity:

ELXON wasn't a secret plan anymore.

It was a hunt.

And she was now part of the story, whether she wanted to be or not.

CHAPTER 5 — High Ground

The ladder vibrated under Mara's hands like a living thing.

Below, the SUVs idled with the patience of predators. Their headlights pinned the ladder in white light, turning every rung into a spotlighted confession. Mara climbed anyway, because stopping was the same as falling.

Wren was above her, climbing fast but not smoothly. Fear made you clumsy. Fear made you skip rungs and slip, made your breath come too sharp, too loud. "Keep three points," Mara whispered through clenched teeth. "Hands and a foot, always." Wren didn't answer. She just climbed.

A second gunshot cracked the air. Metal sparked again, this time above Mara's head. She ducked instinctively and nearly lost her grip. The rung bit her palms. Her heart hammered so hard she tasted it.

Jalen climbed below them one-handed, faster than seemed possible, his other hand raised toward the ground, as if weighing whether to fire back. He didn't. Not yet. "Stop shooting!" Jalen shouted down, voice raw. "You want this quiet? Then keep it quiet."

The speaker's voice replied, calm as a therapist. "Captain Royce. We don't want anyone hurt."

"Then stop trying to hunt people in a small town," Jalen snapped and climbed again.

Mara didn't look down. She couldn't. The only safe direction was up. The grain elevator's side was cold concrete under her shoulder when she pressed close, climbing as she could, merging with it. The wind above them had teeth. It hooked into Mara's jacket and tried to pull her away from the ladder. Her numb feet had graduated into stabbing pain.

Wren reached the top first. Mara saw her hands disappear over the lip of a narrow catwalk, then her legs, then her whole body as she rolled onto metal grating and lay there a moment, panting. Mara climbed the last rungs, lungs burning.

Jalen's voice came from below, tight. "Mara. Don't stop. Keep moving."

Mara hauled herself up and rolled onto the catwalk, the metal grid imprinting into her palms. The world swung for a second, the sudden height, the sudden wind. She forced herself to look. Kansas spread out under them, dark fields, a few sleepy streets, the hospital lights in the distance, a pale green smear still lingering along the horizon like the sky hadn't fully decided to stop warning them.

Wren crawled to the inner edge of the catwalk and pressed her back against the elevator's structure, trying to make herself small. Her eyes were huge, shining, frantic. "Mom," she breathed. "Oh, my God."

Jalen climbed over the edge a beat later, pulling himself up with a sharp grunt that sounded like pain he refused to honor. He rolled to his feet immediately, shoulders squared, gaze sweeping.

Below them, one of the SUVs had pulled closer to the base of the elevator. A man stood near the ladder, looking up, face upturned into the light. Another moved toward a side door set into the elevator's base—maintenance access. "They're going inside," Mara whispered.

"Of course they are," Jalen said. He pulled the jammer out again and flicked it on. The faint hum returned, a vibration in the air felt more than heard.

Wren flinched. "That thing… It's like a mosquito in my skull."

"Good," Jalen said. "It means it's working."

Mara wiped wind tears from her eyes and tried to breathe like a person who wasn't being hunted. "Where do we go from here?"

Jalen pointed along the catwalk. "There's a stairwell on the far side. Leads down into the upper galleries. Control room should be—"

A loud metallic bang echoed from below as the maintenance door slammed open.

"They're in," Mara said.

Jalen started moving. "Then we don't stay on the ladder's line. Come on."

They moved along the catwalk in single file. The metal grating clanged under their feet despite their careful steps. Wind pushed at them from the open side, hard enough that Mara kept one hand on the rail. The rail was cold metal, rough with frost. Wren's breath came in quick bursts. "This is unbelievable."

"Welcome to the new normal," Jalen said without looking back. At the far end of the catwalk, a small structure jutted out—an enclosed access box, like a little shack clinging to the giant elevator. A door with a faded warning sign: **AUTHORIZED PERSONNEL ONLY.** Jalen tried the handle. Locked. He swore under his breath. "Of course."

Wren's voice rose. "So, what now?"

Jalen looked at the lock like it had personally insulted him. Then he reached into his pocket and pulled out a small set of tools, thin picks, and a tension wrench.

Mara stared. "You—"

"Don't ask," Jalen muttered. "Just watch the stairs."

Mara turned and looked back along the catwalk. Below, movement flickered at the base as flashlights cut across concrete. They were inside, climbing. She could hear it faintly now, metal footsteps in the elevator's hollow belly, echoing upward like the building itself was breathing in strangers.

Wren pressed closer to Mara. "How are they so fast?"

Jalen worked the lock with quick, practiced motions, his face calm but his eyes hard. "Because they've done this before. They just usually do it in cities where it's easier to make people disappear in crowds."

Mara's stomach lurched. "Jalen…"

The lock clicked. Jalen yanked the door open and shoved it inward. "Go."

Wren slipped through first, then Mara. The space inside smelled of dust and cold metal. It was narrow, an access tunnel leading to a stairwell that spiraled downward along the elevator's inner structure. The wind died here, replaced by the deep, low groan of the building shifting. Jalen swung the door shut behind them and, after a brief pause, slid a bolt into place.

"Will that hold?" Wren asked.

"Long enough," Jalen said.

They started down the spiral stairs. The air was warmer inside, stale with grain dust and machine oil. Mara's bare feet slapped metal steps, every contact sharp pain. Wren glanced down. "Your feet—"

"Later," Mara said, and kept moving.

The stairwell opened into a wide upper gallery, catwalks crisscrossing the interior like a steel skeleton. Below, the elevator's cavernous belly yawned into darkness. Somewhere, machinery ticked softly. The place felt abandoned, yet alive. Jalen led them across another grating walkway toward a small room with a windowed door. Inside, dimly lit, were monitors and security feeds, stacked in a grid.

Mara's pulse jumped. "Cameras."

Jalen nodded. "Told you. High ground and eyes." He tried the door. Unlocked. They slipped into the room. The monitors glowed like a wall of surveillance, grain bays, loading docks, stairwells, exterior views of the elevator, and surrounding streets. A few angles showed the town's quiet, oblivious grid. One camera faced the ladder they'd climbed. Another faced the base door where the men had entered.

Mara leaned in, breath catching.

On the base-door feed, three figures were visible now, two men from the SUV and a third, broader, moving with a different kind of authority. The third man wore no coat, just a dark sweater, and held a tablet as if it were an extension of his hand. He looked up once, directly into the camera, as if he knew it was there and knew someone was watching.

Wren whispered, "That one… he looks like—"

"Like he does this for a living," Jalen finished.

The tablet man spoke to the others, and one of them nodded and started toward the interior stairwell. Toward them.

Mara's mouth went dry.

Jalen's gaze flicked across the monitors, mapping. "They're coming up the same stairwell we came down. They'll hit this level in—" He glanced at his watch. "—two minutes."

Wren's voice rose. "Then we leave! Where? The hospital? The police? Someone—"

Jalen shook his head once, hard. "Police won't help. Not because they're evil, but because they'll be told 'federal' and they'll step aside."

Wren added, "Same as the receptionist. Same as the hospital."

Mara nodded. "Then tell us what to do."

Jalen's eyes met hers, and in them Mara saw the weight of the decision he'd been carrying alone for a long time.

"We use the cameras.

Wren frowned. "To see them coming?"

"To show them," Jalen said. "To show everyone."

Mara stared. "Broadcast?"

Jalen nodded. "This elevator still ties into the co-op's office network. It's old, but it's connected. If we can get into the right interface, we can push a live stream."

Mara's pulse spiked. "You said not to connect—"

"I said don't connect from your house," Jalen snapped, then softened. "This is different. This is a controlled burn."

Wren stepped closer. "You want to go live from a grain elevator?"

"Yes, because once you say the word ELXON out loud with proof on screen, it's not just a rumor anymore."

Mara's mouth went dry. She looked at the monitors again, at the men climbing. At the tablet, a man who moved like he owned time. She imagined the story if she stayed quiet: she'd be erased. The image would be erased. Kofi would be warned. Wren would be frightened into silence. ELXON would keep selling its salvation rides and building its arks while the planet tore. But she also imagined the story if she spoke: panic. Stock markets crashing. People stampeding. Cities burning. Her stomach twisted.

Wren saw the hesitation on Mara's face and grabbed her arm. "Mom. Truth doesn't have to mean chaos." Mara blinked at her.

Wren's voice trembled, but her eyes were fierce. "You always taught me that people can handle hard things if you don't lie to them."

Mara took in a deep breath. "Wren…"

"People panic when they feel manipulated," Wren said. "When they're treated like animals. But if someone tells them the truth, with dignity, then they might surprise you."

Mara's eyes shone with tears, not from wind this time.

Jalen watched them, expression tight. "You don't have to do this," he said to Mara, quietly now. "I can."

Mara looked at him. "But they called for me. They're here because of me."

"They're here because you're credible. Because you're a scientist with clean hands and a normal life. I'm a conspiracy theory to them. You're a problem."

Mara's throat tightened. "I don't want—"

A sound echoed from the stairwell outside the control room. Footsteps. Close. The men were on their level.

Jalen moved fast. He grabbed a headset hanging on the wall and some old radio gear and shoved them toward Mara. "Decide," he said. "We have seconds, not minutes."

Mara stared at the headset as if it weighed a hundred pounds.

On a monitor, the tablet man stopped at the base of a stairwell, looked down, and spoke. The other man nodded and continued up. Coming for them.

Wren whispered, "Mom."

Mara's mind raced. If she broadcast now, she might save the truth—but sacrifice her daughter. Put Wren's face in the story. Paint a target on her forever. If she didn't broadcast, ELXON might bury everything. And her silence would become complicity. Moral dilemmas weren't dramatic speeches. They were split-second choices, tinged with blood. Mara took the headset, shaking with trembling hands.

Jalen slid into the chair at the console and started typing, fingers flying. "I can route the elevator cams to an outgoing stream," he muttered. "Old system… I can spoof the admin… come on…"

Wren stepped to the door and pressed her ear against it, listening. "Footsteps," she whispered. "Two. Maybe three."

Jalen didn't look up. "They'll try the door."

Mara's heart pounded. "Can you lock it?"

Jalen jabbed at a switch. A red light above the door blinked. "Mag lock engaged, but it won't hold forever."

Mara looked at the monitor showing the interior hallway outside. Two men appeared, moving briskly. They stopped at the control room door. One reached for the handle. It didn't open. He tried again. Then he leaned close to the door and spoke, voice muffled but audible through the thin metal.

"Dr. Keene," he said, calm as before. "We need you to step out."

Mara's skin went cold. The voice sounded different up close, smooth, professional, as if he'd practiced persuasion the way surgeons practiced cuts.

Jalen hissed, "Ignore him."

The man outside continued, voice still calm. "You have information you don't fully understand. You are in danger."

Mara's mouth went dry. *You are in danger.* Not a threat. A fact.

Wren's hands trembled at her sides. "Don't listen."

The man outside paused, then said something that made Mara's stomach clench. "Your daughter is with you."

Mara froze.

Wren turned toward her, eyes wide with horror. "How does he—?"

Jalen's face went hard. "Thermal," he muttered. "Or hospital cams. Or cell data. They tracked you."

The man outside spoke again, now gentler, like a teacher addressing a frightened child. "We don't want to involve her," he said. "But you did when you brought her. Open the door. We'll make this easy."

Mara's hands shook so hard the headset rattled.

Wren stepped close to Mara and whispered, "Mom, he's trying to make you feel like it's your fault."

Mara nodded, throat tight. "It is my fault."

Wren shook her head. "No. Their choices are theirs."

Jalen slammed the key. A small window popped up on the console screen: **LIVE OUTPUT READY.**

He looked at Mara. "If you're doing it, do it now."

Mara's mouth went numb. The man outside tried the handle again, harder. Then a new sound, metal scraping.

"They're prying," Wren whispered, panic rising.

Mara looked at the monitors, then at her daughter, then at Jalen. And suddenly, she knew what she had to do—because it wasn't just about saving herself or saving the truth. It was about how the truth entered the world.

She placed the headset on. "Jalen," she said, voice shaking. "Point the camera at me."

Jalen flicked a toggle. One monitor shifted to show the control room camera angle, grainy, slightly distorted. Mara's face appeared on screen, pale, eyes too wide.

Wren grabbed Mara's hand, squeezing hard. "I'm right here."

Mara took a breath that felt like swallowing glass.

Jalen hovered over the final button. "Once I push, it's out. We won't be able to pull it back."

Mara nodded. "Do it."

Jalen pressed **GO LIVE**. A counter appeared on screen: **STREAM ACTIVE.** For a heartbeat, nothing happened. Then a small notification flashed: **VIEWERS: 12** Then: **38** Then: **112.**

The door shuddered from something slamming into it from outside. Mara flinched but forced herself to stay facing the camera. "Hello," she said, and her voice sounded strange in the small room, amplified by the headset, recorded by the camera, carried out into whatever network Jalen had hijacked.

"Hello," she said again, steadier now. "My name is Dr. Mara Keene. I'm an atmospheric physicist."

The viewer count jumped: **1,004**

Mara's breath caught. She kept going. "I'm speaking from the grain elevator in—" She paused, realizing saying the town's name would put a target on every person here. "—in central Kansas."

She swallowed. "I'm doing this because something is happening to Earth's atmosphere, and people in positions of power have chosen not to tell you."

The viewer count surged: **8,317**

Wren stared at the number, hand over her mouth. Behind them, the door groaned under pressure.

Mara wanted to raise the folded printout, except she didn't have it. It was still in her microwave at home. Panic flashed. Then she remembered: the USB drives. One was with Wren. One was in Jalen's hand.

"Jalen," Mara whispered quickly out of the corner of her mouth, without breaking her forward posture. "Put the image on screen."

Jalen nodded and slammed keys, pulling up the file. The monitor beside the camera view shifted to show Earth from orbit. The thin blue halo. And the wound. Mara heard Wren inhale sharply like she'd been punched.

Mara looked into the camera again. "This image," Mara said, "shows an atmospheric density anomaly, an area where the protective layer around our planet is thinning at an accelerating rate."

Viewer count: **21,004**

The door outside boomed again harder.

Mara's voice shook but held. "There is a private continuity program called ELXON. They are preparing evacuation for a small, selected group, while the rest of the population is being kept in the dark."

A furious banging. The lock light above the door flickered.

Mara continued anyway, because the words were finally out, and there was no putting them back. "If you are seeing auroras where you've never seen them before. If you're seeing unusual sunburns, UV warnings, communications glitches— these may not be random."

The viewer count leaped again: **53,889**

Jalen's eyes widened. "It's spreading," he whispered.

Wren's voice trembled. "Mom, people are listening."

Mara forced a small nod. "I don't know how long we have," Mara said, and her throat tightened around the truth. "But I know this: you deserve to know. And you deserve to be treated like human beings, capable of dignity, capable of kindness, capable of facing reality together."

The lock light blinked red… then went dark. Jalen's head snapped up. "Lock's failing." The door handle turned violently.

Mara kept her eyes on the camera. "There are people who will tell you to panic," voice firm now. "Don't give them that power. Gather your families. Help your neighbors. Prepare in practical ways, water, medicine, warmth, but most importantly, prepare in moral ways. Choose each other."

The door buckled inward a fraction. A voice roared from the other side, no longer polite. "TURN IT OFF!"

Mara flinched but didn't stop. "And to the people hunting us right now," Mara's voice suddenly cold, "I want you to understand something."

Viewer count: **84,112**

"We are not alone in knowing this. And we are not alone in sharing it." She glanced at Wren briefly, just long enough to see her daughter's face: frightened, yes, but lit with something else too. Resolve.

Mara faced the camera again. "This is a beginning. Not an end. Don't let anyone sell you salvation."

The door burst open. Metal screamed. The bolt snapped. The door swung inward, hard. Two men surged into the room.

Jalen moved like a blade. He shoved Mara sideways behind the console and slammed the jammer switch off and on, flooding the room with a harsh hum. One of the men flinched, hand to his ear. Wren screamed. Mara grabbed her daughter's wrist and yanked her down.

The camera kept rolling. On screen, the viewers saw chaos: the control room shuddering, the feed jarring, shadows moving, Jalen's body blocking the lens for a moment.

One of the men lunged for the console. Jalen punched him, fast, brutal, efficient. The second man grabbed for Mara. Mara grabbed a metal clipboard and swung hard, connecting the man's shoulder with a sharp crack. He grunted, staggered.

Wren crawled toward the console, eyes wild. "Mom, what do I do?"

Mara's brain snapped into clarity. "The drive!" she shouted. "Your pocket!" Wren fumbled, pulled out the USB drive. Mara pointed. "Put it in your shoe. Now!"

Wren blinked. "What?"

"DO IT!"

Wren shoved her foot into her shoe awkwardly, jamming the USB drive down into the toe space like contraband.

Jalen shouted, "Mara! The stairs…move!"

Mara grabbed Wren and ran toward the open door. The men were recovering quickly. They were angry now and fully unleashed.

As Mara and Wren burst out into the upper gallery, the wind and height hit them again like punishment. They sprinted along the interior catwalk, metal clanging under their feet. Behind them, Jalen slammed the control room door shut and threw his weight against it, buying them seconds.

Mara's headset, still on her head, crackled with the sound of the stream still active. She could hear her own breathing amplified. The truth was out. But now they had to survive long enough to keep it out. They reached the far stairwell, a vertical drop into darkness.

Wren grabbed the rail, trembling. "Where does this go?"

"Down," Mara said. "To ground."

"And then?" Wren cried.

Mara looked down into the elevator's hollow depths and felt the impossible weight of the next question. Because "down" was easy. "After" was the whole book.

Above them, the control room door exploded open again, echoing across metal and concrete like a gong. Jalen's voice rang out, sharp and urgent. "GO!"

Mara pulled Wren into the stairwell, and as they descended into the dark, the livestream still running, the viewer count still climbing somewhere beyond their reach, she realized something that made her chest ache with terror and hope at the same time.

The world now knows about ELXON. And the world, if it chose to, might not accept them leaving quietly.

CHAPTER 6 — The Thousand Small Leaks

The stairwell swallowed them.

It wasn't a clean descent. There was no graceful spiral into safety. It was a steep metal spine bolted inside the elevator, vibrating with every footstep, every echo, every slammed door above. Mara's bare feet skidded on the steps. Pain shot up her legs like an electric shock.

"Slow down," Wren gasped, gripping the rail so hard her knuckles went white.

"We don't have slow," Mara hissed and kept pulling her daughter downward.

Above them, the upper gallery rang with noise, boots on metal, voices sharp and urgent, the reverberation of a hunt happening inside a hollow tower. Each sound amplified, multiplied, made monstrous by the elevator's cavernous belly.

Mara's headset still pressed against her scalp, a ridiculous detail in the middle of collapse. Static crackled in her ear. Then, faint, layered voices. Not the men chasing them. Not Wren. Other voices. Distant. Public.

"—is this real—" "—that's Earth—" "—ELXON—what's ELXON—" "—share it now—" "—don't let them delete—"

Mara's throat tightened. The stream was still alive. The world was watching. People in pajamas. People on night shifts. People awake for reasons unrelated to the end of the world.

They were seeing the wound. Hearing her voice. Passing the truth hand to hand like fire.

Below, a door with a green EXIT sign appeared—**LEVEL 3: GALLERY ACCESS**—and Mara yanked it open. Cold air hit them again. The space beyond was a wide interior platform lined with pipes, grain chutes, and rusted warning signs.

Wren's chest rose and fell like she'd run miles. "Mom, my shoe—" Wren blurted, then shoved the words back down as if she suddenly understood what "quiet" really meant.

Mara nodded, breathless. "Good. Keep it there."

They moved across the platform, hugging the wall, searching for another stairwell, another way down. The elevator's interior felt like a maze never meant for human panic. A clanging sound above made Mara flinch. Jalen. She pictured him fighting at the top—blocking, buying time, doing what he'd always done: absorbing the danger so others could move.

Guilt surged in Mara's chest so violently it felt like nausea.

"We can't leave him," Wren whispered, reading Mara's face.

Mara fought to keep her voice steady. "He told us to go."

"That doesn't mean—"

"It means he knew what this cost," Mara snapped softly. Then, quieter: "And he chose it anyway."

They reached another door—**MAINTENANCE STAIR**—and Mara tried the handle. Locked. Mara cursed under her breath, then tried again with more force, as if anger could open metal. Nothing.

Wren's eyes darted around the platform. "There," pointing. A ladder descended into a darker shaft, narrower than the one they'd climbed. A service ladder, vertical and unforgiving, disappearing down into the elevator's guts.

Mara rushed to it and looked over the edge. The shaft dropped into blackness. She couldn't see the bottom.

Wren's voice shook. "You want us to go down *that?*"

Mara listened. Boot steps above, closer now. Voices tightening like a noose. "We don't have choices," Mara said.

Wren stared at the ladder like it was a dare from God. Then she nodded, jaw clenched. "I go first?" Wren asked, voice thin.

Mara shook her head. "I go first. You follow."

Wren opened her mouth to argue, then shut it again and gripped the ladder.

Mara swung onto it and began to climb down, hands cold on metal. Her muscles burned. Her feet screamed. She forced herself to move anyway. Halfway down, her headset crackled again. A new voice, clearer than the layered public noise, sharp, familiar.

"Mara," it said. Kofi.

Mara nearly slipped. "Kofi?" she whispered, breathless.

"Don't answer loud," Kofi hissed in her ear. "I'm on the stream. I'm watching you. Dear God, Mara—"

Her chest tightened. "It's still live?"

"Yes," Kofi said. "And it's everywhere now. People are screen-recording. Mirroring. Posting. There are already copies on servers outside the country. They can't pull it back."

Mara's throat closed with relief so intense it almost hurt. Wren's boots clanged above her as she descended, trembling. "Kofi, they're chasing us. We're inside the grain elevator. We're going down a service ladder—"

"I know," Kofi said. "Listen. Your face is on the stream. Wren's face, too."

Mara flinched.

"I'm sorry," Kofi added quickly, as if he could soften the blade. "I'm not saying it to blame you. I'm saying it because you need to move like the world already knows you. You're not a private person anymore."

More concerned now, Mara asked, "what's happening out there?"

Kofi's voice sped up, adrenaline making him crisp. "News stations picked it up within minutes. ELXON accounts are already posting 'misinformation' statements. There's a spin, some 'charity foundation' nonsense. But the image, Mara, the image speaks louder than any press release."

Mara blinked into the dark shaft. "Are people panicking?"

A pause, just long enough to feel heavy. "Not like they expected," Kofi said quietly. "It's… weird. People are shocked.

Angry. But it's more like grief than riot. They're asking questions. They're calling representatives. They're sharing practical prep tips. There are pastors on livestreams telling people to stay calm. There are nurses making lists of meds to refill. It's… organized."

Mara's eyes stung. Wren's earlier words echoed: *Truth doesn't have to mean chaos.*

Kofi's voice cracked slightly. "Mara, you were right. People can handle hard things if you don't lie to them."

Mara swallowed past the tightness in her throat. "We have to get out."

"Yes," Kofi said. "And you need somewhere to go. Somewhere with allies."

Mara reached the bottom of the ladder and felt her feet hit concrete. She nearly collapsed with relief. She looked around. The shaft opened into a narrow service corridor that smelled of damp concrete and grain dust. A low light flickered overhead. At the far end, a door with an old push bar. Mara put a hand on it, hesitating. Footsteps above, closer. Voices, harder now, not polite.

"They're on the level below us," Wren whispered, landing behind Mara, her breath loud in the tight space.

Mara pressed her finger to her lips. In her ear, Kofi said urgently, "Mara—someone just contacted me."

Mara's stomach clenched. "Who?"

"A man named Silas Crane. He's a billionaire, apparently, but he's not ELXON. He says he's been trying to warn people quietly. He says he can get you out."

Mara froze. Silas Crane. The name tickled something in her memory, an article, maybe, about a reclusive philanthropist who funded climate research and refused to appear on camera. The kind of rich person people joked about because he didn't act like a cartoon.

"How did he contact you?" Mara whispered.

"He reached out after your stream," Kofi said. "He already knew who you were. He's offering a safe route and a place to regroup. Mara, he says he can prove he's real."

"Prove how?" Mara's voice trembled.

"He just sent me a code phrase. He says Jalen will recognize it."

Mara's heart stuttered. "Jalen—"

"We can't wait for Jalen," Wren whispered, voice breaking.

Mara nodded, pain flaring behind her ribs. "Kofi, tell me the phrase."

Kofi inhaled. "Okay. He says: **Blue lens, black seam.**"

Mara's breath caught. Jalen had used the word *lens*. He had described the atmosphere as a blue lens. And the wound as a seam unraveling. That wasn't a phrase you guessed. That was a phrase you earned. Mara pressed her hand to the door bar. "Kofi," she whispered, "where is he?"

"He says he has a driver two blocks from the elevator. A gray Suburban. Kansas plate. He says they'll be in an alley behind the co-op offices on Maple. He says they'll wait seven minutes and then leave. He says the driver's name is Nadine."

Mara's head snapped up. Nadine. Jalen had mentioned an insider in the outline of her fear, an ELXON leak.

Wren's eyes widened as if she'd heard the same warning in the air. "Nadine… like the woman you talked about?"

Mara nodded slowly.

Kofi continued, "Mara, there's more. People online are calling you 'the Kansas scientist.' They're creating hashtags. It's spreading faster than any takedown. But ELXON is already pushing legal threats and claiming it's deep-fake orbital imagery."

Mara's mouth went dry. "Of course."

"So, you need to disappear," Kofi said. "Not forever, just long enough to build your chain. A thousand small leaks, remember? You started it. Now we keep it moving."

Above them, a door slammed. A voice echoed down the shaft, tight, angry.

"Down here!"

Wren flinched. Mara's pulse spiked. "They're coming," Wren whispered.

Mara pushed the service door open. Cold air hit her face. They stepped out into the base level of the elevator, an industrial space with conveyors and bins and the smell of old grain. The main lights were off, but emergency lamps cast dim pools of visibility. The open loading bay yawned ahead like a mouth.

Mara scanned left. A stairwell. Right. A corridor leading toward the exterior. She chose right. They ran, footsteps muted by dust and grit.

Behind them, boots pounded. Flashlights swung, slicing through shadows. "STOP!" someone shouted.

Wren's breath hitched. "Mom—"

"Don't stop," Mara said, voice fierce. They burst through a side door and into the open night. The wind slapped them. The town lay quiet, unaware that history was sprinting through its alleys in the early morning hours.

Mara grabbed Wren's hand and pulled her between buildings, away from the main street. Her feet screamed with every step, but fear was stronger than pain. Behind them, the elevator door banged open again. Light poured out. Voices spilled into the alley.

Mara hid behind a dumpster, holding Wren against the wall. They listened as they caught their breath. The men didn't run. They moved methodically, scanning, as if they had time. And maybe they did. Because they weren't chasing just two women anymore, they were chasing a story.

In Mara's ear, Kofi whispered urgently, "Maple Street. Two blocks. Seven minutes." Mara nodded, even though he couldn't see it. She waited until the flashlight beams swept past, then pulled Wren forward and sprinted again, down Maple, past a closed florist with frost on its windows, past a row of dark offices with a single security light buzzing like an insect.

The co-op offices appeared: a flat building with a faded sign, and a narrow alley behind it. Mara skidded into the alley and froze.

A gray Suburban sat there, engine running, headlights off. The driver's window was down. A woman leaned slightly out, watching them approach with an intensity that wasn't fear so much as focus. She wasn't dressed like a chauffeur. She wore a dark hoodie and a knit cap, and her eyes were sharp. "Mara Keene?" she called softly.

Mara didn't answer. She couldn't, not without proof. The woman lifted one hand, palm out, and said, very clearly: "Blue lens. Black seam."

Mara's knees almost buckled with relief. Wren's breath released in a shaky sob. Mara grabbed the rear door handle and yanked it open. "Get in," she whispered. Wren climbed in first. Mara swung in after her.

The driver looked at Mara in the rearview mirror. "I'm Nadine," she said. "We have about ninety seconds before they realize you didn't stay inside the elevator."

Mara's voice trembled. "Who sent you?"

"Silas Crane."

The name felt like a door opening.

Nadine shifted into drive. As the Suburban rolled out of the alley, Mara looked back through the rear window. At the end of Maple Street, a dark SUV turned the corner slowly, headlights sweeping. Searching.

Nadine didn't speed. She didn't panic. She drove like a person who knew panic got you killed. She took a series of turns, right, left, right again, like she'd memorized the town as a map of escape routes rather than streets.

Wren sat rigid beside Mara, hand pressed to her shoe where the USB drive hid.

Mara's headset crackled one last time. Kofi's voice, urgent and soft: "Mara, are you in?"

Mara answered. "Yes."

"Good," Kofi said, and Mara could hear the tremor of relief in him. "Listen, don't trust anyone easily. But if Silas is real, he might be the counterweight you need."

Mara stared out the side window as dark storefronts slid past. "What about Jalen?" she whispered.

There was a pause long enough to feel like a prayer. "I don't know," Kofi said softly. "But I'm watching feeds. If he gets out, we'll know. He's too stubborn to die quietly."

Mara closed her eyes, pain and hope tangling.

The Suburban crossed the edge of town and headed into open road, the fields opening up around them like a black sea.

Nadine spoke again, eyes on the road. "Silas has a safe house," she said. "Not a bunker. Not a palace. A place with people, supplies, and communications, off-grid. He's building something."

"What?" Wren asked, voice thin.

Nadine glanced at her in the mirror. "A calm network. The opposite of ELXON's panic."

Mara's throat tightened. "Why?"

Nadine's face hardened with something like disgust. "Because ELXON thinks humanity is a resource to harvest and people are inventory," she said. "Silas thinks they are people." Silence filled the car for a moment, only road noise and breathing and the faint hum of the engine.

Then Wren whispered, "Are we safe?"

Nadine didn't lie. She didn't offer comfort she couldn't prove. "No," she said. "But you're moving. And right now, moving is the only kind of safety we get."

Mara looked out at the dark horizon, where the faintest green smear still lingered like the sky couldn't forget what it had shown. She thought of the viewers climbing into the tens of thousands, the truth spreading like sparks. A thousand small leaks were no longer a phrase. It was a strategy.

ELXON had wanted to do it quietly. Now the whole world was beginning to shout. And somewhere behind them, inside the grain elevator's hollow belly, a man named Jalen Royce was either escaping… or being erased.

Mara pressed her hand over the USB drive in Wren's shoe through the fabric, as if she could feel the truth through rubber and plastic. "Hold on," Mara whispered, not to Wren, not to Nadine, not even to herself. To the world. To the thin blue lens. To the torn seam.

And as the Suburban disappeared into the Kansas night, Mara understood something that made her heart ache with fierce clarity: The story was no longer about who got off the planet.

It was about who stayed human while the sky came apart.

CHAPTER 7 — The Man Who Refused

They drove for forty minutes without seeing another car.

Kansas at night had always been a kind of emptiness Mara loved: wide fields, long roads, and the sense that the world had room to breathe. But tonight, the emptiness felt like an ocean that could swallow you without effort.

Nadine kept the headlights low and the speed steady. No reckless swerves. No dramatic acceleration. Just quiet competence.

Wren sat rigidly beside Mara in the back seat, one hand pressed to the toe of her shoe as if the USB drive might try to escape on its own. Her other hand was wrapped around Mara's wrist, a grip that said *don't leave me* without using words.

Mara still wore the headset, though its crackle had faded into silence. She'd turned it off. She couldn't risk another signal. The world could watch the replay; she didn't need to stay live.

Her mind wouldn't stop replaying the door buckling, the calm voice turning cruel, the viewer count climbing like a heartbeat.

And Jalen. Every time she pictured him, she saw him half-lit in the elevator's control room, moving like a ninja, choosing danger with the calm of someone who'd already decided his life mattered less than the truth.

Mara stared out the window at fields slipping by and tried not to let guilt eat her alive.

Mara finally couldn't take it. "Nadine," she said softly.

Nadine didn't look back. "Yeah."

"Why are you helping us?" Mara asked.

A beat of silence. Then Nadine said, "Because I helped build the machine that's trying to kill you."

Wren's head snapped up. "You're ELXON."

Nadine's jaw tightened. "I was."

Mara leaned forward. "Doing what?"

"Security architecture," Nadine said. "Information containment. Tracking. Takedowns. The whole protect the public from panic thing."

Mara's stomach turned.

Wren's voice shook with anger now. "So, you're the reason bloggers disappeared."

Nadine's hands tightened on the wheel. "I didn't disappear anyone."

"That's not an answer," Wren snapped.

Nadine exhaled through her nose, controlled. "I flagged threats. I built systems that route alerts to people with badges and budgets. And then those people did what they do."

Wren's eyes flashed. "So, you pushed the button and told yourself you didn't pull the trigger."

Mara watched Nadine's shoulders stiffen. The words landed. Good. They should. Nadine's voice became quieter. "Yes."

Silence settled again, heavier than before. After a moment, Nadine said, "Silas called it 'moral outsourcing.' He was right."

Mara blinked. "You know him personally?"

Nadine nodded once. "He was on a list."

Wren's grip on Mara's wrist tightened. "A passenger list."

Nadine didn't correct her. Mara's throat went dry. "And he refused."

"Yes," Nadine said. "He refused loudly. They hated him for it."

Wren stared out the window, furious and shaken. "How can anyone refuse and still be alive?"

Nadine's mouth twitched, almost a smile, but bitter. "Because Silas Crane isn't just rich. He's… inconvenient. He has files. Leverage. Donations in the right places. Friends in the right rooms. And he doesn't bluff."

Mara felt her chest tighten. "So, he's protected."

"Protected," Nadine said, "but not safe."

The road curved, and the fields began to change. Fewer farmhouses. More trees. A dark line of cottonwoods and evergreens closes in, hiding the land. Nadine turned onto a gravel road, then onto another road that looked barely used, rutted, narrow, the kind of road you took only if you already knew where it went. Finally, a gate appeared between two posts. Not fancy or even electric. Just metal and chain.

Nadine stopped, rolled down the window, and flashed a small light three times. The gate opened. Manually. Quietly. By a figure who stepped out of the darkness and waved them through.

Nadine drove in, and the figure closed the gate behind them with a slow roll and a soft latch. She turned off the headlights and continued with the dim guidance of moonlight and the faint glow of small path lights set low to the ground. A modest, two-story farmhouse appeared ahead. No mansion. No fortress. Lights warm in the windows. Smoke curling from a chimney.

The sight hit Mara like a punch of normalcy. It was comforting.

Nadine parked behind a stand of trees, hidden from the road. "We walk," she said, already unbuckling. "No car noise right up to the house."

Wren glanced at Mara. "Are we really doing this?"

Mara's voice was tight. "We already did."

They climbed out into the cold air. Mara's feet screamed again on the gravel. She hissed and fought not to limp. Wren looked down at Mara's bare feet and swore softly. "Jesus, Mom."

Mara shook her head. "Later."

They walked along a narrow path through trees. The night felt different here, less open, more enclosed. The wind was softer. The silence was deeper. At the front porch, the door opened before they could knock. A man stood there with a calm face and eyes that looked like they'd seen too much.

Silas Crane. He wasn't young, but he wasn't elderly either, late fifties, maybe early sixties. He wore a plain sweater and jeans, and his hair was silver at the temples. No designer anything. No billionaire costume.

He looked at Mara like he'd been waiting for her for a long time. "Dr. Keene," he said, and his voice was warm but precise. "Thank you for not dying."

Mara blinked. "That's… one way to greet someone."

Silas's mouth curved faintly. "I find sincerity is underrated."

His gaze moved to Wren. "And you must be Wren."

Wren stiffened. "You know my name?"

Silas didn't flinch. "Because your mother's stream is now being replayed on six different networks and at least four hundred thousand personal devices, and people are doing what they always do—pausing, zooming, finding faces."

Wren's cheeks paled.

Silas stepped aside. "Come in. You're freezing. And your mother is bleeding." Mara looked down and realized her hands were still scraped raw, and her feet… her feet were a disaster.

Inside, the house smelled like coffee and woodsmoke. Someone made soup. The scent of onions and herbs rose in the air like a blessing.

The living room was occupied, not crowded, but active. A handful of people moved quietly: a woman in scrubs checking a supply bin, a man setting up a laptop on a dining table, another adjusting a radio antenna by a window. Not servants. A team. They looked up as Mara and Wren entered. Eyes sharp. Bodies ready.

Silas closed the door and turned to them. "No phones," he said gently. "Not yet. We'll give you clean devices. We're not being dramatic. We're being alive."

Wren swallowed. "Who are these people?"

"My people," Silas said. "The ones who refuse to pretend."

Nadine stepped inside behind them, shutting the door and locking it with a practiced motion. She looked… different here. Less guarded. Still tense but not braced for immediate attack. Silas's gaze met Nadine's, and something unspoken passed between them: recognition, respect, shared exhaustion. "Welcome back," Silas said to her.

Nadine's jaw tightened. "I'm not back. I'm just… here."

Silas nodded. "That's enough." He turned to Mara. "I owe you an apology," Silas said.

Mara frowned. "For what?"

"For not reaching you earlier," Silas said. "I knew ELXON would eventually need a credible scientist to silence or recruit. I didn't know they'd move this fast."

Mara's throat went tight. "You knew about ELXON."

Silas nodded. "Yes."

Wren's voice rose, sharp. "Then why didn't you tell people?"

Silas looked at Wren with calm steadiness. "Because telling people without proof gets you labeled unstable. Telling people with proof gets you killed. I've been trying to build a way to tell the truth and keep the truth-tellers alive."

Wren's anger didn't disappear, but it shifted, less accusatory, more desperate. "So, you planned to wait until my mom almost died in a grain elevator?"

Silas's face softened. "No. I planned to create a chain. Your mother did something braver than my plan. She lit the match."

Mara inhaled deeply. "What do you know?"

Silas gestured toward the dining table where screens glowed softly—maps, feeds, orbit diagrams.

"Come," he said. "Before the world catches up with you."

They moved to the table. A young man with a beard slid a chair out for Mara without speaking. A woman in scrubs handed Mara a blanket. Another person crouched at Mara's feet and gently wrapped her toes in warm cloth as if it were a sacred act. Mara almost cried. The kindness felt too big for the terror.

Silas sat across from her. He tapped the laptop and pulled up a document that looked like a spreadsheet: names, tiers, codes. Not all readable at once, but enough to make Mara's stomach turn. "This," Silas said, "is an early ELXON passenger framework."

Wren leaned in, eyes scanning. There were categories:

1: GOVERNANCE TIER

2: CAPITAL TIER

3: TECHNICAL ESSENTIALS TIER

4: CULTURAL STABILIZERS

Wren frowned. "Cultural stabilizers?"

Silas's mouth tightened. "Celebrities. Influencers. People whose faces can sell a new myth to frightened passengers in a metal tube."

Mara's hands clenched. "So, Anika…"

Silas nodded. "A face. A bridge. A brand."

Wren looked sick. "And the 'charity rides'?"

Silas clicked on another file. A glossy brochure appeared. The ELXON logo. A slogan: **HUMANITY'S NEXT HORIZON.** Then, in smaller text buried in "terms," language about *screening, medical clearance, behavioral assessment,* and *confidentiality agreements.*

Wren whispered, "It's a filter."

Silas met her gaze. "Yes."

Mara looked down. "How many?"

Silas leaned back slightly, eyes distant, as if the number had weight. "In the current plan," he said, "they aim for roughly two thousand souls on passenger craft. That's their 'continuity' number—enough to seed a colony and preserve power structures. The support launches are far larger, including cargo, fuel, and infrastructure. But human seats? About two thousand."

Mara's stomach turned. Wren's voice was small. "Two thousand out of... eight billion."

Silas nodded. "Yes."

Mara stared at the tiers and felt her chest tighten with anger so sharp it was almost clean. "And you," Mara said, voice trembling, "you were offered a seat."

Silas nodded once.

Wren leaned forward, eyes hard. "Why did you refuse?"

Silas didn't answer immediately. He looked around the room at his people—at the woman in scrubs, at the radio antenna, at Nadine, at the quiet teamwork of ordinary kindness. Then he looked back at Mara. "Because I couldn't live with myself," he said simply.

Wren scoffed, but it came out more like a sob.

Silas continued, voice steady. "They framed it as self-preservation. As duty. As 'someone must carry humanity forward.' And I thought... if your version of humanity requires abandoning most humans, what exactly are you carrying forward?"

Tears stung Mara's eyes. Silas's gaze held hers. "I'm not interested in saving a species," he said. "I'm interested in saving a soul."

Silence settled over the table like snow. Then Nadine spoke, voice low. "That's why they hate you."

Silas nodded. "Yes."

Mara forced herself to ask the question that mattered. "When," she said. "When do they launch?"

Silas clicked to another map. Dots appeared across the globe: coastal launch facilities, inland spaceports, converted military runways, ocean platforms. "Staggered. They'll begin when the atmospheric disintegration becomes undeniable from high-altitude flight, when commercial pilots start seeing the 'thin line' even without instruments. They've built a trigger into their plan."

Mara's throat went tight. "And what's the trigger?"

Silas's voice was quiet. "When they believe people are too frightened to stop them. And too shocked to organize."

Mara glanced at the screen showing the replay of her broadcast, comment sections moving like rivers, people sharing, arguing, praying, preparing.

"Then I may have ruined their timing," Mara whispered.

Silas's eyes glinted with something like fierce approval. "You did. That's why you're here. And that's why they'll come."

Wren's face tightened. "Let them come."

Silas shook his head once. "Not like that. We don't meet force with chaos. We meet it with strategy."

He leaned forward, voice turning practical. "We build the calm network publicly now," Silas said. "We feed people verified information. We coordinate supplies. We teach communities how to stay steady. And we continue the thousand small leaks, data, images, whistleblowers, until ELXON can't hide behind polished smiles."

Fear rising, Mara asked, "and the atmosphere?"

Silas's eyes softened slightly. "That's the part I can't fix," he said. Then, quietly, "But there's something else you need to know."

Mara's pulse jumped. "What?"

Silas glanced at Nadine. Nadine hesitated, then pulled a small drive from her pocket and slid it across the table. "This," Nadine said, "is from inside ELXON."

Mara's breath caught. "What is it?"

Nadine's eyes flicked toward the window as if she expected it to shatter. "It's their internal orbital feed," she said. "Not the cleaned public one. The real one."

Mara's hands shook as she reached for it. "And?"

Nadine's voice dropped to a near whisper. "And there are… anomalies," she said. "Objects in orbit that aren't ours. Not satellites. Not debris. They move wrong."

Wren stared. "You mean—"

Silas cut in, calm but firm. "We don't leap to aliens. We stay grounded in evidence."

Mara's heart hammered. "Show me."

Silas nodded to the bearded young man at the laptop. "Pull it up."

The file loaded slowly, then resolved into a sequence of orbital images, Earth's curve, the blue rim, and the wound. In the darkness beyond, faint points of light. At first, they looked like stars. Then one of them moved. Not in a smooth orbit arc. Not like a satellite. It shifted, paused, then changed direction. A small, precise angle as if something had decided to look at Earth from a different perspective.

Mara's breath caught. Silas watched her carefully. "They've been there for weeks," he said quietly. "ELXON has seen them. They haven't told the public. They haven't even told most of their own."

Wren whispered, "Why would they hide that?"

Nadine's face hardened. "Because if the public thinks someone else is out there, someone with more power than them, ELXON loses its god status."

Mara stared at the moving light. Her skin prickled. For the first time since the aurora, Mara felt something that wasn't just fear or anger. It was... attention. The sensation of being observed.

Silas's voice was calm, but the words landed heavily. "Dr. Keene, I think Earth's wound isn't the only secret."

Mara fought to keep her voice steady, eyes locked on the screen. "Then we're not just fighting ELXON," she whispered.

Silas nodded once. "No," he said. "We're fighting the lie that we're alone, and that only the powerful get to decide what happens next."

CHAPTER 8 — The Calm Network

The house didn't feel like a bunker.

That was the first thing Mara noticed once the immediate adrenaline drained enough for her body to register the room again. Bunkers were cold, sealed, and built around fear. This place was… human. There were blankets draped over chairs, a stack of board games on a shelf, and a mismatched set of mugs beside a kettle. It felt like a home that had decided to become a headquarters, not the other way around.

Silas Crane stood at the dining table with his hands braced on either side of the laptop, studying the orbit feed like it was a wound he didn't know how to bandage. Nadine hovered near the window, scanning the dark outside with the reflexes of someone who had lived too long inside systems meant to hunt.

Wren sat on the couch with Mara's feet in her lap, wrapping the warm cloth more carefully now. She didn't look up much. Anger still lived behind her eyes, but it had shifted into focus.

Mara's hands were steady again. That scared her more than the shaking. Steady hands meant her brain had begun to adapt to the idea that the world could end.

Silas looked up. "Okay," he said, voice practical. "We do three things right now." He held up one finger. "First: we keep you alive." A second finger. "Second: we stabilize the message." A third. "Third: we build redundancy."

Mara agreed. "Redundancy is how we beat takedowns."

Silas nodded. "Exactly." He turned to the people around the room, not assistants, not guards, but ordinary professionals with extraordinary calm.

"Jaya," he said to the woman in scrubs, "medical check. Feet, hands, hypothermia risk." Jaya nodded and crossed the room with a small bag that looked like it had been packed by someone who thought in outcomes. She knelt in front of Mara and gently unwrapped the cloth Wren had tied.

Mara's toes were pale and angry, scratched and bruised. Jaya clicked her tongue softly. "You ran barefoot across Kansas in December?"

Mara managed a weak smile. "Wouldn't recommend."

Jaya glanced up, eyes kind but firm. "I'm going to recommend you never do that again."

Silas continued, assigning tasks like a conductor. "Eli," he said to the bearded young man, "capture the stream from every available mirror. Save it offline. Burn it to physical media. Make copies we can hand people."

Eli nodded. "Already running."

"Mark," Silas said to the man by the radio antenna, "get me a clean line to the outside network. Ham, shortwave, anything that doesn't rely on commercial infrastructure."

Mark lifted two fingers in acknowledgment. "On it."

Silas looked at Nadine. "You and I will prepare."

Nadine's expression tightened. "For what?"

Silas's voice dropped. "For the next wave. They'll come for her credibility first."

Mara's stomach tightened. "How?"

Silas's gaze held hers. "Smear," he said. "Deep-fake accusations. Mental health narratives. Attempts to frame you as unstable, political, religious, and profit-driven. Anything to make the public dismiss you before they must engage the evidence."

Mara's throat went dry. "They'll say I'm lying."

"They'll say you're wrong," Silas corrected. "Then they'll say you're dangerous. Those are different tools."

Wren's head snapped up. "Can they do that? Just, just decide my mom is crazy, and people believe it?"

Silas's expression softened slightly. "Not everyone," he said. "But enough to slow the spread. Enough to fracture the response."

Nadine spoke, voice quiet and sharp. "ELXON doesn't need everyone to doubt. They only need *enough* doubt that people hesitate."

Mara stared at the screen showing her own face mid-broadcast, eyes wide, hair blown, the image grainy but undeniable. "I didn't say anything political," Mara whispered, almost pleading.

Nadine gave her a look that held no comfort. "They'll make it political. They always do. Politics is the fastest way to turn truth into a team sport."

Silas raised a hand, calming the room. "We don't fight their narrative with anger," he said. "We fight it with clarity. Dr. Keene, you're going to record a second message."

Mara blinked. "Another broadcast?"

Silas nodded. "Short. Calm. Practical. You give people something to do besides panic. You give them a checklist, not a prophecy."

Wren's eyes filled with something like pride and fear. "Like emergency prep."

"Exactly," Silas said. "And you also say something else."

Mara's stomach clenched. "What?"

"You tell the truth about the moral dilemma. You tell them ELXON exists, yes, but you also tell them people are refusing it."

Wren's voice hardened. "They don't get to rewrite the world as 'only the rich survive.'"

Silas nodded. "And we don't allow it. We elevate the human response."

Mara took a breath. "Okay."

Silas gestured toward a small side room off the living area, an office with a desk, a lamp, and a camera tripod already set up.

Eli spoke without looking up from his laptop. "Lighting's ready. Audio is clean. We'll record to three devices."

Mara stood carefully, wincing as her feet protested. Jaya touched Mara's knee gently. "You can do this seated."

Mara exhaled. "Thank you." Wren helped her into the office. The small room felt oddly intimate, like a confessional. The camera lens looked too patient. Mara sat in a chair, blanket around her shoulders, hands folded in her lap.

Eli adjusted the tripod. "Whenever you're ready," he said softly.

Mara stared at the lens. In her head, she saw the viewer count climbing. She saw the door buckling. She saw men in dark coats, and the way their voices tried to sound kind until kindness wasn't useful anymore. She inhaled. And she spoke.

"My name is Dr. Mara Keene," she said calmly. "If you're seeing this, you've likely already heard part of what I said earlier today." She paused, steadying herself.

"I want to say something very clearly," Mara continued. "Truth does not need chaos. We can face hard realities together without turning on each other."

She felt Wren behind the camera, quiet and present. "First, here are practical steps you can take right now, without panic."

She lifted a sheet of paper Eli had placed beside her, a simple list. "Make sure you have water. Basic medications. A way to stay warm. Charge power banks. Check on elderly neighbors. Identify who in your community has medical training. Plan to communicate if cell networks are unstable."

Her voice remained even, controlled.

"Second," she continued, "do not rely on rumors. Rely on evidence. If you see unusual auroras, UV spikes, or communications disruptions, document them. Photograph them. Share them with timestamps. Elites don't own science."

A pause.

"Third," Mara said, voice tightening slightly, "there is a program calling itself ELXON. It is being marketed as philanthropy and inspiration. It is also being used as a selection mechanism for evacuation capacity. I cannot promise every claim you'll hear about ELXON is true. But I can promise this: the existence of a plan to preserve a chosen few is real." She steadied herself.

"And now the most important thing," Mara said quietly. "You are not helpless. You are not disposable. Don't let anyone convince you that your worth is determined by your bank account or your access to a seat."

She let the words land.

"People are refusing ELXON. People with resources. People with skills. People who have been offered an escape and have said no, because they choose humanity over self-preservation."

Mara's eyes stung, but she didn't let her voice wobble. "If you feel anger," she said, "turn it into action: organize, prepare, and protect each other. The opposite of ELXON is not revenge. It is community."

She held the camera's gaze. "I will continue to share verified information as long as I'm able. Please, stay calm. Stay kind. Stay awake."

Eli held up a hand. "Cut."

Mara exhaled hard, like she'd been holding her breath for years. Wren stepped around the camera and hugged her carefully, face pressed to Mara's shoulder. "I'm sorry," Wren whispered. "For being angry."

Mara wrapped her arms around her daughter, trembling slightly. "You get to be angry," she whispered back. "Just don't let it steal you."

They stayed like that for a moment until Silas's voice called from the other room. "We have a problem."

Mara and Wren stepped back into the living room. Silas stood at the dining table, now looking at a tablet, brows knit. Nadine stood beside him, jaw tight. Eli's fingers flew over the keyboard.

"What?" Mara asked.

Silas turned the tablet toward her. A news clip was playing. A sleek anchor in a studio, smile strained. Behind him, on a screen, was Mara's face from the livestream, frozen mid-sentence. Under it, a headline:

"VIRAL 'ATMOSPHERE HOLE' VIDEO DEBUNKED: EXPERTS SAY IT'S A DEEP-FAKE"

Mara's stomach dropped.

The anchor continued, voice smooth: "Several online accounts are circulating a dramatic video claiming Earth's atmosphere is disintegrating and accusing a so-called 'ELXON Foundation' of planning a mass evacuation. Atmospheric agencies have not confirmed these claims, and digital forensics experts suggest the orbital imagery may be manipulated."

Silas's voice was quiet. "They're moving fast."

Nadine snorted. "Told you."

The clip cut to a forensics expert in a crisp suit, with a confident tone. "Deep-fakes have become increasingly convincing," the expert said. "We urge the public not to share sensational content."

Wren's eyes flashed with fury. "That's—"

"A lie," Mara said, voice flat.

The anchor shifted. "In other news, a statement from the ELXON Foundation assures the public its 'Next Horizon' initiative is purely philanthropic, offering a limited number of civilian suborbital experiences to fund climate research…"

Sickened, "They're wrapping it in climate research," Mara whispered.

Silas nodded grimly. "Because it's the easiest cover. It sounds noble."

Eli spoke quickly. "We have mirrored copies on multiple servers already. But they're building a counter-story: Mara Keene is unstable, chasing attention, pushing misinformation."

Mara's throat tightened. "How do we stop that?"

Silas's eyes held hers. "We don't stop them," he said. "We outlast them."

Nadine tapped the tablet. "They're also doing the second part."

Mara frowned. "Second part?"

Nadine swiped to a screenshot: a social media thread, already viral, with captions like:

"She's a disgruntled former professor." "She was fired." "She's selling prep kits." "It's a doomsday cult." "Follow the money."

Wren's face went pale. "Mom…"

Feeling disgusted, Mara emphatically denied it. "None of that is true."

"That doesn't matter," Nadine said. "The point isn't truth. It's noise."

Silas leaned forward. "We counter with the opposite: documentation."

He looked at Eli. "Release the raw sensor logs. Time-stamped, unedited. Release a technical explanation from Kofi. Bring in independent atmospheric scientists who can verify the physics. Make it boring enough that only serious people will argue with it."

Eli nodded. "Already texting Kofi."

Mara's mind raced. "And the orbital image?"

Silas looked at Nadine. Nadine hesitated, then said, "We need another source."

Mara's stomach clenched. "Another satellite feed?"

Nadine nodded. "Independent. Public. Something ELXON can't fully control. Or we get someone inside."

Wren's eyes widened. "Inside ELXON?"

Silas's gaze sharpened. "Yes."

A radio crackled from the corner where Mark sat. He raised his head. "We've got chatter," he said. "Encrypted bursts. Someone's moving."

Silas stepped closer. "Who?"

Mark listened, adjusting dials. "Could be ELXON comms. Could be military. Hard to tell. But there's a phrase repeating."

Silas's face tightened. "What is it?"

Mark frowned, focusing. "Sounds like… 'Phase Gate.'"

Mara's stomach lurched. "Phase Gate? Like… a launch phase?"

Nadine went still. "No," she said quietly. "That's not their standard launch language."

Silas's eyes narrowed. "Where have you heard it?"

Nadine's voice was tight. "In a compartmented file once. A subproject." She swallowed. "A contingency."

Wren stared. "A contingency for what?"

Nadine didn't answer right away. Then she said, very softly, "For when the atmosphere can't be repaired."

Mara's throat tightened. "So, they've escalated."

Silas nodded once. "Yes."

Jaya, still kneeling near Mara's feet, looked up. "Then we assume they're coming here."

Silas's gaze turned hard. "They will."

Mara's voice shook. "Then why are we still in one house?"

Silas's expression softened, but only slightly. "We won't be," he said. "Not for long."

He looked at Mara. "You stop being one target. You become many."

Mara blinked. "What?"

Silas gestured to the team. "We split. Nodes. Safe houses. People carrying pieces of proof. We make it impossible to erase the truth by erasing you."

Wren's eyes widened. "You're sending her away?"

Silas looked at her with quiet respect. "I'm sending both of you into a network that can survive."

Mara's heart pounded. "And Jalen?" Mara asked, voice tight.

Silas's gaze flicked to Eli. Eli hesitated, then said, "We got a message. On a dead channel. It's… him."

Mara's chest seized. "Thank goodness"

Eli nodded. "He barely made it. He's injured. He says he escaped into the fields, same as you, but he's not clear. ELXON has his face now. They'll label him a terrorist."

Mara felt the room spin slightly.

Wren whispered, "Where is he?"

Eli swallowed. "He didn't say. He just said one thing."

Mara leaned forward, breath held.

Eli looked at Silas, then at Mara. "He said," Eli read from the message, "'tell Mara the lights in orbit are not ours. And they're moving closer.'"

Silence slammed into the room. Mara's skin prickled. On the laptop at the table, the orbital feed glowed faintly. The moving point of light hovered in the darkness beyond Earth, like an eye that had shifted its gaze toward them.

Silas's voice was quiet. "Then the timeline just changed again," he said.

Wren swallowed hard. "Better or worse?"

Silas looked at Mara with a steadiness that felt like a hand on her shoulder. "For truth," he said finally. "Truth changes everything."

CHAPTER 9 — The Inspiration Ride

Silas didn't call it an escape. He called it a **handoff**.

That word mattered because it kept the story from turning into a chase scene in Mara's mind. Chases were reactive. Handoffs were planned. Handoffs meant you were still choosing your moves.

He gathered everyone in the living room as dawn began to thin the darkness outside. The sky had gone from black to the bruised gray-blue of a winter morning, and for a moment it looked almost normal, like the world hadn't cracked open in the night. But the aurora's aftertaste still hung low on the horizon, pale green, like a secret refusing to leave fully.

Silas stood near the fireplace with a folded map in his hand. "We're splitting," he said, voice calm. "Not because we're afraid. Because networks survive what single points don't."

He pointed to the people around the room. "Node One: communications," he said, nodding to Mark and Eli. "Your job is to keep the story alive. Trusted journalists, scientists, mirrors, radios, and printed documents. If something goes down, you go around it."

Mark nodded. Eli's fingers were already moving, copying, compressing, encrypting.

"Node Two: medical and supplies," Silas continued, looking at Jaya and another woman named Rosa, who had quietly stocked a pantry all night. "Communities will need practical stability. You're going to work with clinics and churches. Quietly. No panic, just preparation."

Jaya's gaze was steady. "We've got lists ready."

Silas nodded, then turned toward Mara and Wren. "And Node Three," he said softly, "is measurement." Mara's throat tightened. "You," Silas said, meeting her eyes. "You keep gathering data. You keep producing evidence that doesn't rely on one orbital image. UV readings. Ozone proxies. Magnetometer curves. Anything that a thousand amateur scientists can independently confirm."

Wren blinked. "You want my mom to… keep doing science while the world collapses."

Silas's mouth twitched. "Yes. Because science is the one language ELXON can't fully edit if enough people speak it."

Nadine stepped forward. "And because the moment ELXON lies, data becomes a weapon."

Mara understood the weight of it. "And where do we go?" she asked.

Silas unfolded the map on the table. "A farm outside Salina," he said. "Not fancy. Quiet. It belongs to a retired weather service technician named Howard Rook. He's been collecting atmospheric data for forty years. His barn has an old ham setup, a generator, and a field station you can expand. He's trustworthy."

Wren frowned. "What are you basing that on?"

Silas's gaze sharpened. "Because he refused an ELXON contract two years ago when they tried to buy his station. He called them 'well-dressed cowards' and told them to go to hell."

Wren almost smiled despite herself.

Silas turned to Mara, voice lower. "And Mara… you'll be safer there than here. ELXON will search for you near your origin point first. They'll assume you'll run to family, or a city, or a place with coverage."

Thinking out loud, Mara noted, "but Wren has to work. She can't just disappear."

Silas's expression softened. "She can if she chooses. And if she stays, she becomes leverage."

Wren's jaw tightened. "I'm not leaving my mom." Mara started to argue. Wren cut her off. "Don't. You didn't ask me before. You don't get to decide now."

Mara's eyes stung. She nodded once and let the moment stand as the truest form of consent they'd had all night.

Silas handed Mara a small, foam-lined, hard-plastic case. "Clean devices," he said. "Phone, laptop, radio beacon. No personal accounts. No biometric unlock. Use only what we give you."

Mara's fingers curled around the case. It felt heavier than it looked.

Then Silas handed her another object. A thin bundle wrapped in cloth. "More important," he said quietly. Mara unwrapped it. A small metal cylinder no longer than her hand, sleek, matte, with a tiny lens-like circle at one end. She looked up. "What is this?"

Nadine answered before Silas could.

"An atmospheric spectrometer," she said. "Portable. Better than your homemade setup. ELXON-grade."

Mara's pulse jumped. "Where did you get—"

Nadine's eyes didn't flinch. "From them."

Staring at the device, Mara was half-awed, half-nauseated.

"You will collect better data now," Silas said in a steady voice. "And you will share it in a way they can't dismiss."

Wren hugged herself. "And if they catch us?"

Silas didn't lie. "Then we make sure your proof outlives you," he said quietly.

The room fell silent. Then Eli lifted his head. "We have movement."

Everyone turned. Eli tapped his laptop, bringing up a live news feed. A glossy studio. Bright smiles. The same anchor from earlier, the one who'd called Mara's image a deep-fake, now wearing a look of excitement. "—and in a historic moment for private space innovation," the anchor said, "the ELXON Foundation will conduct a live-streamed suborbital flight today at 10:00 a.m. Eastern, featuring a group of philanthropic supporters and cultural ambassadors, including global icon Anika Sato."

Wren's face tightened. "They're doing it again."

"They're countering the narrative, "Nadine said through clenched jaws.

Mara leaned forward. "They want to show the sky is fine."

Silas nodded. "They want a controlled image. A curated 'view' that excludes the wound."

On the feed, footage rolled: polished rockets, smiling faces, VIP lounges. A montage of luxury wrapped around the idea of salvation.

Then Anika appeared, hair perfect, smile warm. "People are scared," she said into a microphone. "And fear spreads fast online. That's why I'm doing this. To show everyone we're okay. To show them Earth is still beautiful."

Mara felt sick. Silas's gaze hardened. "They're using her."

"Or she's letting them," Wren said with a voice shaking with emotion.

Nadine turned to Silas. "They'll curate altitude. Camera angle. Spectrum filters. Anything to hide atmospheric thinning?"

Mara's mind snapped into science mode. "If they go high enough," Mara said, "they might accidentally show the rim. Even if they try not to."

Silas nodded. "That's why we watch." He pointed at Eli. "Record it. Every frame. Every telemetry readout they accidentally leave visible." Eli's fingers flew.

"Silas," Mara said as she stood slowly, wincing at her feet, "if they're launching a public ride, it means something else too."

He looked up. "What?"

"It means they're confident," she said. "Confident enough to flaunt. Or… confident because they're about to move into the final phase."

Nadine's face darkened. "Phase Gate."

Silas's eyes flicked to the orbital feed still open on another monitor. The moving light. Still there. Still shifting and not orbiting like a machine. Watching like a mind. Silas spoke quietly. "We leave now."

Within minutes, the house came to life. Mark loaded radios into a bag. Jaya packed medical supplies. Eli handed Silas a stack of drives labeled with careful handwriting: **STREAM MIRROR 1–12**.

Silas hugged no one. He didn't have time. But he looked each person in the eyes, and the look said what hugs usually said: *Stay alive.*

"You're with me," Nadine said, nodding at Mara.

Wren stepped forward. "I'm with my mom."

Nadine hesitated, then nodded once. "Of course, but you do what I say when I say it."

Wren's mouth tightened. "Same."

For a moment, Nadine's eyes flickered with something like reluctant respect.

They left by the back door, three at a time, moving into the morning's gray light. Two vehicles waited under trees: the gray

Suburban and an older pickup that looked like it belonged to a farmer who hated new technology.

Silas climbed into the pickup with Mark and Eli, heading in one direction.

Nadine drove Mara and Wren in the Suburban in another direction. Before Nadine pulled out, Silas leaned into their window. "Mara," he said quietly. "One more thing."

Mara looked up. "What?"

Silas's expression softened. "You did the hardest part," he said. "You told the truth."

Mara drew in a deep, steady breath. "And now I have to live with it."

Silas nodded. "Now you have to *keep* it."

Then he stepped back, and the pickup rolled away into the trees.

Nadine drove them down a narrow gravel road lined with frost-bitten weeds. The world looked almost peaceful, the way it did when your eyes wanted to lie to you.

Wren stared out the window. "How long until they find Silas?"

Nadine kept her eyes on the road. "They already know he exists. They didn't take him seriously until your mom."

Mara's throat tightened. "And now?"

"Now," Nadine said, "they will."

They drove for an hour, switching highways twice, then turning onto smaller roads and back roads. Nadine avoided tolls, avoided cameras, and avoided predictable routes. Finally, she turned off onto a dirt track bordered by bare trees and old fencing. A farmhouse appeared, plain, weathered, with smoke from a chimney. A large barn sat behind it, and next to the barn, a tall antenna mast rose like a thin metal tree.

A man stood at the end of the drive, hands in his pockets, wearing a heavy coat and a hat pulled low.

Howard Rook.

He didn't wave. He just watched them approach with the stillness of someone who'd seen storms coming long before anyone else believed him. Nadine rolled down the window.

Howard stepped closer and peered in at Mara. "You're the Kansas scientist," he said bluntly.

Mara gave a tired half-smile. "Apparently."

Howard grunted. "Well. Come on. You look like hell."

Wren bristled. "She's been hunted all night."

Howard glanced at Wren and softened by half a degree. "Then you're stubborn," he said. "Good. We'll need that."

He turned and gestured them toward the barn. Inside, the barn wasn't full of hay. It was full of equipment. Old weather station gear. Radios. Shelves of batteries. A workbench lined with sensors and wires. A small generator in the corner. Maps on the wall with hand-written notes and dates.

Mara's eyes widened despite herself. "This is…"

"A hobby," Howard said. "A habit. A way to not be surprised."

He pointed to a table where a screen displayed real-time atmospheric readings. "And last night," Howard added, voice grim, "my instruments went damn near vertical."

Mara's pulse jumped. "You saw the spike, too."

Howard grunted. "I saw a spike. I saw an aurora. And I saw my neighbor's grandkid get sunburned feeding chickens."

"So, it's everywhere," said Wren, inhaling sharply.

Howard shook his head. "Not everywhere. Yet. But it's moving."

Mara set Silas's spectrometer case on the table as if it were sacred. "We can measure better," she said.

Looking at Nadine, Howard asked, "And you are…?"

Nadine didn't flinch. "Someone who helped build the lie. Now I'm trying to undo it."

Howard stared at her a beat longer than polite, then nodded once. "Fair."

Howard pointed toward a chair. "Sit," he ordered. "You're bleeding, and your feet are a mess."

Mara sat. Wren crouched at her feet again, protective and fierce.

Howard pulled up the live feed on another screen. "Here," he said, tapping. "Their ride starts in two hours."

Leaning in, Mara watched. The ELXON countdown graphic glowed, slick and confident. Anika's face appeared again, smiling into a camera as if she were selling perfume, not a curated view of the planet's collapse.

A cold certainty settled in Mara's chest. They weren't doing this to calm the public. They were trying to gauge public opinion. Measuring how many would believe the deep-fake story. Who would accept reassurance, and who would be confused long enough for ELXON to finish Phase Gate?

Mara looked at Howard's instruments. Then at Silas's spectrometer. Then, at the live countdown to the inspiration ride.

"We capture their data," Mara said quietly. "Then compare it to ours."

Howard nodded. "Already started a baseline."

Nadine moved to the door, scanning the horizon through a crack. "We assume they'll show the world anyway," Nadine said. "By accident or by arrogance."

Wren whispered, "And if they show it, people will know Mom told the truth."

Mara's throat tightened. "Yes," Mara said softly. "And then the world decides what kind of species we are."

Outside, morning light strengthened, pale and cold. Inside the barn, screens glowed with numbers, curves, and the thin blue line of a planet under examination.

And somewhere above Earth, a light moved against the stars, too deliberate to be debris, adjusting in tiny, precise angles as if it had noticed humanity.

Mara stared at the feed and felt something settle into her bones like a warning:

ELXON was about to perform for the world. And the world was about to see more than ELXON intended.

CHAPTER 10 — The Thin Blue Line

By 9:45 a.m. Eastern, the world revolved around a countdown.

Howard's barn smelled like coffee and soldering flux, the scent of weather stations and long nights. Radios crackled softly. Screens glowed in clusters. Outside, the winter wind dragged across fields as if it were searching for something.

Mara sat wrapped in a blanket, feet propped on an old crate. Jaya had insisted, via a voice message relayed through Eli before the network split, that she treat frostbite as a real threat, not an inconvenience. Mara hated that she needed the reminder.

Wren sat on the floor beside her with the laptop open, refreshing the stream mirrors. Her earlier fury had cooled into focus. She looked older than she had two days ago. She had stopped waiting for adults to make things safe.

Nadine stood near the barn door with binoculars, scanning the horizon every few minutes. Howard said little, but his hands moved constantly; adjusting dials, logging readings, tapping notes into a weathered notebook as if writing the world down could keep it from disappearing.

On the largest screen, ELXON's broadcast began. Sleek graphics. A polished "mission control" set. Smiling hosts in branded jackets. The ELXON logo: an X inside a circle, rotating as if it were a promise.

A woman's voice, warm and confident: "Welcome, everyone, to an extraordinary moment. Today, we bring you a view of Earth from the edge of space, an experience that inspires unity, wonder, and hope."

Mara thought, her jaw tightening, curated hope.

The camera cut to the launch site: a coastal platform with a gleaming white vehicle standing upright against a blue sky that looked normal enough to be insulting. It looked too clean, too staged.

A banner on the screen read: **NEXT HORIZON: LIVE.**

Wren whispered, "They're really doing it."

"They're measuring the crowd," grunted Howard.

Lowering her binoculars, Nadine remarked, "They're also signaling to the insiders: The plan continues."

Mara watched the broadcast but kept half her attention on Howard's instruments. Two truths at once: the story on screen and the physics in the barn.

ELXON's host introduced the passengers with the tone of an awards show.

"A visionary investor and humanitarian…"

"A pioneering tech leader…"

"A cultural ambassador beloved worldwide—Anika Sato…"

Anika stepped into the frame wearing a sleek suit with the ELXON emblem. Her smile was so calm it made Mara's skin crawl. Anika waved at the camera. "I know many of you have seen frightening things online," she said gently. "But I'm here to show you something true. Something beautiful. We're okay."

Wren's hand tightened around her mouse. "She's lying."

"Or she's telling herself a story," Mara offered.

Howard pointed to a small monitor showing UV readings. "That story doesn't match the numbers."

The broadcast moved quickly into spectacle: cabin shots, slow-motion boarding, a countdown overlay in clean white text.

T-minus 3:00

Mara said softly, leaning forward. "Howard, they'll cut away from the external cameras at max-Q."

He nodded in agreement. "I know. That's where the public doesn't get to look."

Nadine said, "They'll also filter the window feed."

Mara's voice went flat. "We don't need their window feed."

Looking up, Wren asked, "What do we need?"

Mara pointed to the stream's telemetry corner, small, almost invisible numbers most viewers would ignore. "Altitude," Mara said. "Time. Acceleration. If they leave those, we can model what they *must* have seen."

Howard's eyes gleamed faintly. "Now you're talking."

The countdown hit **T-minus 0:10.**

The host's voice rose with excitement. "Here we go!" The vehicle's engines ignited with a bright white flame and a clean roar. The rocket lifted with a smoothness that felt too perfect.

Wren whispered, "That's… beautiful."

Mara didn't let herself be seduced by it. She watched the telemetry numbers. Altitude climbed. Speed climbed.

The host spoke over it, smiling, selling wonder like a product. At **T+1:12**, the feed cut briefly. A "technical overlay" appeared—ELXON logo, upbeat music, a message: **"SIGNAL STABILIZING."**

Mara's eyes narrowed. "There it is."

Fingers flying across his keyboard, Howard reported, "Recording every frame." When the video returned, the camera angle had shifted, still showing the vehicle, but now from a lower perspective: more sky, less horizon.

Mara was seized by a cold certainty. "They're trying to keep the rim out of frame," she said.

Wren's voice shook. "Why would—"

"Because the rim tells the truth," Mara said.

At **T+4:08**, the feed switched to an internal cabin view.

Passengers strapped in, laughing a little too hard. Anika floating slightly, hair drifting, the perfect image of weightlessness and joy. Behind her, a window. But the window didn't show Earth clearly. It was… muted. A gentle blur. A soft blue glow like a screensaver.

Nadine's eyes narrowed. "That's not raw."

"That's an overlay," Howard said in disgust.

Throat tight, Mara exclaimed, "They're faking the view."

Wren stared. "Can they do that?"

"Easily," Nadine said, voice grim. "You stream what you want people to see."

Anika smiled into the camera. "Look," she said softly. "Isn't it beautiful?"

Mara's hands clenched.

Howard tapped a different screen. "Our magnetometer just spiked again."

Mara's stomach turned. "In real time?"

Howard nodded. "Right now. While they're up there."

"So, the sun is—," began Wren.

"Pushing," Mara said. "And the shield is… compromised."

On-screen, the host said, "We're now approaching peak altitude, just at the edge of space!"

Mara leaned in, heart pounding. If the passengers looked out, if the overlay glitched, if the vehicle's system hiccupped, there might be a fraction of a second of raw.

Howard muttered, "Come on. Come on…" As if the universe could be coaxed.

At **T+7:42**, Anika turned her head slightly toward the window. Her smile faltered for half a heartbeat. Then she smiled again, wider, too perfect.

Mara saw it. Not the wound, not yet. But the flicker of real fear behind a rehearsed face.

Wren whispered, "She saw something."

Nadine's jaw tightened. "Yes."

The broadcast cut again. **"SIGNAL STABILIZING."** The overlay lasted longer this time.

Pulse racing, Mara cried, "They're losing control."

"Or they're hiding something," said Howard.

When the feed returned, it wasn't the cabin view. It was an exterior camera mounted beneath the vehicle, pointing downward.

Earth filled the frame, curved, gorgeous, cloud-swirled. The blue rim glowed at the edge. For one second, it seemed like the world held its breath. Then Mara saw it. A thinness. A bruise in the rim. A place where the blue halo didn't glow evenly.

Not as stark as Jalen's image, but there. The wound.

Wren's hand flew to her mouth. "Oh no."

Howard's eyes widened. "There!"

Nadine's voice was harsh. "Record it. Record it."

Mara's throat tightened with vindication and grief. The feed lasted for two seconds. Then the image glitched, pixelated, with edges tearing. And in the glitch, something else appeared.

Not on Earth. Beyond Earth. A point of light that moved wrong. It slid into frame like a deliberate intrusion, too smooth, too fast, then it stopped as if it had realized it was being seen.

Mara froze.

"That's not a satellite," whispered Howard.

Nadine's face went pale. "No."

"What is that?" stared Wren, wide-eyed, voice shaking. The point of light shifted, an angular movement, a tiny adjustment that looked like intention.

Then the broadcast cut so violently that the screen went black. For a full second, there was nothing. Then the ELXON logo returned with upbeat music and a calm message:

"THANK YOU FOR WATCHING. TRANSMISSION COMPLETE."

Silence filled the barn. Even the radios seemed to hush.

Mara stared at the black screen where the point of light had been. Her skin prickled. The sensation wasn't fear exactly. It was unexplainable.

Howard broke the silence first, voice hoarse. "Well."

"They just proved you right," Wren said weakly.

Nadine spoke quietly, controlled. "And they just showed something they didn't mean to."

Howard turned to his computer and replayed the captured frames, isolating the glitch. He zoomed in. There, near the edge of the frame, was the point of light. It wasn't a flare. Not a lens artifact. It had a faint geometry around it, a shape that suggested edges and symmetry.

Mara caught her breath while Wren whispered, "It looks like…a tear in the sky."

Howard shook his head slowly. "No. It looks like something is watching the tear."

"ELXON will have seen that too," Nadine said in a tight voice.

Mara's mind raced. "They're not just hiding the wound," she whispered. "They're hiding whoever or whatever is out there."

Wren's voice shook. "Why?"

"Because if there's someone with more power, ELXON loses its leverage." Nadine's gaze was hard.

Mara stared at the frozen frame. The thin blue line, damaged. The point of light, deliberate. And something else, so faint it was almost nothing, an edge of color near the light. Not green. Not blue. A pale gold shimmer, like a whisper of aurora in space.

Her breath caught in her throat.

Silas had said: *We don't leap to aliens. We stay in evidence.*

But evidence was piling up like storms. Howard finally looked at Mara, expression grim but steady. "Doc," he said, "you just got your second proof."

Mara gulped. "And now ELXON will hit back harder."

"Yes," Nadine agreed, eyes already scanning outside the barn again.

Wren's voice was small. "What do we do?"

Looking at the replay, then at Howard's instruments, then at the spectrometer case on the table. Her voice came out quiet but firm. "We measure everything," Mara said. "We publish it everywhere. And we build the calm network until the truth is stronger than their spin."

Howard nodded once. "Good."

Nadine's phone, one of the clean devices Silas had provided, buzzed on the table. Nadine picked it up, eyes scanning. Her face went still.

"What?" Mara asked.

"ELXON just issued an emergency statement," Nadine said, voice flat, "They're claiming the 'Kansas scientist' is part of a coordinated disinformation attack… and they're offering a reward for information leading to her location."

Wren's face drained of color. "A reward?" Mara's chest tightened.

Nadine continued, and her voice was hard. "And they used your full name, Wren." Mara felt the room tilt.

"They're making us targets," said Wren quietly.

Howard's eyes narrowed. "Then we stop being where they expect."

Mara stared at the still frame of the point of light beyond Earth. Millions had seen the wound. And the watcher had been seen too, if only for a second. The game had changed. Not just because the public now had proof.

But because something beyond Earth had just entered the story in a way no one could control, it was no longer possible. Not ELXON, not Silas, not Mara. But Mara understood, with a cold clarity that settled into her bones: ELXON wasn't just racing against the atmosphere. They were racing against time.

And against whoever was arriving.

CHAPTER 11 — Wanted

The reward poster hit the internet the way a match hits dry grass.

It wasn't a "wanted" poster, not officially. ELXON didn't have police powers. But they didn't need police power when they had what worked better: money, influence, and a narrative machine.

Howard pulled it up on a screen and let it sit there, ugly and bright. A flattering photo of Mara from an old university webpage, cropped, cleaned, and softened. Under it, bold text:

INFORMATION REQUEST Mara Keene **Potentially Connected to Coordinated Orbital Imagery Manipulation**

Below that, smaller text dripped with faux responsibility:

"If you have credible information that may assist in protecting the public from harmful misinformation, contact the ELXON Foundation Integrity Hotline."

Then, in a neat box:

REWARD: UP TO $500,000

Wren stared at it like it was a monster wearing a tie. "They're putting a price on my mom," she whispered.

Howard's mouth twisted. "They're putting a price on certainty."

Nadine's face was hard. "They're also baiting the desperate. That's who rewards are for."

Mara's throat was tight, but her mind had gone strangely calm—like a storm eye forming inside her chest. "They're trying to flood us with noise and make it dangerous to help us."

Nodding, Howard added, "So, we make it safer to help each other than to betray."

Fear and fury tangled together in Wren's face. "How?"

Before Mara could answer, Howard's instruments chirped. The alert tone cut too sharply through the barn's quiet.

Leaning toward his monitor, he narrowed his eyes. "That's not normal."

Blanket slipping from her shoulders, Mara rose. "What did you find?"

On the screen, a graph spiked in a way that didn't match the earlier patterns. Howard tapped the curve. "UV-B," he said. "Rising faster than it should at this latitude. It's late morning, yes, but this curve…" He shook his head. "This curve is wrong."

Mara's stomach clenched. "How wrong?"

A clean baseline from last year appeared beneath today's jagged climb, shadowing it like a ghost. "Twenty percent above expected," Howard said, then his voice dropped. "And climbing."

Wren's expression tightened. "So, the wound is… getting worse."

Nadine's clean phone buzzed again, once, twice, three times. She ignored it until the fourth buzz came like an insistence.

A glance at the screen changed her expression.

"What?" Mara asked.

Nadine held up the phone. "Silas."

A jolt ran through Mara. "Is he okay?"

With a single tap, Nadine answered and lifted the phone to her ear without turning on the speaker. "Talk," she said.

Silas's voice came through faintly, distorted by encryption and distance, but unmistakably calm. "They found the house," he said.

Mara's breath caught.

Nadine's jaw tightened. "How?"

"Doesn't matter," he replied. "They didn't catch us. But they're escalating and using local law enforcement proxies. 'Public safety.' 'Misinformation threat.' All very clean."

Wren went pale. "They're using cops?"

"Not all police. Not knowingly." Silas's tone sharpened just slightly. "They're feeding a story. Most people follow stories when a uniform wears them."

"Are you safe?" Mara asked.

"A moving target," he said. "Which is what you need to be now. Mara, Howard's location is compromised by association. Not yet, but soon. Your stream put Kansas on the map. ELXON will comb this region."

Listening from the table, Howard muttered, "They can comb to their heart's content."

Silas continued, "We're activating Node Four."

Mara frowned. "There wasn't a Node Four."

"There is now." Grim humor brushed his voice. "We didn't plan for the 'reward' move at this speed."

Nadine's eyes narrowed. "What's Node Four?"

"Public counterweight," Silas said. "A face they can't easily smear."

Mara's stomach twisted. "A celebrity?"

"No. A survivor."

Everything in her went still.

"Jalen," she whispered.

Silas exhaled. "Yes."

Wren's hand flew to her mouth. "He made it?"

"He's alive," Silas said, his voice softening by a fraction. "Injured. And furious."

Nadine's eyes closed briefly, like she'd been holding her breath for hours.

Relief nearly buckled Mara's knees. "Where is Jalen now?"

Silas paused. "Close enough to be dangerous."

She gulped. "What does that mean?"

"It means he's coming to you."

Howard's brows lifted. "To my barn?"

"To your node," Silas corrected. "Which needs to move. Today."

A scowl crossed Howard's face. "I don't run."

Silas didn't argue with his pride. He treated it like weather: real, to be respected, not negotiated.

"I'm not asking you to run," Silas said. "I'm asking you to reposition. Temporary. You can come back when the hunt isn't hot."

Howard grunted, unhappy.

"Mara, one more thing before you leave," Silas continued. "Release the frame capture of the inspiration ride glitch showing the wound and the moving object."

Mara nodded slowly. "That will explode."

"Good, Explosions can be controlled if they're deliberate."

Wren's voice shook. "And the reward?"

His tone hardened. "We counter it publicly as harassment. We frame it as what it is: an attempt to silence whistleblowers. We also distribute your second message, which includes practical guidance. People rally around action."

Mara's chest tightened. "ELXON will say we're inciting panic again."

Silas replied, calm and sharp. "Then we keep refusing to panic."

A pause.

"And Mara," Silas added quietly, "the orbital lights…"

Her skin prickled. "What about them?"

"They moved again."

Mara's stomach clenched. "Closer?"

"Yes. Not directly toward Earth. But toward the wound."

Howard muttered, "Like flies to blood."

"Or doctors to injury," Silas offered.

The words tightened in Mara's throat.

"We intercepted chatter," he continued. "ELXON is calling it interference. They're not afraid. of the public. They are afraid of losing control of the narrative entirely."

Nadine's voice was low. "So, they'll accelerate Phase Gate."

Silas didn't deny it. "Yes. Which is why you move now."

Mara drew in a breath. "Where?"

"A mobile node near rural Manhattan, not the city," he said. "A church basement with ham gear and a farmer's back lot for equipment. It's staffed by people who don't want money. They want the truth."

Howard snorted. "Church folks."

A faint smile touched Silas's voice, "Sometimes stubbornness comes with hymns."

Wren looked at Mara. "We're moving again."

She nodded, then forced her mind into tasks. "We need to pack the instruments, duplicate the logs, and—"

"Already duplicating," Howard cut in.

Eli had taught them speed by example: you didn't wait to be told twice.

Nadine ended the call with Silas and looked at Mara.

"Two hours," she said. "That's how long we have before someone with a half-million-dollar incentive decides to be 'helpful.'"

Wren's face tightened. "We can't trust anyone."

"We can trust patterns," Mara said quietly. "And we can trust people who have nothing to gain from betraying us."

A hard case hit the table with a thud.

"This is your spectrometer," Howard said. "And this," handing her a small notebook, "is my baseline logs. Forty years. If you're going to be the face of truth, you better have history on your side."

Mara's throat tightened. "Howard… this is your life."

He shrugged as if it were obvious. "So's the sky."

Wren pulled off her shoes and shook the USB drive out into her hand. She held it up. "We still have this."

Mara nodded. "And we make sure we always have more than one."

At the barn door, Nadine scanned the road. The winter landscape looked harmless: fields, trees, a distant line of telephone poles. But now every car could be a hunter. Every person could be an opportunist. Every friendly question could be bait. "We leave in five," she said, turning back. "No debate."

One last glance went to the biggest screen, where the captured frame of the moving light beyond Earth, frozen mid-shift. That strange sensation came again, like a gaze. Not human. Not ELXON. Something else. Something that didn't care about rewards or press releases. Something that responded to wounds. Mara whispered, mostly to herself, "If you're out there…"

Wren looked at her. "What?"

Mara shook her head, swallowing. "Nothing."

But it wasn't nothing. When the world started hunting truth-tellers, it was easy to believe the universe was indifferent. And yet, somewhere beyond the thin blue line, something had moved *toward* the damage, not away from it.

They loaded the cases into the Suburban. Howard insisted on bringing his own truck too, refusing to abandon his equipment entirely. He moved like a man packing for a storm he'd predicted all his life.

Nadine started the engine. As they rolled down the dirt track away from the farmhouse, Mara looked back at the barn, at the antenna mast, the instruments, the quiet place where truth had been measured with ordinary hands.

"Do you think we'll ever come back?" Wren asked quietly.

Mara's chest tightened. "I don't know," she admitted. Then, after a beat, she added something she surprised herself by believing. "But we're not alone in this anymore."

Wren frowned. "You mean Silas?"

Mara stared out at the pale winter sky. "I mean, everyone who saw the wound. And everyone who chose not to panic."

As the Suburban merged onto the highway, moving toward the next node and the next wave of conflict, the new reality settled in place:

ELXON had placed a bounty on her name.

But the truth had placed something else in the sky:

A watcher.

A responder.

And it was about to be *found*.

CHAPTER 12 — Basement Hymns

The church didn't look like a resistance cell.

It looked like every church Mara had ever driven past without thinking twice: white siding, a modest steeple, a parking lot with faded lines, and a hand-painted sign that still said **WELCOME** like welcome was a fact, not an invitation.

But the moment Nadine turned down the gravel lane behind it and killed the headlights, Mara understood what Silas meant by *nodes*. Nodes weren't dramatic. Nodes were ordinary places with extraordinary readiness.

They parked behind a line of cedars, hidden from the road. Howard pulled in behind them with his truck, jaw set like he'd rather fight the sky than relocate again.

Wren opened her door and looked around. "So… this is it?"

Nadine nodded. "This is it. Quiet. Uninteresting. The kind of place people don't think to hunt first."

Howard snorted. "They will now."

"Not if we move smarter than their assumptions," Nadine said.

They carried the hard cases through the back entrance. A single porch light glowed, dim and warm, and before Nadine could knock, the door opened.

A woman stood there holding a thermos like a weapon. She wasn't armed. She wasn't young. She didn't have a tactical vest or a radio clipped to her collar. She had silver hair pulled into a loose bun, sensible shoes, and eyes that had seen grief and still chosen kindness.

"You're late," she said.

Nadine blinked. "Hello to you too."

The woman tipped her chin toward Mara. "Dr. Keene?"

Mara nodded carefully. "Yes."

Her expression softened by a fraction. "Good. I'm Pastor Lila Hart. And before you panic, yes, I'm the pastor, and yes, I know what a magnetometer is."

Howard muttered, "Well, I'll be damned."

Lila stepped aside. "Come in. You're freezing, and someone's going to try to sell your names for money. We don't do that here."

Inside, the church was quiet, but not empty. They moved through a hallway and down a narrow stairwell into the basement, which smelled faintly of old hymnals, coffee, and the settled dust of potlucks and tornado shelters. Then the basement opened up.

Tables had been cleared and rearranged. Extension cords snaked across the floor. A ham radio rig sat on a folding table beside a laptop, an antenna line running up through a window well. A whiteboard on the wall was covered in neat handwriting:

- **VERIFIED DATA ONLY**
- **NO PANIC POSTS**
- **COMMUNITY CHECK-INS**
- **SUPPLY COORDINATION**
- **LISTEN FIRST**

A few people looked up as they entered: two farmers, a teenage boy with a laptop and a look of intense concentration, a nurse in scrubs who gave Mara a quick nod, and an older man in a weathered NOAA jacket worn like armor.

The realization hit Mara all at once: This wasn't a safe house run by money. This was a safe house run by *people*.

Lila took the spectrometer case from Mara's hands as if it mattered as much as communion. "Set it here," she said, pointing to a table already cleared.

Wren hovered close, scanning faces.

Quietly, Nadine asked, "Any visitors?"

Lila's expression tightened. "One."

"Who?" Mara asked, pulse jumping.

Instead of answering directly, Lila nodded toward a curtained corner of the basement where a cot had been set up. "Someone came in through the back field at dawn," she said. "Collapsed in my kitchen. Said he knew you."

Mara's throat tightened.

Behind her, Wren whispered, "Jalen."

Nadine's jaw set. "Of course it's him."

Mara moved toward the cot before her brain could catch up. The curtain was half drawn. She stepped around it. Jalen Royce lay on his side, one arm wrapped around his ribs, face pale. A bandage crossed his eyebrow. His lips were cracked. His eyes were closed but not relaxed. Not restful. Exhausted. He looked smaller than he had on the grain elevator catwalk. Not weak, just human.

Mara's chest ached. She lowered her voice. "Jalen?"

His eyes snapped open instantly, sharp as a blade. He sat up too fast, winced, then steadied himself with a tight breath. "Keene," he rasped. His voice sounded like it had been scraped raw. "You're alive."

Throat tight, Mara nodded. "So are you."

His mouth twitched in something that wasn't quite a smile. "Barely."

Wren stepped into view behind Mara. Jalen's gaze flicked to her and softened by a fraction. "Wren."

Her eyes widened. "You… you know my name."

His expression turned grim. "Everyone knows it now."

Mara crouched beside the cot. "What happened after we left?"

For half a second, his eyes went distant, as if he had to force the memory into words. "They tried to pin me in the elevator," he said. "I went down through the grain chutes. Cut my side on metal. Lost a lot of blood." He touched his ribs carefully. "Not enough to die. Enough to be angry."

Nadine stepped closer, arms crossed. "Did they see you?"

His gaze sharpened. "They know my face. They'll call me violent. They'll use me as your 'proof' that this is a coordinated extremist thing."

Mara's stomach turned. "So, they'll paint us as terrorists."

Jalen nodded. "They already started. And they'll do worse."

Standing at the edge of the curtained area, Howard muttered, "Worse than a bounty?"

Jalen looked at him, then at Mara. "They're accelerating," he said quietly. "Phase Gate is real."

Mara's pulse jumped. "What is Phase Gate supposed to be?"

He exhaled slowly. "It's the switch from 'public philanthropy' to 'final logistics.' Once they flip it, the rides stop being rides. They become seat allocations. Full lockdown protocols. Quiet martial agreements. Restricted airspace. Then launch."

Wren's voice trembled. "How long?"

Jalen's eyes held Mara's gaze. "Soon."

She forced herself not to flinch. "Days?"

A hesitation. Tiny. Terrifying. "I don't know," he admitted. "But it's no longer 'months.' They've moved too many assets for that."

Lila entered the curtained space carrying a mug of coffee, as if it were a peace offering. "You can scare people later," she said briskly. "Drink. Talk. But you don't do it like you're narrating the apocalypse. You do it like you're planning a storm response."

Jalen blinked at her, then gave a small, grudging nod and took the mug. "Thank you," he rasped.

Her eyes narrowed in approval. "You're welcome."

Mara stood and turned back to the main basement area. "We have work to do."

Howard was already setting up equipment on one table, his notebook open, pen moving. The NOAA-jacket man approached Mara and stuck out his hand. "Ed," he said. "Retired meteorologist. I ran models for thirty years. I watched your first stream and thought, 'Well, that's either the best deep-fake I've ever seen or we're about to learn humility."

Mara shook his hand. "And what do you think now?"

He nodded toward Howard's monitor. "Your numbers are matching ours. Deep-fakes don't spike UV."

Something inside Mara loosened just a little.

At a nearby laptop station, Wren sat down and pulled off her shoe. She shook the USB drive free and placed it on the table as carefully as if it were alive.

Nadine's eyes flicked to it. "We duplicate it now."

Wren's jaw tightened. "We do. But no one takes it away from me."

For a second, Nadine looked ready to argue. Then she stopped. "Fine. You keep the original. We copy." That tiny concession felt like a trust.

Mara opened the spectrometer case and powered it on. A soft tone sounded—clean and precise. She felt her hands steady. Science steadied her. The truth didn't feel less terrifying, but it felt… more navigable.

Howard leaned over, eyes gleaming. "That thing's a beauty."

"ELXON-grade," Nadine said quietly, almost like a confession.

Mara looked at the machine, then at the people around her, and thought: *We're doing this in a church basement.* The world was ending, and salvation, real salvation, looked like folding tables and coffee and stubborn humans refusing to become monsters.

Then Eli's voice crackled through a speaker on the table, carried by the ham radio relay. "Node One to Node Three," he said. "You there?"

Lila tapped the radio. "We're here."

Mara leaned in. "Eli, it's Mara."

A pause, then relief. "Thank God. Okay, listen. The inspiration ride glitch is spreading fast. People saw the wound. People saw the light."

Mara's throat tightened. "So, it wasn't just us."

"No," Eli said. "And ELXON is panicking quietly. They're claiming it was 'a lens artifact' and 'space debris.' But the movement didn't move like debris."

From the cot, Jalen spoke sharply. "Tell him to send the raw capture to every independent astrophotography group."

Eli paused. "Who is that?"

"Jalen," Mara said. "He's alive."

A long exhale came through the speaker. "Of course he is." Relief washed over him. "Sending out raw data now. Stay safe and stay in touch."

Mara looked at the people around the room. "We're going to release a packet. Not a rant. A packet."

Ed nodded. "Technical appendix. Lay summary. Data graphs. Timestamped."

"And a calm message," Lila added. "What to do, how to help, where to verify."

Wren lifted her head. "And what about the bounty?"

Nadine's eyes narrowed. "We flip it."

Mara blinked. "How?"

"With precision," Nadine said. "We make the bounty the story, not you. Harassment designed to silence evidence. We get civil rights lawyers involved. Press advocates. Whistleblower organizations. Make it legally radioactive for any platform to boost it."

"Will that work?" Wren asked.

"It will slow it," Nadine said.

The spectrometer chimed softly. Mara glanced at the readout, and her stomach dropped. The ozone proxy wasn't just low. It was **dropping** at a steady decline that didn't match any normal diurnal pattern.

Howard stepped close, saw the number, and went still. "Okay," he murmured. "Okay, that's... new."

Her throat closed up. "It's accelerating."

Ed leaned in, eyes narrowing. "How fast?"

The math automatically calculating in Mara's head—rate of change, slope, extrapolation—and she felt cold spread through her chest. "Fast enough that we'll see symptoms sooner."

Wren's voice trembled. "What kind of symptoms?"

"UV burns. Crop stress. Respiratory irritation. More auroras. Power instability," said Mara.

"And fear," added Lila.

Mara looked at her. "Yes."

A steady hand on Mara's shoulder, grounding her. "Then we keep people calm," Lila said. "We give them truth and tasks. That's how you keep fear from becoming violent."

A sudden burst of static snapped through the ham radio, sharp and louder than before. It wasn't Eli. It wasn't Mark. It was something else. It was a pure tone, repeating.

Three short pulses. A pause. Three short pulses again.

Ed froze. "That's not atmospheric."

Howard's eyes widened. "That's not solar either."

Nadine moved instantly, leaning over the radio like she could intimidate it.

Despite the pain, Jalen sat up straighter.

The pulses repeated. Precise. Identical each time.

Then, beneath them, a faint pattern appeared: not random noise, but modulation. Something was shaping the static.

Mara's skin prickled.

"Is that… a signal?" Wren whispered.

Howard's hands shook slightly as he adjusted the dial. "If it is, it's strong."

Ed swallowed. "From where?"

The pulses changed. This time, four short bursts. A pause. Then one long, steady tone that vibrated through the basement like a held note.

Jalen went pale. He looked at Mara and spoke so quietly that the words seemed to hurt. "That's the same pattern I heard in orbit," he said. "Before my 'accident.'"

Silence slammed into the room.

Lila's voice was barely a whisper. "You never told anyone that."

His eyes stayed on Mara. "Because no one would've believed me. And because ELXON did."

The radio crackled again, the tone shifting as though it were searching, adjusting, aligning. Then, beneath the static came a third layer. A sound that wasn't a voice but wasn't noise either.

A shape. A pattern. A presence.

The hair rose on Mara's arms. Not fear. Not exactly. Recognition, like the moment you realize someone is standing behind you in the dark and they've been there longer than you thought.

Lila backed up a step, one hand over her mouth.

Wren stared at the radio as if it were a doorway.

Nadine's face went tight with something like awe and dread tangled together.

Howard whispered, "They're… talking."

"Or knocking," Jalen said hoarsely.

Eyes fixed on the pulsing meter, Mara pushed down the lump in her throat.

Outside, above the church, the sky looked normal. Inside the basement, the air felt charged, alive, like the world had leaned closer to listen.

And with cold clarity, Mara understood: ELXON's bounty had made her a target on Earth. But whatever was sending that signal, whatever had moved closer to the wound, had just made her a point of interest in the sky.

And it wasn't asking politely. It was calling.

CHAPTER 13 — The Knock

No one spoke for a full minute.

The basement held its breath around the radio rig like the entire church had become an ear.

The signal repeated with precise pulses, then the long tone that vibrated through the metal table legs and into Mara's bones. It wasn't loud enough to be painful, but it was steady enough to be undeniable. Like a fingertip tapping glass, again and again, with patience that didn't belong to humans.

Howard adjusted the dial in microscopic increments. The static thinned, thickened, thinned again. Ed leaned in so close his breath fogged the screen. Wren sat rigid, hands clenched in her lap. Nadine didn't move at all. Her stillness was the kind trained people used when motion could be fatal. Jalen watched the meters like he expected them to bite.

Lila broke the silence first, voice low but firm. Pastor-quiet, the tone you used in emergencies when you wanted fear to sit down and behave. "Okay," she said. "We're going to treat this like anything unknown: we observe, we document, we don't worship it, and we don't panic."

A breath escaped Howard, a sound of relief. "Amen." Wren blinked at him. He shrugged. "I'm not religious. I just like the word."

Mara forced herself to breathe. "Howard," she said softly, "can you record the raw waveform?"

He nodded without looking up. "Already capturing. Multiple formats. Timestamped."

At last, Nadine moved, drawing a small, handheld, sleek device from her pocket. "ELXON built these for hunting hidden comms," she said quietly. "Let's see what we're dealing with." She clipped it to the radio output, eyes narrowing at the screen. The analyzer displayed the frequency and the modulation pattern—an elegant set of spikes that looked too intentional to be atmospheric. "This isn't noise," she said.

Ed swallowed. "So, it's… engineered."

"By who?" Wren questioned.

No one answered because the only honest answer was that *we don't know*. The tone shifted again. Short pulses now, faster, like an adjustment. Then it stopped. For half a heartbeat, the basement fell into ordinary silence. Mara's ears rang with the absence.

And then, a new signal appeared.

Not the same frequency. Higher. Cleaner. Narrow. The spectrum analyzer jumped like it had been slapped.

Nadine's eyes widened. "They changed channels."

Howard's mouth went dry. "Like they're responding."

"To what?" asked Wren in a shaky voice.

Mara stared at the analyzer, brain sprinting. "To our listening," she whispered.

Wincing with pain, Jalen sat up straighter. "In orbit, it did that too," he said. "It would pulse, then go quiet, then come back closer in frequency, like it was… searching for a receiver that could understand."

Lila's face tightened. "Like knocking until someone opens a door."

The new signal pulsed once. Then twice. Then came something no one expected. Not a word. Not language. A sound pattern—like a chord broken into parts. Three tones layered, then repeated with slight changes, like someone playing the same note sequence and adjusting the spacing, testing.

Mara's skin prickled. It reminded her of a scientist calibrating an instrument. Repeating, refining, finding the right alignment.

"That's… structured," Howard whispered.

"It's musical," Ed said, barely above a breath.

Wren swallowed hard. "It sounds… sad."

Sharply, Mara turned toward her daughter. "Sad?"

Wren kept her eyes on the radio rig. "Like… like when you hear a siren in the distance, and you don't know who it's for." Mara's throat tightened. The tones repeated again, but this time one dropped lower and lingered longer, like a breath held too long.

Nadine's analyzer beeped. She stared at the screen, then looked up at Mara, face pale. "It's synchronized," Nadine whispered. "With—"

"With the magnetometer." Howard cut in, staring at his own monitor.

Mara's heart slammed. Howard's magnetometer line, normally jagged with solar noise, had begun to show tiny regular spikes aligned with the pulses. Not huge. But there. Like the signal wasn't just traveling through the air, it was interacting with the planet's magnetic field.

"That's not possible," Ed said, his voice shaking.

"It is if the transmitter is… powerful," Mara said. Or close. Or both.

Jalen's gaze fixed on Mara, and something in his eyes looked like fear trying to become a warning. "They're not just sending a radio signal," he said hoarsely. "They're tapping the shield."

Silence hit again. Then the basement lights flickered. Once. Twice. The same way Mara's porch light had flickered the night it all started, as if the electrical system were being nudged.

Wren's breath caught. Howard swore softly. "Oh, that's new." Lila's hand went to the wall switch reflexively, like she could stop the world flickering by asserting control over it.

The lights steadied. The tone continued. Ed's hands trembled slightly. "This is… real."

Mara's voice came out quietly. "Yes."

Nadine's face hardened. "ELXON will notice." As if summoned by her words, the clean phone on the table buzzed again. This time, it sounded violent and insistent. Nadine snatched it up and scanned the message. All expression left her face.

"What?" Mara asked quietly.

Nadine looked at Jalen. "They're moving assets," she said. "Multiple launch sites. Silent convoys. Airspace restrictions are being drafted under 'national security' language."

Jalen's jaw clenched. "Phase Gate."

A grim nod. "They're flipping it."

Howard slammed his notebook shut. "Then we broadcast again."

Lila's eyes sharpened. "Not in panic."

He glared. "No, *with evidence*. You've got their glitch frame. You've got your local spikes. Now we've got—" He gestured at the radio rig like it was a live wire. "—whatever this is."

Ed exhaled. "If we claim aliens, we lose half the public instantly."

"We do not claim aliens," Lila said firmly.

Wren's voice came tight and clear. "But we can say we received an anomalous signal."

Mara looked at her, surprised. "That's actually the right phrasing."

Wren lifted her chin. "I'm learning fast." Something like pride cut through Mara's fear.

On the analyzer, the repeating pattern changed again. The tones shifted into a different sequence, faster now, more urgent.

And Mara experienced it, not just in her ears but also in her chest. The long tone vibrated through the room and into her ribs. It wasn't just sound. It was… insistence.

Howard's face went pale. "It's getting stronger."

"It's closer," Jalen whispered.

Then Lila did the most unexpected thing in the room. She took a slow breath, walked to the radio rig, and placed her hand gently on the table beside it, as though grounding herself. Her voice was steady when she spoke. "If you're trying to reach us," she said softly, speaking not into the microphone but into the air itself, "we're listening."

Mara's pulse spiked. "Lila—"

Without looking back, Lila raised one hand. "We can listen without surrendering our minds," she said.

The signal stopped. Instantly. Complete silence. Everyone froze.

"Did you—" Wren's voice cracked.

Howard stared at the meters. "It stopped the moment she—"

The cleanest tone returned, one long note, steady, almost gentle. Then three short pulses. Then a pause. Then, unmistakably, something shaped like a response. Not words, but a repetition of Lila's cadence: long, short-short-short, pause.

A mirror.

Nadine's face went white. "My God."

"It's… answering," Ed whispered.

Awe prickled across Mara's skin, dangerous in its force. Awe made people stupid. Awe made them worship. Awe made them stop thinking. She forced her brain back into discipline. "Record everything," Mara said, voice firm.

Howard nodded, hands shaking as he checked the capture logs.

Wren's eyes were huge. "So, it can hear us."

"Or it can detect our emissions when we speak into the rig," Jalen said hoarsely.

Lila looked at Mara, calm as stone. "Either way," Lila said quietly, "we are no longer only talking to each other."

Mara stared at the steady tone and felt the world tilt again, less from fear, more from the realization that the universe had just leaned toward them and tapped back.

Nadine's phone buzzed again, but she ignored it.

"What do they want?" Howard whispered.

Watching the spectrum analyzer Mara admitted. "I don't know, but they're not sending this to ELXON."

Wren's voice was small. "How can you tell?"

Mara pointed at the frequency readout. "This is old-band ham range," she said. "It's messy. It's human. ELXON would be listening on higher, more secure bands and encrypted channels. This signal chose a place where ordinary people could hear it."

Lila's eyes softened. "Then maybe it's not looking for power," she said. "Maybe it's looking for—"

"Willingness," Jalen finished quietly.

The tone shifted again. A new pattern emerged: three tones, then a descending line, then a pause, then a soft burst like a sigh. Howard stared at the analyzer and whispered, "It's... mapping something."

"Or pointing," Ed said, eyes widening.

Mara leaned closer to the screen, heart pounding. And then she saw it. The signal wasn't random. It carried a modulation that matched something they already had: the spectrometer's last scan of the aurora's strange spectrum. The same faint gold shimmer near the moving light in orbit. The same frequency signature in the ultraviolet edge. It was subtle. But Mara's whole life had been built around catching subtlety. Mara's mouth went dry. "It's the same signature," she whispered.

Nadine stared. "Same as what?"

Mara looked up, voice barely steady. "Same as the light we saw beyond Earth," she said. "Same as the gold shimmer."

Wren's breath caught. "So, the light and the signal are connected."

Jalen's face went tight. "Meaning it's not random debris."

"Meaning it's a craft," Ed said, swallowing hard.

Howard's voice shook. "Meaning they're here."

The basement lights flickered again, softer this time, like a gentle tap. Then the radio rig emitted one final sequence, three short pulses, one long tone, and then a new sound layered beneath it: A faint, rhythmic vibration, like something heavy moving through air far above. Not a plane. Not thunder. A presence.

Everyone in the basement felt it at once. A subtle pressure change, the way the air seemed to thicken, as if the building itself had become aware of the sky. Nadine moved to the window well, looked up through the glass, and went utterly still.

"What?" Wren whispered, rushing to her.

For a moment, Nadine didn't answer. Then, barely audible. "There's a light. Directly above us."

Mara's heart slammed. Howard joined them first. Lila followed, calm but pale. Wren pressed close. Ed leaned in behind them. Outside, the winter sky was gray-blue and innocent. Except for one thing.

A point of pale gold, too bright to be a star in daylight, too steady to be a plane, hovering high above the church like an eye that had found what it was looking for.

It didn't blink. It didn't drift. It simply held position. Watching. Waiting.

And Mara, staring up through the basement glass, understood the terrifying and exhilarating truth: The knock had been real.

And now the visitor had arrived.

CHAPTER 14 — The Test

The first thing Mara noticed was how quiet the world became.

Not silent, cars still passed on the distant highway, the church furnace still hummed, someone upstairs still moved a chair, but the *texture* of the noise changed. Like the air had absorbed the sharp edges.

The pale gold point above the church didn't flare or pulse. It simply stayed. A held breath in the sky.

In the basement, no one moved for a long moment. Even Howard, who never stopped moving, stood with his hands on the window well ledge as if he let go, the planet might slip away.

Wren pressed her forehead to the glass, eyes wide. "It's… right there."

Behind her, Nadine scanned the sky with a practiced gaze, searching for the telltale blinking of aircraft, the subtle wobble of a drone, the streak that could still be explained. She found nothing. "It's stationary," she whispered. "At least from this angle."

"Stars don't show up in daylight like that," Ed said, his voice thin.

Then Lila did what she always did when the room threatened to spin out. She grounded it. "Okay," she said calmly, turning away from the window and facing the group. "Nobody runs outside. Nobody starts filming with their personal phones. Nobody posts anything yet."

Howard bristled. "Why not? This is the biggest—"

Lila lifted a hand. "Because we don't know what it reacts to," she said, firm. "And because if ELXON has ears everywhere, and they do, then our first move needs to be wise, not loud." Mara noticed her throat tighten with appreciation. Lila wasn't denying the moment. She was managing it.

With a quiet grunt, Jalen eased himself off the cot, one hand pressed to his ribs. He moved more slowly than he wanted to, but his eyes were sharp. "That light," he said, "is the same tone I heard in orbit."

Wren turned to him. "So, it followed you?"

His expression tightened. "Or it found us because we started shouting."

Mara looked back at the radio rig, at the meters still twitching with residual energy. "It's responding to the signal," she said quietly. "And possibly… to intention."

A soft snort came from Nadine, though it wasn't mocking. It was disbelief trying to hold itself together. "Intention isn't measurable."

Mara met her gaze. "Neither is panic. But it changes outcomes."

Howard's mouth opened, then shut. Even he couldn't argue with that.

Lila stepped closer to the radio rig and looked at Mara as if she were handing her a heavy responsibility. "Dr. Keene," she said, "if this is contact, you're the one with the clearest head in the room."

Mara's stomach dropped. "I don't feel clear."

"You are," Lila said. "You stayed calm in a grain elevator while men tried to drag you into silence. You can do this."

Wren's hand found Mara's wrist. A grounding grip. A reminder: *you're not alone.* Mara found her strength and inner calm, then nodded once. "Okay," she said. "If we respond, we respond the same way we've responded to everything else, carefully, with documentation, with restraint."

Ed blinked. "Respond... how? Like... radio?"

She glanced at the rig. "That's one channel. But it might not be the safest first channel."

"Because it's traceable," Nadine said, eyes narrowing.

"Because ELXON is listening," Mara corrected. "If we transmit something that confirms contact, and they intercept the transmission, ELXON will weaponize it."

Howard let out a low growl. "They'll claim it as theirs."

Nadine nodded grimly. "Or they'll attempt to provoke it."

"Or they'll try to shoot it," whispered Wren.

The room went cold. Jalen's jaw clenched. "They won't shoot it. Not if they're smart."

A harsh laugh slipped from Nadine. "Power isn't smart. Power is arrogant."

Mara's chest tightened. "Then our first response has to do two things: confirm we're listening and protect the public from ELXON turning this into a crown."

Lila nodded. "Agreed."

Howard rubbed his face like he was trying to wake up from the world. "So, what do we say?"

Mara stared at the rig. The signal had repeated Lila's cadence. That mattered. It meant pattern recognition. It meant mirroring. Maybe it meant… language building. Taking a slow breath, she said, "We start with something universal."

Wren's eyebrows lifted. "Such as?"

Mara looked toward the spectrometer, still humming softly on the table. "Math."

Ed let out a shaky laugh. "Of course you'd say math."

She didn't smile. "Not because it's magic. Because it's stable. Because it reduces misinterpretation."

Jalen nodded slowly. "In orbit, the pattern felt… calibrated. Like they were trying to align."

Nadine's eyes sharpened. "So, we give them a clean reference."

Howard leaned in, suddenly intensely focused. "Prime numbers," he said, almost eager. "Classic."

Mara hesitated. "Prime numbers are classic for humans. We're assuming too much."

Lila's voice was gentle. "Then start simpler."

Mara nodded. "Binary pulses. A simple count. One, two, three. Then a pause. Repeat."

Howard already had his hand on the keyer. "I can do that."

"No," said Nadine, raising her hand.

Howard glared at her. "Why not?"

Her answer was controlled. "Because the moment we transmit on an open ham band, anyone listening can triangulate. ELXON will know our location within minutes." Howard's shoulders slumped slightly. He hated it, but he heard it.

Mara looked at the window well again, at the pale gold point hovering steadily above them. "If it's directly overhead," Mara murmured, "it may already know where we are."

Nadine narrowed her eyes. "That doesn't mean we invite ELXON to know."

Wren swallowed hard. "How do we stop them?"

Mara's brain turned through possibilities: Options. Consequences. Ethics. Science. Then she remembered something so ordinary it almost felt ridiculous: **light.** If the visitor was above them, holding position, and had already used the radio, it could perhaps sense electromagnetic changes.

Howard had mentioned a spotlight upstairs. Church maintenance equipment. Exit sign. Practical things. Mara turned to Lila. "Do you have a strobe? Emergency lights? Anything we can control from inside?"

Lila blinked, then nodded. "We have a maintenance closet. There's a portable work light, and the sanctuary has an old stage dimmer."

Howard's eyes widened. "Optical communication," he whispered.

"Like Morse code with light," Ed said, staring.

"Not Morse," Mara said. Not our language. Just a pattern. A count. A response that says: *We noticed you.*"

Nadine's jaw tightened. "Less traceable than radio."

"Still traceable," Mara said. "But slower."

Lila moved instantly. "I'll get the light." She returned minutes later with a portable work light, a bright, harsh white light, and a long extension cord. She plugged it in near the window well. Mara registered the absurdity and the beauty of it: the possible first contact between species, mediated by a church work light and an extension cord.

"This feels insane," Wren whispered.

Mara glanced at her. "It's human."

Howard took a breath. "What's the pattern?"

Closing her eyes for a second, Mara thought it through. Then she opened them. "One flash. Pause. Two flashes. Pause. Three flashes. Pause. Repeat."

"A simple count," Ed said, nodding.

"We're not claiming anything," Mara said. "We're not inviting anything. We're just acknowledging." Lila's hand hovered over the work light switch.

Mara's chest tightened. "Wait." Everyone froze. Mara looked at Jalen. "Tell us about the last time you heard this in orbit?"

Darkness crossed his face. "The ELXON liaison team called it interference," he said. "Then they rerouted feeds and told us not to talk about it."

"And after that?" Mara asked.

His eyes met hers. "After that, my capsule 'malfunctioned.'" The room went still.

Wren's voice was small. "They tried to kill you."

Jalen didn't deny it. He just said, "They didn't want witnesses."

Cold anger settled into Mara's bones. Then she looked at Lila's hand on the switch. "Okay," Mara said, voice steady. "Do it. But we document everything. And we keep the radio rig recording."

"Recording," Howard said.

Nadine's analyzer sat ready. "Recording."

Ed glanced at his laptop. "Recording."

Lila took a slow breath, and her eyes lifted as if she were about to pray without saying the words. Then she flipped the switch. The work light flared bright in the window well, shooting a hard beam upward through the glass.

One flash. Pause.

Two flashes. Pause.

Three flashes. Pause.

Repeat.

The basement was filled with the subtle reflection of the light on faces, making everyone look like they were in a storm cellar waiting for the tornado to decide. After the third cycle, nothing happened.

Wren's breath hitched. "Did it—"

Then the light above the church shifted. Not moving like a plane. Not drifting like a balloon. It *tilted,* causing a subtle change in brightness, as if it had turned an eye.

Mara's skin prickled.

"It reacted," Howard whispered.

The radio rig crackled faintly. Not the earlier pulses. A new tone, so clean it almost didn't sound like it belonged in the messy human band. It came in as a single sustained note, then broke into a pattern that matched the light flashes:

One. Pause.

Two. Pause.

Three. Pause.

A mirror again.

Wren's eyes filled with tears. "It's copying us."

Mara's throat tightened. "It's learning."

"Or testing," Nadine said, face pale.

"Both," Jalen said hoarsely.

For the first time, Lila's hands trembled as she lowered the work light. "What does it want?"

Mara kept her eyes on the analyzer where the tone held steady, then changed. This time, after the count, the signal added something else—four pulses, then one long tone. A question mark made of sound.

Her mind raced. Four. Long. Four… long… She turned to Howard. "Do you have the last aurora spectrum file?"

He pulled it up instantly.

At the edge of the UV spike, the gold shimmer carried a cadence too: faint, subtle, repeating.

Mara compared the patterns, and her stomach tightened. They matched. The visitor wasn't just learning human patterns. It was presenting *its own*. A signature. A fingerprint. A way to say: **This is us.**

Nadine's clean phone buzzed again. She ignored it. It buzzed again. And again. Finally, she snatched it up, scanned the message, and her face went hard. "ELXON just issued airspace restriction notices over multiple regions," she said. "And they're deploying 'security drones' around rural infrastructure."

Howard's jaw clenched. "They're hunting nodes."

"They'll come here," Ed said, swallowing.

"Yes," Nadine said.

Mara looked up toward the pale gold light, still steady above the church, and felt the collision of two realities: one presence in the sky that mirrored and assessed. Another on

Earth that hunted and silenced. Two forces moving toward the same wound for very different reasons.

Wren grabbed Mara's hand. "Mom… what if this is our only chance?"

Mara's throat tightened. "Only chance for what?"

Her daughter's eyes shone. "To ask for help."

"We shouldn't ask aliens to fix our mess," Nadine said sharply.

Lila's reply was calm and quiet. "We can ask without surrendering responsibility."

Jalen's eyes stayed on the light, haunted. "It won't help the unworthy," he murmured, echoing the future premise like it was already written into the air. "Not until the negative energy clears."

Mara froze. "What did you just say?"

He blinked, as if he hadn't meant to speak it aloud. "I heard a phrase," he said slowly. "In a translation attempt, ELXON ran. They… they thought the signal carried semantic layers. The phrase they got—whether it's real or their algorithm hallucinating—I don't know. But it kept repeating."

Mara's pulse spiked. "What phrase?"

Jalen swallowed. "*Wait until the weight lifts.*"

The room went cold.

"Weight… like…" Wren whispered.

"Like greed," Lila said quietly. "Like fear."

Nadine shook her head, jaw tight. "Or like human noise."

Mara stared at the light above the church and felt the story crystallize into its next terrible shape:

This wasn't a rescue yet. It was a test. A measuring. Just like ELXON measured the public with an inspirational ride. The visitors were measuring humanity with a knock.

And now Mara had to decide how to answer a question she couldn't fully understand, while ELXON tightened its grip on the planet like a fist. The radio signal pulsed again: four short bursts, one long tone. Question.

Mara steadied herself. She reached for the work light switch again. "Okay," she said softly. "We answer."

Nadine's eyes widened. "With what?"

Her voice trembled but held. "With the only thing we can offer without lying." She looked around at the basement—at the people who had refused money, refused panic, refused cruelty. Then she looked up through the window well toward the pale gold point in the sky. And she said, barely above a whisper:

"We answer with who we choose to be."

CHAPTER 15 — Who We Choose to Be

Mara didn't touch the switch right away.

In Lila's hands, the work light hummed softly, hot and ordinary, the kind of tool you used to find a dropped key under a pew. And yet they were using it like a microphone pointed at the universe. The radio rig crackled once: four short pulses, then a long tone, then held a clean note as if waiting. Question.

Mara forced herself to breathe slowly. "What do we actually *say?*" Wren whispered.

Nadine's eyes stayed sharp. "We don't say anything that gives ELXON leverage."

Howard muttered, "ELXON can leverage air."

Lila's hand tightened around the work light. "We say something we would say even if ELXON weren't listening."

From the cot, Jalen leaned back, face pale, and jaw tight. "We say something true enough to survive misuse."

Mara's mind slid toward the familiar: measurement, calibration, repeatability. But this wasn't physics. Not entirely. This was ethics under pressure. Mara looked around the basement. At Ed's NOAA jacket faded with years of storms. At Howard's notebook packed with forty years of stubborn attention. At Lila's calm, which refused to let fear drive the room. At Nadine, built by ELXON, now breaking herself into something better. At Wren, young and furious and refusing to be used as leverage. And something in that vision steadied her like a hand on her spine.

If this were a test, then the answer wasn't a clever signal. The answer was a **demonstration**. Not of power. Of intent. Mara spoke quietly. "We can't ask for rescue."

Wren blinked. "But—"

Mara held up a hand. "We don't plead. We don't bargain. We don't worship. We show… willingness."

Nadine's mouth tightened. "Willingness to what?"

Mara's throat tightened. "Willingness to choose each other."

Howard stared at her. "How do you flash *that* with a work light?"

Her eyes went to the whiteboard on the wall.

VERIFIED DATA ONLY

NO PANIC POSTS

COMMUNITY CHECK-INS

SUPPLY COORDINATION

LISTEN FIRST

She pointed towards it. "We flash those,"

Ed frowned. "Those are words."

"Not the words," Mara corrected. "The structure." She walked to the whiteboard and uncapped a marker with a sharp snap.

"Okay," she said, thinking out loud now, the way she always did when she needed others to trust the architecture of an idea. "We've already done count patterns. One-two-three. They mirrored."

She drew three short marks, then a longer line. "They introduced four-and-long," she continued. "A question." She drew: ●●●●—

"A question mark made of sound," Wren whispered.

Mara nodded. "If it's a question, we answer with an offer."

Across the room, Nadine folded her arms. "Offer what?"

The marker hovered over the whiteboard for a moment. "Transparency," Mara said. She wrote one word on the whiteboard: **TRUTH.** Then another: **CALM.** Then another: **CARE.**

Howard snorted. "We're going to send greeting-card words to a craft in the sky?"

Steady, Mara looked back at him. "We're going to send an organized pattern that indicates we value cooperation over domination."

He opened his mouth to argue, then shut it again. Because the alternative was what ELXON did: domination wrapped in soft language.

Lila stepped closer. "How?"

Mara drew a simple mapping:

- **1 pulse** = TRUTH

- **2 pulses** = CALM

- **3 pulses** = CARE

She held up the marker. "We establish a code. We repeat it. And we include the count as a legend."

Ed's eyes widened. "We teach them our intention."

Nadine shook her head. "Assuming they interpret it."

Mara's voice stayed calm. "They don't have to interpret it perfectly. They only have to recognize we're attempting alignment, not exploitation."

Wren swallowed. "So, we start with the legend again, one, two, three, then we repeat the meaning?"

"Exactly."

Howard rubbed his hand over his face. "This is crazy."

Lila's eyes were gentle. "So is hiding in a church basement while billionaires plan to abandon the planet."

Howard exhaled. "Fair."

Mara turned back to the window well. The pale gold point remained steady above the church, as if it had pinned them with quiet attention. Her heart hammered.

She nodded to Lila. "Let's do it."

Lila raised the work light to the window well and angled it upward. Howard hovered near the radio rig, recording everything. Ed had his laptop running Capture. Nadine's analyzer screen glowed with clean spikes. Wren sat close to Mara, her hand gripping Mara's, a lifeline.

Under her breath, Mara began to count. "One flash. Pause. Two flashes. Pause. Three flashes. Pause." Legend.

Lila flashed it precisely.

Then Mara continued, voice steady.

"One flash—pause." **TRUTH.**

"Two flashes—pause." **CALM.**

"Three flashes—pause." **CARE.**

She repeated the sequence twice more, slow and deliberate. The basement filled with the rhythm of light: blink, pause, blink-blink, pause, blink-blink-blink, pause.

At first, Mara felt ridiculous. And then she didn't. Because the rhythm no longer felt like a code. It felt like a vow.

The radio rig crackled. A tone responded, clean, steady. Then it pulsed: One. Pause. Two. Pause. Three. Pause. Legend mirrored.

Wren's eyes filled with tears. "It's copying again."

The signal continued. One pulse. Pause. Two pulses. Pause. Three pulses. Pause. And then: Four pulses. Long tone. Question again. But this time, the question didn't feel like "Do you exist?" It felt like—

Do you mean it?

Mara's throat tightened. Nadine's voice was low. "It's escalating the exchange."

Howard whispered, "It wants confirmation."

"Or consistency," Ed said on a long breath.

Mara nodded. "Then we repeat. Same. Stable." She nodded to Lila again. They repeated: **TRUTH. CALM. CARE**. Again.

The signal held steady. Then it changed. Beneath the clean tone, something new emerged: faintly layered, not words exactly, but an image-like structure in modulation, the way a fax machine once carried crude pictures through sound.

Howard's eyes widened. "It's sending data."

Ed leaned closer. "Can we decode?"

With a slight tremor in his hands, Howard routed the audio through a decoder tool. It wasn't designed for alien modulation, but it could approximate a pattern into shape. The screen flickered. Lines appeared. A shape slowly formed, blocky, low-resolution, but unmistakable. It looked like a curve. A line. A thin arc.

Mara's breath caught. Earth's horizon.

Then another line appeared, thinner and uneven. The rim. The wound.

Wren's voice broke. "It knows."

Mara agreed in amazement. "Yes."

The image shifted again. Another form took shape. A cluster of points near the wound, like flecks. Then the flecks gathered into a pattern. A web. A net. Something like… scaffolding.

"Is that… repair?" Howard whispered.

"Or containment," Ed said, eyes wide.

Nadine's face tightened. "Or harvesting."

Mara stared, heart pounding. Then the image changed again. This time, the net/web shape moved away from the wound and toward a cluster of darker points, moving together.

Cold spread through Mara's chest. "ELXON," she whispered before she could stop herself.

Wren turned to her sharply. "What?"

Mara pointed at the darker cluster. "That's not natural," Mara said, voice tight. "Those are… vessels. Human-made. Many of them."

Howard went pale. "Launch assets."

"Stations," Nadine said, jaws clenched.

Ed swallowed hard. "They're showing us ELXON."

The signal pulsed again: four short bursts, one long tone. Question.

Mara stared at the crude image of the swarm. "What are they asking?"

From the cot, Jalen answered in a hoarse voice but certain. "They're asking who we're choosing."

Mara turned to him, heart hammering. "How do you know that?"

He looked haunted. "Because ELXON asked me the same thing." He swallowed once. "They asked: Are you with us, or are you in our way?"

Mara looked back at the signal's question pattern. Four short. One long.

Then the image returned: Earth, wound, swarm, net. As if the visitor were saying: "We can repair." **But not while the swarm controls the wound.** *Or* maybe: **We can repair. But we won't repair for predators.**

Lila's voice was quiet. "That's the weight," she whispered. "The weight that has to be lifted."

Nadine's expression tightened. "Or it's coercion."

Mara's throat tightened too, but her mind stayed disciplined. "We don't assume motive," Mara said. "We answer with our intent again."

Wren's voice trembled. "How?"

Mara stared at the whiteboard mapping. Then she wrote another word beneath the others. **REFUSE**

Howard blinked. "Refuse?"

She nodded, and her voice came out steadier than she felt. "We add a fourth concept," she said. "Refuse exploitation."

Nadine's brows lifted. "And you map it how?"

Mara wrote:

- **4 pulses** = REFUSE

Wren whispered, "Four pulses… that's their question number."

Mara nodded slowly. "Then we take their symbol and make our meaning." She looked at Lila. Lila's hand hovered over the work light switch, trembling slightly.

Mara drew a breath. "Legend," Lila flashed: one-two-three. Then Mara spoke the code: One flash. **TRUTH.** Two flashes. **CALM.** Three flashes. **CARE.** Four flashes. **REFUSE.**

She repeated it. Then again. The basement felt charged, as if the air itself were listening. The radio rig went silent. Then it responded.

One. Two. Three.

Then four.

Four pulses, sharp, decisive.

Then the long tone held… and in that long tone, the lights in the basement flickered softly in a slow wave, not like failing electricity, but like the building itself was breathing. Wren grabbed Mara's hand so hard it hurt.

"That's… feedback," Ed exclaimed.

Howard's voice shook. "Or acknowledgment."

The signal shifted once more. A new image formed on the decoder screen. Earth's horizon. The wound. And then, descending toward it in crude lines, a new shape. Not a net. A ring. A circular structure around the damaged area, like a brace placed on a cracked bone. Mara's breath caught.

"That looks like a patch," Howard said.

"Or a lock," Nadine said, face tightening.

Lila's voice was barely audible. "Or a healing bandage."

Then the image changed again, this time showing the ring hovering *above* the wound, not touching it. Waiting.

As if the visitor was saying: **We can. But we won't… yet.**

The radio signal ended with a final pattern: Four pulses. Long tone. Then… silence. The pale gold point above the church dimmed slightly, still there, but less bright. As if it had done what it came to do.

Knock. Listen. Measure. Mirror. Ask. Receive.

Mara stared at the last frozen image on the decoder screen: a ring poised above Earth's wound like a hand held back.

"So, they can fix it," Wren whispered.

Mara barely shook her head. "I think they can," she said quietly.

Nadine's voice was cold. "And they won't until something changes."

Across the room, Jalen looked exhausted. His eyes were heavy with pain and understanding alike. "Until the weight lifts."

Lila stared at the whiteboard where the words now stood like a creed:

TRUTH. CALM. CARE. REFUSE.

She whispered, "Then the test isn't whether they can save us." Her eyes lifted toward the pale gold point still hanging in the sky. "It's whether we can become worth saving."

Mara's clean phone buzzed, this time with a different tone: a priority alert from Node One. Nadine snatched it, scanned it, and her face went hard. "ELXON just declared a global continuity emergency," she said. "Lockdown protocols. Airspace restrictions. Launch windows opening. Passenger transfers starting."

Howard's jaw clenched, staring at the alert. "They're doing it."

Wren went pale. "They're leaving."

Mara looked back at the words on the whiteboard. Truth. Calm. Care. Refuse. The visitors had offered a possibility. Not a rescue. A condition.

Now humanity had to decide, quickly, whether it would cling to ELXON's escape fantasy…

Or refuse it and become something else.

CHAPTER 16 — The Calm Network Goes Loud

By afternoon, the church basement was no longer a hiding place.

It was a **switchboard**.

Word spreads the way truth always spreads, once enough hands carry it: not as a single viral explosion, but as thousands of small movements. It was shared through Screenshots. Recordings. Reposts. Radio relays. Text chains. Community boards. Printed flyers taped to grocery store doors.

ELXON had wanted a single narrative. Instead, the world became a chorus.

At the center of one table sat Howard's decoder printout, crude but undeniable: the ring hovering above the wound, waiting.

Mara kept her eyes on the data, not the wonder. Wonder could make you sloppy. Data kept you honest.

At another table, Ed's NOAA-style models ran on an old laptop that whined like it resented being asked to predict the end of civilization. He fed it UV readings from Howard's station and ozone proxies from Mara's spectrometer, and with every passing hour, the projections tightened like a noose.

Wren moved between stations like she'd been born to manage chaos without becoming it. She managed duplicate drives, verified timestamps, cross-checked mirror links, and, most importantly, prevented people from posting unverified content.

"Not that," she snapped at a teenage boy who was about to upload a grainy video claiming he'd filmed a ship over Topeka.

The boy bristled. "But it's real!" Wren didn't yell. She didn't shame him. She did what her mother had taught her without ever naming it: She respected him enough to require honesty.

"Then prove it," Wren said, voice firm. "Time, location, direction, device metadata. Or it doesn't go up."

The boy deflated, but he nodded. "Okay."

Nadine watched Wren for a moment with a look Mara couldn't read—something between regret and admiration.

Jalen sat at a table with his ribs taped, one arm braced in a sling. He should have been lying down. He wasn't. Stubbornness was still doing half the work of medicine. Speaking into a handheld mic connected to the ham rig, he relayed short, controlled packets to other nodes.

"Node Three to Node Six: confirmed ELXON convoy sighting near Wichita, three black coaches, two unmarked escorts, time-stamped at 14:12 local… repeat, verified convoy…"

Through it all, Lila moved around the basement like a calm tide. She didn't micromanage or preach. She did what real leaders do best in emergencies: She watched people's faces. She stepped in when fear spiked. She made coffee as exhaustion began to turn kindness into sharpness and kept the room from becoming a cult.

At 3:07 p.m., Mark's voice crackled through from Node One. "Lila," he said, urgent but steady. "We have confirmation: ELXON has initiated Phase Gate."

The room stilled. Mara's stomach dropped.

Lila tightened her grip on her mug. "Define 'initiated.'"

Mark inhaled. "They're moving passenger groups under 'continuity emergency' orders. Private jets, chartered buses, secure trains. They're restricting airspace corridors and rerouting civilian flights under 'solar activity' advisories."

Howard muttered, "Solar activity. Convenient."

"And they're beginning synchronized launch windows," Mark continued. Smaller craft first, then the main carriers."

Wren's face tightened. "So, it's happening."

Mara looked at Ed's model lines on the screen. The atmosphere wasn't collapsing in some distant future. It is degrading **now**. She braced herself. "How many are they moving?"

A brief hesitation came over the line. "We estimate… around two thousand primary passengers. Tiered. Plus, essential crew."

Mara's throat tightened.

"Two thousand," Wren whispered.

Jalen's jaw clenched. "Two thousand who think they're the seed of humanity."

Nadine's reply came flat and cold. "Two thousand who are the seed of the same disease."

Lila held up her hand. "Careful," she warned gently. "We don't become what we hate." Nadine looked away, jaw still tight.

Mara crossed to the whiteboard where their four words still stood like a spine: **TRUTH. CALM. CARE. REFUSE.** She stared at them until the pressure in her chest eased enough for breath to return. Then she turned. "We go loud."

Howard blinked. "We already are."

"Not like this," Mara pointed to the ham rig. "We need a coordinated message, simple, repeatable, practical, broadcast through every channel we have."

Ed frowned. "Another video?"

Mara nodded. "Yes. But not just me. Not just a Kansas scientist."

Wren's eyes widened. "You want… a group message."

Mara met her gaze. "Yes."

Jalen sat up straighter. "You want faces."

Again, Mara nodded. "Faces that don't look like a conspiracy. Faces that look like the world."

"A pastor," Lila said, stepping forward.

"A meteorologist," Ed added.

Howard grunted, "A farmer."

Nadine's lips pressed into a line. "A former ELXON operative."

"And me," Wren said.

Mara's heart tightened. "Wren—"

Wren's eyes were steady. "They already used my name. I'm already in it." She took a shaky breath. "I want to choose how." Staring at her daughter, grief and pride collided in Mara's chest.

Lila nodded once. "Then we do it together."

They set up the camera in the basement, angled so the whiteboard was visible behind them, displaying those four words like a banner. They didn't make it dramatic. No music. No montages. Just people on folding chairs, tired faces, steady eyes.

Eli had taught them to make redundancy, and now redundancy itself would become the message: a video that could be cut into clips, transcribed into flyers, relayed over the radio, and shared neighbor to neighbor.

When Mara finally looked at the lens, she didn't feel brave. She felt responsible. She spoke first. "My name is Dr. Mara Keene," she said. "You've seen me on video already. You've also seen people trying to discredit what you saw with your own eyes."

She let the words settle before continuing. "I'm here with people who have nothing to gain by lying to you. A pastor. A retired meteorologist. A lifelong weather observer. A former security architect for ELXON. And a citizen, my daughter, who refuses to be treated like collateral."

Wren's jaw tightened, but her eyes didn't waver. "This is what we can verify today," Mara went on. "Atmospheric readings are changing rapidly. UV exposure is rising. Communications disruptions are increasing. And ELXON has initiated a continuity plan to evacuate a selected group." She held up a folder of printed data, boring, undeniable.

Lila followed, her calm carried through the screen, weighted with something larger than charisma. "If you are scared," she said, "you are not weak. Fear is a normal response to abnormal truth. But fear does not have to become chaos."

Next came Ed, practical and measured. "Check your UV index," he said. "Not once but do it daily. Protect skin. Protect eyes. Monitor the elderly and children. Prepare water and medications. Community planning is more effective than individual hoarding."

Howard looked almost irritated to be on camera, which made him perfect. "I've watched weather patterns for forty years," he said gruffly. "This is not normal. If anyone tells you it's 'just a cycle,' ask them for data. Then ask them why they won't show it."

Then Nadine spoke. Her voice was controlled, but the truth inside it shook the room. "I helped build systems that silence people," she said. "I did it because I thought I was preventing panic. I was wrong. Panic doesn't come from truth. Panic comes from being lied to."

She swallowed, eyes hard. "ELXON is not salvation. It's choice. If they offer you a seat, ask who they're leaving behind.

And if they threaten people who speak, recognize the threat for what it is.

Wren came last. She didn't sound rehearsed. She sounded like a young person refusing to be manipulated. "My name is Wren Keene," she said. "ELXON used my name in a reward notice because they think fear will make people turn on each other."

Her voice trembled, but she kept going. "Don't do it. Don't become their tool. If you see someone targeted, protect them. If you have resources, share them. If you don't, share information and kindness. You are not powerless."

Tears stung Mara's eyes, but she kept her face steady. Then Mara finished with the four words behind them. "Truth," Mara said. "Calm. Care. Refuse. Repeat those to yourself if you feel overwhelmed. Because those are the choices that keep us human."

From the rig, Eli's voice crackled faintly as he listened remotely. "We've got it," he said. "We'll distribute."

They ended the recording. For a brief moment, the basement was nothing but people breathing. Then the clean phone buzzed. Nadine glanced at it, and her face tightened.

"What now?" Jalen asked, voice rough.

She looked up slowly. "ELXON is blaming the calm network," she said. "They're calling it a coordinated destabilization effort."

Howard snorted. "Destabilization. That's rich."

Nadine continued, voice flat. "And they just announced the first 'continuity launch' will occur tonight."

Silence slammed into the basement. Tonight. Not weeks. Not later. Tonight. Wren's hand found Mara's again, squeezing hard.

Mara's mind raced. "If they launch tonight, they're leaving before the public can organize."

"Or because the public *is* organizing," Jalen said.

Lila swallowed, but her gaze held steady. "Then we have hours."

Ed's face tightened. "Hours to do what?"

Mara looked at the whiteboard, then at the recorded image of the ring above the wound. It was the visitors' "waiting hand." The symmetry of it hit her with cruel clarity: ELXON racing upward to flee, while something above was waiting to repair, if humanity proved itself.

When she spoke, her voice quietly carried weight. "Hours to choose," she said.

Howard frowned. "Choose what?"

Her voice didn't shake. "Whether we let ELXON take the future," she said, "or whether we refuse them the right to define humanity."

Outside the church, daylight faded toward winter evening. Above it, the pale gold point still hovered, steady and watchful. Not rescuing and not interfering. Just observing what humans did when they knew the truth and had very little time left to live with it.

And in that gaze, Mara sensed something both terrifying and strangely hopeful: The visitors were watching the choices ripple outward, neighbor to neighbor, town to town, like light spreading in the dark.

The "negative energy" wasn't a mystical fog. It was greed. It was secrecy. It was betrayal.

And if it thinned at all, it would be because ordinary people decided to be extraordinary.

CHAPTER 17 — Launch Night

The sun went down as if it didn't know what it was leaving behind.

A winter dusk slid over Kansas, pale and slow, the kind of evening that usually meant casseroles and early bedtimes. Tonight, it meant a countdown that no one had voted on.

In the church basement, every screen carried a different piece of the same unfolding: satellite-tracking overlays, livestream mirrors, radio chatter relays, social feeds that had become emergency bulletins. The calm network moved like a nervous system; signals firing, rerouting, adapting.

Mara sat with the spectrometer on her lap, watching the ozone proxy tick lower in tiny increments that felt like sand slipping through a glass.

Under his breath, Howard swore every time the UV curve rose when it shouldn't.

Nearby, Ed's models updated in brutal little steps.

Jalen kept his hand pressed to his ribs and refused to lie down.

At her laptop, Wren filtered posts and forwarded only verified sightings, jaw locked tight. She had started labeling everything the way professionals did:

CONFIRMED

UNCONFIRMED

DEBUNKED

NEEDS METADATA

Nadine paced in short lines, eyes flicking between the door and the screens like she could physically keep danger out by watching hard enough.

Through it all, Lila moved among them, calm as a metronome, distributing coffee, quiet words, and reminders to breathe.

At 8:11 p.m. Central, Mark's voice came through the radio from Node One. "First launch window is open," he said. "Multiple sites."

The room stilled. Mara looked up. "Which sites?"

His voice tightened. "Coastal platform in the Atlantic. A converted airbase in Nevada. Offshore rig in the Pacific. And two we didn't know about, suborbital rail-launch setups."

Howard muttered, "Of course. Hidden in plain sight."

Ed's jaw clenched. "They built redundancy into the escape."

With a knot in her throat tighten, Mara asked, "how many vehicles?"

Mark exhaled. "As of now? We estimate twenty-three human-capable craft initiating launches or launch attempts. More cargo in the background."

"Twenty-three," Wren whispered.

For one strange second, Mara remembered the early numbers she had once imagined in her own outline. Then she felt almost sick at the realization that reality was always worse. Rich people didn't make one plan. They made ten.

"They're scattering, so failure doesn't matter," Jalen said in his hoarse voice.

Nadine nodded grimly. "They expect losses."

Lila's eyes sharpened. "Losses of what?"

The answer came from Nadine, quiet and cold. "Of people."

The first video feed they received wasn't a livestream. It was shaky cellphone footage from a beach. A bright column rising over water, the rocket's flame reflecting off the waves like a second sun. The person filming wasn't cheering. They were crying. A voice over the recording said, "They're leaving us."

Mara's chest ached.

Wren didn't look away. She tagged the clip **CONFIRMED**, then forwarded it through the calm network with a short caption: **VERIFY: Coastal launch observed 8:17 p.m. CT. Stay calm. Document. Help neighbors.**

The second feed came from Nevada, security-camera footage leaked from a roadside gas station, showing a distant plume and a low rumble strong enough to shake the frame.

Then the third. Then the fourth. Bright lines in the sky. Quick flashes. The sound of low thunder wasn't thunder. By

8:29 in the evening, the entire planet seemed to be watching its elites climb into the dark.

Mara fought down a surge of nausea. Ed murmured, almost to himself, "This is what it looks like when a civilization abandons itself."

Howard's face was gray. "And calls it progress."

Then Nadine's phone buzzed with a message from an unknown node: **UNCONFIRMED: Launch failure—Atlantic. Explosion.**

"Metadata?" Wren snapped, sharper than she meant to. The reply came back: coordinates, timestamp, three angles. Her face tightened. "It's real." She sent it to Mara and Howard.

Howard pulled up the footage. It was distant, but unmistakable: a bright ascent, then a sudden blossom of white light, then debris raining down like burning confetti. The sound came later, delayed by distance, one ugly boom that made the person filming scream.

Mara's breath caught. "They died," cried Wren.

Jalen's jaw clenched. "Not all of them. But enough."

"ELXON planned for acceptable losses," Nadine said flatly.

Gripping her mug, Lila said, "There's nothing acceptable about that."

Another message hit: **CONFIRMED: Pacific platform launch successful.**

Then: **CONFIRMED: Nevada launch successful.**

Then: **UNCONFIRMED: Rail launch misfire, Germany.**

Then: **CONFIRMED: Rail launch failure, Germany Casualties unknown**

The calm network did what it had promised to do. It did not sensationalize. It documented. It verified. It shared practical guidance.

And still, grief rolled through the feeds like a storm. Across the country, people posted goodbye videos to the sky. Parents stood outside with their children, trying to explain why the people leaving were not heroes.

But something else was happening too, something ELXON hadn't planned for. The calm network wasn't just spreading evidence. It was spreading **behavior.**

People began filming themselves helping each other. A woman in Missouri posted a clip of her neighborhood gathering water jugs for elderly residents. A nurse in Dallas recorded a short video on UV protection and distributed it to local clinics. A pastor in Ohio live-streamed a message that was almost identical to Lila's: *Truth doesn't require chaos.* A mechanic in Detroit offered free repairs for anyone trying to get to their family.

It wasn't glamorous. It didn't trend as panic did. But it spread.

Watching the posts, Mara had hope. Maybe the visitors were right. Maybe "negative energy" wasn't mystical at all. Maybe it was simply the sum of choices that made a world unbearable. And maybe those choices could shift.

At 9:03 p.m., Howard's magnetometer spiked hard. Not like earlier. Hard enough that the line jumped and stayed high. Howard's eyes widened. "That's—"

Ed leaned in, face pale. "That's massive."

The spectrometer chimed too, an alarm tone sharp enough to turn Mara's stomach. She stared at the screen. The UV proxy surged. The ozone proxy plunged faster, like the numbers had tripped over a ledge. Her chest tightened. "The disintegration is accelerating."

Wren looked up, eyes wide. "Because of the launches?"

Nadine's face hardened. "Or because they're launching *because* it's accelerating."

Through clenched teeth, Jalen exhaled. "They saw a tipping point."

Outside, a low rumble passed through the earth, subtle but unmistakable. Not a truck. Not wind or thunder. The lights in the basement flickered. Howard whispered, "There it is again."

Mara's skin prickled. They all looked toward the window well. The pale gold point in the sky was brighter now. Not pulsing and not flashing. Just… more present. As if it had leaned closer. As if it could no longer pretend it was merely observing.

Lila whispered, "It's watching the launches."

Nadine's voice was tight. "It's watching the wound."

"Or it's watching *us*," Ed said, swallowing hard.

Jalen spoke quietly, voice raw. "ELXON thinks tonight decides who gets a future."He looked at Mara, eyes haunted. "But tonight, might be deciding something else."

Mara's throat tightened. "Worthiness." Jalen nodded.

At 9:14 p.m., the next thing happened so fast it didn't feel real at first. A new feed appeared on Wren's screen showing a live camera from a highway overpass in Florida, pointing toward the ocean. In the corner of the screen, the viewer count climbed so fast it blurred. A rocket rose, bright, clean. Then, to the left of the rocket's plume, the sky… bent. Not like a cloud or heat shimmer. It looked more like space itself had curved. A pale gold ring appeared, faint at first, then clearer, hovering high above the horizon, massive and silent.

The rocket kept climbing. The ring didn't move. It simply… existed. Wren's voice cracked. "That's the ring."

Howard's hands shook. "That's what we saw in the decoded image."

"That's impossible," Ed whispered.

Nadine stared, face pale. "It's here."

The rocket's plume angled, slightly off course, then corrected, as if the guidance system had hiccupped. Then the livestream cut. Black screen. ELXON logo. **"SIGNAL STABILIZING."**

Mara's stomach turned. "They cut it. The moment it appeared."

Jalen's jaw clenched. "They don't want the public seeing a bigger power." But the public had already seen enough.

Because the ring was visible in multiple feeds now, different angles, different states, even a shaky clip from a fishing boat in the Atlantic. The ring wasn't everywhere. It was near the wound. Holding position like a brace. Waiting.

And the launches continued. Some streaked upward into the dark. Some exploded. Some vanished mid-ascent in ways that made physics feel suddenly optional.

At 9:37 p.m., a clip circulated. It was grainy and distant, but horrifying: A rocket rising from a desert base and then… disappeared as if it had slipped behind an invisible curtain. No explosion. No debris. Just absence.

Wren stared at it, terrified. "What just happened?"

"Interdiction," Nadine said quietly.

Ed's face went pale. "They stopped it."

"Or redirected it," Howard suggested.

The idea landed in Mara like ice: The visitors weren't only watching. They were beginning to act. Not loudly. Not violently. Selectively.

Lila's voice was quiet. "They're not stopping all of them."

"No," Jalen said, eyes fixed on the screen.

Holding her breath a bit too long, Mara whispered, "they're measuring."

Howard's whisper barely carried. "Who they let through?"

"Based on what?" Wren asked, her voice shaking.

Silence pressed in. Then, from the radio rig, a tone emerged, faint at first, then clean and steady. The same signature they'd heard earlier.

The same gold-spectrum fingerprint. It pulsed once. Then twice. Then three. Legend. Then four pulses. **REFUSE**. Then the long tone held, and the basement lights flickered in that slow wave once more, as if the building were breathing.

Mara's throat tightened. It felt like a message. Not in words. In alignment. A reminder of what mattered. Truth. Calm. Care. Refuse. Outside, the sky carried streaks of fire, hope, and betrayal.

Inside the church basement, something else was launching. Something that didn't leave the planet at all. A launch of conscience.

And with painful clarity, Mara understood: ELXON was trying to escape Earth's end.

But the visitors were asking a different question:

Who was escaping *humanity*?

And who was finally becoming human enough to stay?

CHAPTER 18 — The Leader Who Stayed

By 10:12 p.m., the world had stopped pretending.

Even the people who wanted to believe ELXON's "deep-fake" story couldn't hold it anymore. Not with rockets carving the night sky, not with the aurora crawling south like a living bruise, not with the UV alerts flashing on phones in places where UV had never mattered after sunset.

Truth had weight. And the weight was finally breaking through the lies.

The church basement became louder, not with panic, but with traffic. Messages. Calls. Relays. People are asking for guidance instead of gossip.

Wren's laptop chimed every few seconds. She didn't flinch anymore. She had learned what triage looked like in the digital world: you couldn't save every message. You could only save the ones that mattered most.

Howard's radios carried voices from other nodes, short, clipped, efficient. "Node Seven: supplies route established…" "Node Two: clinic coordination underway…" "Node Nine: verified sighting of ring near the Atlantic wound…"

Nearby, Mara's spectrometer beeped again, then again. Numbers shifted in uncomfortable ways, not catastrophic yet, but trending like a cliff you were walking toward.

Across the room, Ed's models ran and re-ran, narrowing toward the same conclusion every time: Hours mattered now.

Near the basement stairs, Nadine stood like a guard, her eyes flicking to the door every time headlights swept across the church windows. The bounty had changed everything. It turned desperation into a predator.

Jalen sat with a microphone in his hand, listening to the world's pulse through wires.

And Lila—steady Lila—moved among them, saying the same words in different forms: "Breathe." "Verify." "Check your neighbors." "Don't run alone."

Watching her, Mara understood something she hadn't fully named until this moment: The calm network wasn't held together by science alone. It was held together by *leadership*. The kind that stayed regardless of personal gain and safety.

At 10:26 p.m., the call came. It wasn't from Silas. It wasn't from Mark. It was from a number labeled **UNKNOWN — VERIFIED PATH**, one of Eli's emergency routes.

Nadine answered on the first ring, voice flat. "Talk." A familiar voice came through: ragged, older, and unmistakably public. Not a billionaire. Not a celebrity. Not an ELXON spokesperson. A former astronaut, one of the few whose name everyone recognized, not for wealth, but for courage. Commander Ruth Calder.

Mara's breath caught. Ruth Calder was the woman who had walked out of NASA five years earlier in a quiet "retirement" that never made sense to anyone who loved space. She'd vanished into private life, rumor-magnet life, *what happened to her* life?

Now she was back, alive, urgent, and angry. "I need Dr. Keene," Ruth said. "Now."

Mara stepped forward so fast her blanket slipped. "I'm here."

Relief and exhaustion tangled in Ruth's exhale. "Thank God. I've been trying to reach you for hours. They jammed my channels. I had to bounce through a ham relay in Iowa run by a teenager who thinks I'm a conspiracy."

Wren looked up, wide-eyed. "We have a teenager, too."

"Commander Calder, how have you heard about me?" asked Mara.

A bitter laugh. "Because your face is on every screen I can still access. Because ELXON put a bounty on you like they're the sheriff of Earth. And because you're saying what I've been holding in my throat for years."

Mara's throat tightened. "You knew."

Ruth didn't deny it. "I saw it."

Silence hit the basement like a sudden pressure drop. Mara's voice came out quietly. "The wound."

"Yes," Ruth said. "Not today. Not yesterday. I saw the thinning start in orbit months ago. Subtle. Explainable, until it wasn't."

Mara's stomach clenched. "Why didn't you tell the public?"

Ruth's voice sharpened. "I tried." A pause, then quieter: "They made me disappear politely. They offered me a seat, Mara. They offered my family a seat."

Wren's breath caught. Ruth continued, her voice breaking slightly. "They said I could be remembered as a hero… or buried as a lunatic."

"ELXON," Nadine said, jaw tightening.

"Yes," Ruth replied, her tone going cold. "Different name then, same machine."

Mara braced herself. "Commander… what do you want?"

The exhale that came back sounded like a decision hardening into shape. "I want to speak," Ruth said. "To the world. Not a press conference. Not a studio. A raw message. Unfiltered. Truth."

Lila stepped forward, voice gentle but firm. "Why now?"

Ruth didn't hesitate. "Because the launches started. Because the ring appeared. And because if we don't anchor the public in truth right now, ELXON will rewrite the story as 'necessary sacrifice' and walk away with the future."

Mara's heart pounded. "You'll be targeted."

Ruth gave a grim laugh. "I've already been targeted. They just did it quietly."

Jalen leaned forward, voice rough. "Where are you?"

A brief pause. "I'm in Texas."

Mara blinked. "Texas?"

"Keller," Ruth said. "A friend's ranch. There's a small airstrip nearby. And there's a camera."

Mara's chest tightened. Keller. Too close to the kind of airspace ELXON could control, but also close to people. To infrastructure. To the places truth could still travel.

"We can route your message," Lila said quietly.

"Good," Ruth snapped. "Because I'm going live in fifteen minutes."

Wren's eyes widened. "Fifteen minutes?"

Ruth didn't apologize. "The sky is falling. We don't schedule."

Mara experienced a flicker of panic. "Commander, what will you say?"

For the first time, Ruth's voice softened. Only slightly. "I'm going to say I stayed."

Mara's throat tightened.

"They offered me the escape," Ruth went on. "They offered my grandchildren the escape. And I said no."

Silence filled the room. Wren whispered, "Why?"

When Ruth answered, her voice came out steady, carrying a strength that felt like steel wrapped in skin. "Because I looked down at Earth from orbit," she said, "and I realized the planet isn't a resource. It's a home. And you don't abandon your home and call yourself noble."

Mara blinked fast.

Ruth continued, "I'm going to tell them about the wound. About the secrecy. About the selection. And I'm going to tell them something else: that the public isn't failing. The public is being *kept blind.*"

"Not anymore," Nadine muttered.

"Exactly," Ruth's voice sharpened again. "And I'm going to ask people to do one thing: stay calm and stay human. Because if there's any chance of help, any chance at all, it will come to the version of us that isn't feral."

Mara's skin prickled at the echo. The visitors. The ring. The condition. Mara leaned toward the radio mic. "Commander Calder... we received a signal."

A pause sharp. Ruth's voice went quiet. "Say that again."

Mara chose her words carefully. "An anomalous, structured signal. A ring-shaped presence near the wound. It appeared on multiple feeds. And... we believe it's responding."

Silence on the line for a full second. Then Ruth exhaled. "I knew it," she whispered.

Wren's eyes widened. "You knew about them, too?"

Ruth's voice dropped low. "In orbit, we saw lights that weren't ours. NASA called it debris. ELXON called it interference. I called it what it was." She paused. "Attention."

Mara's chest tightened. "Why didn't you say anything?"

Ruth's voice cracked with something like old rage. "Because I couldn't prove it without being erased."

"We have crude decoded imagery now," Mara said.

Ruth's voice steadied. "Then I'm not speaking alone," she said. "I'm speaking with you behind me."

Mara's pulse spiked. "Commander—"

Ruth cut in, firm. "I'm not putting your location on blast. But I am putting the *truth* on blast. That's the point."

Lila looked at Mara, eyes serious. "This is the leader stepping up." Mara nodded slowly.

Then Ruth spoke again, calm and resolute now. "Dr. Keene, I'm going live with a message that includes your four words if you'll allow it."

Mara blinked. "Four words?"

Ruth's tone softened. "Truth. Calm. Care. Refuse."

A knot formed in the throat. "Yes."

Ruth exhaled. "Good. Then the world has a spine."

Suddenly, Nadine's analyzer beeped sharply and urgently. Nadine looked down, then up, her face gone pale.

"What?" Mara asked.

"The gold signature is increasing."

Howard stared at his magnetometer. "So is the field disturbance."

Ed's face went white. "It's getting closer."

"While ELXON launches," Lila said.

Outside, the church windows glowed faintly with reflected aurora, green and pale gold tangled together like the sky was writing something.

Ruth's voice cut through the line again, fiercely. "Listen. Whatever is out there, whatever is watching, this is the moment we show who we are."

Mara's pulse spiked. "I'm going live now," Ruth said. "Route it. Mirror it. Spread it. And if they try to silence me—" Her voice hardened like a blade. "—make the silence louder than their lies."

The line clicked dead. For a second, everyone in the basement just stared at each other.

Wren moved first, fingers flying. "We can route her through our mirrors."

Ed nodded. "We can cross-post to independent stations."

Howard grunted. "Ham relay too."

"We do it all," Lila said, steady as ever.

Nadine looked at Mara, eyes hard but oddly human. "This," Nadine said quietly, "is how you beat them."

Mara's chest tightened. Not with sabotage. Not with violence. With a leader who stayed and made staying look like courage instead of failure.

On the biggest screen, Ruth Calder appeared. She stood outdoors under a darkening Texas sky, wind tugging her hair, face lined with years and stubborn truth. No studio. No makeup. Just a woman who had seen Earth from above and refused to let the powerful steal the story.

She looked into the camera and spoke the words that would either steady the world… or ignite it. "My name is Ruth Calder," she said. "I've been to orbit. I've seen what they didn't want you to see."

Mara's breath caught. And all at once, the calm network leaned forward as one.

Because this was the moment the truth stopped being a leak.

It became a river.

CHAPTER 19 — The River

Ruth Calder's voice didn't sound like panic.

It sounded like gravity.

In the church basement, her image filled the largest screen. The picture was grainy with wind-noise crackling, and the sky behind her was an unsettled purple-gray. She stood with her feet planted like the earth mattered, like she wasn't trying to float above consequences.

"My name is Ruth Calder," she said again, slower this time, letting the words root themselves into the moment. "I flew orbital missions. I trained astronauts. I have held my breath inside a machine and trusted it to bring me home."

She looked straight into the camera.

"And I have never been more afraid than I am right now. Not because the sky is falling, but because powerful people believe you can't handle the truth."

Mara was overcome with emotion. Beside her, Wren's hand clenched around hers.

Ruth continued, voice steady. "You have been lied to. Not out of love. Out of convenience." She paused, eyes sharp. "I saw thinning in the upper atmosphere months ago," she said. "Subtle changes at first there were UV anomalies, electromagnetic disruptions, the kind of things you can call 'cycles' if you need to sleep at night."

A sad smile flickering at the corner of her mouth, "But it stopped being subtle. And when it did, the response from the people who claim to protect you was not transparency."

Her face hardened. "It was secrecy."

In the basement, Howard muttered, "Tell it."

Ruth continued, "A private initiative, known now as ELXON, began consolidating resources to evacuate a selected group. World leaders. Billionaires. Technical specialists. And yes, celebrities."

A beat passed. "They called it continuity. They called it duty. They called it the only way."

Her voice sharpened. "They did not call it what it is."

Leaning closer to the camera, she let the wind slap at the microphone like the sky itself was trying to interrupt. "It is abandonment."

On Wren's screen, the viewer count rose so quickly it ceased to feel real. Five million. Eight million. Twelve.

The calm network mirrored Ruth's message everywhere, with clipped videos, transcripts, radio summaries for people without internet, and flyers printed in church offices and stapled to community boards.

A river.

Still holding the camera's gaze, Ruth said, "If you are watching this, and you feel anger, I understand. If you feel grief, I understand. If you feel fear, I understand."

She drew in one steady breath. "But I am asking you to do something that will feel impossible: Stay Calm."

Now her eyes softened. "Not because this isn't serious," she said. "It is. But because chaos is the currency of people who want to control you."

Lila lay her hand gently on Mara's shoulder, a quiet yes.

Ruth raised one hand, palm open to the camera as if taking an oath. "I am not telling you to trust me blindly. I am telling you to trust evidence. Trust the scientists who share real data. Trust the people measuring UV spikes and ozone changes. Trust your own eyes when the aurora appears in places it never belonged."

Her jaw tightened. "And when someone tells you it's a deep-fake, ask yourself: why are they working so hard to keep you asleep?"

The comments beneath Ruth's broadcast weren't all in agreement. There were arguments, conspiracies, and people screaming in caps lock. But something else stood out, something Mara hadn't expected. There were thousands of comments that read like this:

"Okay. Tell us what to do." "Where can we verify?" "How do we protect kids from UV?" "I have elderly neighbors—what should I check on?" "I'm scared, but I'm listening."

People weren't erupting into a riot. They were asking for instructions. Truth had given them something ELXON never intended to give them: dignity.

Quietly, Ruth continued. "I was offered a seat. My family was offered a seat."

Wren's breath caught.

Ruth's eyes glistened, but her voice never broke. "I said no. Not because I'm brave. Because I couldn't live with myself if I stepped onto a ship built from everyone else's silence."

She exhaled, then spoke the words that rippled outward like a spine strengthening. "Truth," Ruth said. "Calm. Care. Refuse."

The church basement went utterly still.

Again, slower this time. "Truth. Calm. Care. Refuse." Then Ruth did the thing Mara hadn't realized the world most needed.

She named the moral choice without shaming anyone. "If you are offered a seat on ELXON," she said, "you will be tempted to tell yourself it's your right, your reward, your survival. I'm not here to call you evil."

Her voice was gentle now. "I am here to ask you: what kind of humanity do you want to carry forward?"

A pause, long enough to be a door. "Because if you carry forward a humanity that abandons its own," Ruth said quietly, "then you are not preserving life. You are preserving a disease."

In the basement, Nadine's jaw tightened as if she'd been struck.

Ruth finished with brief and specific practical steps, then looked into the camera one last time. "I will not be silenced. And you don't have to be either. Choose each other. Help each other. Protect truth-tellers. Protect the vulnerable. Don't let the rich turn you into a weapon against your neighbor."

Then, in a lower voice, she added: "And if there is anyone out there watching how we respond, let them see something worth saving."

The broadcast ended. For one heartbeat, the basement was silent. Then the world answered. Phones lit up. Radios crackled. Laptops refreshed. Not with screaming. With movement.

Reports poured in:

- Neighborhood groups forming UV check teams to help parents and the elderly

- Hospitals sharing guidance on respiratory irritation and UV burns

- Churches and community centers opening their doors for supplies and shelter

- Teachers making calming, honest lesson plans for children

- Amateur astronomers posting verified comparisons of the ring sightings near the wound

And something else began happening, quieter but seismic. ELXON passengers start to speak. At first, it came anonymously, with faces blurred and voices altered, giving shaky confessions. "I was invited," one said. "They called it continuity. They made me sign a nondisclosure. They told me not to tell my parents."

Another voice: "They offered my company a Tier Two seat allocation if we donated. It felt… disgusting."

Then a video surfaced, unblurred, face fully visible. It was a tech executive Mara recognized from magazine covers. His hands shook as he spoke into the camera. "I'm refusing," he said. "I don't know if it matters. But I'm refusing."

Wren's eyes filled with tears. "People are listening."

Mara looked at the images with pride. "People are choosing."

Then Nadine's analyzer beeped sharply. She looked down, then up, face pale. "The gold signature," she whispered. "It's increasing again."

Howard's magnetometer line rose like a slow tide. Not spiking. Building.

Ed stared at his model, then lifted his eyes toward the window well. "Something's happening."

They crowded to the glass. Outside, the sky had changed. The aurora was no longer only green. A pale gold seam ran through it now, subtle at first, then clearer, as if the atmosphere itself had been threaded with a new frequency.

Wren whispered, "That's the signature."

Mara's heart hammered. "Yes."

Above the horizon, toward the invisible location of the wound, the ring had brightened. Not dramatically. Not like a spotlight. Like a tool powering up.

Howard's voice went hoarse. "It's activating."

Ed's hands trembled. "In response to—"

"In response to us," Lila finished softly.

Jalen stared at the sky, haunted. "They waited," he whispered.

Mara's throat tightened. "For what?"

Barely audible, he answered, "For the weight to lift."

As if on cue, messages flooded the calm network from across the world:

- **Celebrity refuses ELXON seat, gives statement**

- **Astronaut leaks internal NASA memo—confirms anomaly**

- **Government official resigns, cites secrecy**

- **Crowds remain calm at launch site protests—singing, not rioting**

The "negative energy" wasn't evaporating like magic. It was being **chosen against**, one refusal at a time.

Mara stared at the brightening ring and felt awe rising in her again, dangerous and holy.

Then a new message popped up on Wren's screen. It was short and verified, from a node near the Atlantic.

CONFIRMED: Ring interacting with upper atmosphere. Local readings stabilizing by 2–4%.

Mara's breath caught. "Stabilizing?"

Howard's eyes widened. "That fast?"

Ed leaned in, scanning. "It's localized, near the wound. But yes, stabilization."

Almost disbelieving, Nadine's voice was tight, "They're starting."

Lila closed her eyes briefly, and when she opened them, they were wet but steady. "Not because we earned it," she whispered. "Because we finally stopped proving we didn't deserve it."

Mara looked around at the people beside her: the basement crew, the calm network beyond them, the wider world outside, choosing truth over panic. And she felt the story pivot on its hinge.

ELXON was still launching. There were ship still escaping. Some were failing. But above the wound, the ring was no longer merely waiting. It was **working**.

And then Mara understood: the visitors weren't here to save a planet.

They were here to save the possibility of a different humanity.

And that work had only just begun.

CHAPTER 20 — The Claim

ELXON moved the moment the ring began to work.

Not with public statements at first, those came later, polished and smiling, but with the quiet violence of systems able pivot faster than human conscience.

In the church basement, Nadine's analyzer kept chirping, a steady warning song. The gold signature line had risen and held. Stable now, as if the ring had found a frequency and locked into it.

Howard's instruments confirmed the same thing from a different language. According to external node reports, the ozone proxy had stopped falling so quickly. Not healed. But **stabilized**. A pause in the freefall.

The relief washed over Mara. But it was like a dangerous drug. Relief could make you careless.

Lila, sensing it too, didn't let anyone drift inside it for long. "Okay," she said quietly. "We can't celebrate yet."

Howard frowned. "Why not? It's—"

"It's the first breath after drowning," Lila said. "You don't throw a party in the water. You keep swimming."

Mara nodded. "She's right."

Across the room, Ed was already running a comparative model, pulling readings from nodes near the Atlantic rim and comparing them with inland proxies.

"It's real," he murmured. "Localized, but real. Something is altering the field properties above the wound. Like—"

"Like a brace," Mara said softly.

Wren's face was pale with hope. "So, they're saving us."

Nadine's voice cut in, flat. "Don't say that yet."

Wren bristled. "Why?"

"Because the moment the public believes 'aliens are saving us,' people stop doing the hard human part. And ELXON will exploit that. They'll frame it as proof they were right."

Pale but upright, Jalen gave a grim nod. "They'll claim it." As if his words summoned the proof, Wren's laptop chimed with a breaking alert from a major network.

A studio anchor, calm yet excited, spoke over footage of a bright ring hanging near the Atlantic. "—unconfirmed reports of an unusual atmospheric phenomenon," the anchor said. "Sources connected to the ELXON Foundation suggest this may be a controlled geoengineering demonstration designed to stabilize upper-atmospheric conditions in response to increased solar activity."

Howard stared at the screen. "Geoengineering demonstration."

Ed's mouth fell open. "They're taking credit."

A cold, slow anger was crawling through Mara's chest. "They're trying to make the ring their product."

Nadine's jaw tightened. "Because if the ring becomes 'ELXON tech,' they control the narrative again."

The broadcast continued with smooth graphics and synthetic reassurance: *ELXON ATMOSPHERIC STABILIZATION INITIATIVE*—a shiny title slapped onto something nobody on Earth had built.

Then the anchor smiled. "ELXON representatives assure the public that advanced stabilization systems are being deployed in coordination with international partners. The Foundation emphasizes that calm and cooperation are essential…"

Wren barked a humorless laugh. "Now they want calm and cooperation?"

Lila's eyes narrowed. "Calm without truth is control."

Jalen's voice came out hoarse. "They'll use the calm network's language to keep people docile."

"We respond with evidence. Not outrage," Mara said, forcing herself to breathe.

Howard muttered, "Outrage would be appropriate, though."

She glanced at him. "Yes. But we can't afford to be predictable."

Turning to Wren, Mara said, "Pull the clips. Find where they mention 'controlled demonstration.' We counter with our own measurements. We use timestamps, independent node readings, and the gold signature spectral match. And we make it clear: ELXON didn't create this." Wren nodded, fingers already flying.

Nadine added, "And we highlight that the ring appeared before their statement. They're reacting, not initiating."

Ed gave a sharp nod. "We also show the anomalies in orbit predating Phase Gate."

Quietly, Lila said, "And we remind people: stay calm does not mean stay silent."

Mara's clean phone buzzed with a message from Silas. Nadine grabbed it first, then handed it to Mara without reading, a small gesture, but a significant one. Mara opened the message.

SILAS: *ELXON is issuing emergency legal threats to any outlet sharing the "ring as non-human" claim. They're also mobilizing teams toward rural nodes. Assume they'll attempt to seize your equipment and drive you into silence. Do not stay in one place.*

Her chest tightened.

Watching her face, Jalen said quietly, "They're coming."

Howard clenched his jaw, but he said nothing.

Nadine's expression turned grim. "They won't come politely. And they'll use local authorities where they can."

Wren swallowed hard. "We can't keep moving forever."

Mara looked at her daughter and felt the ache of it: Wren wanted an ending. A stable point. A home. Mara wanted that too. But the story didn't care what they wanted. It cared about what they chose.

Lila stepped closer, voice steady. "Then we do what we've been doing. We become many."

Ed nodded. "More nodes."

Howard grumbled. "More damn work."

A faint smile touched Mara's lips. "Yes."

Wren's laptop chimed again. This time it wasn't a network alert. A message came from an unknown sender, routed through three relays. The text was blunt:

LOOK UP. NOW.

Mara's skin prickled. They rushed to the window well. Outside, the aurora had intensified, the pale gold seam brighter now, stitched through green like thread pulled through torn fabric.

But it wasn't the aurora that stole Mara's breath. Above the church, closer than before, the pale gold point had changed. It was no longer a point. It had become a shape. Not fully visible, not like a ship you could point at and say *there*. More like the outline of something enormous refracting the air. An arc. A curve. A faint geometry that made the sky itself look slightly wrong, as if the atmosphere had begun to reveal the thing it had been hiding.

Wren whispered, "Oh my God…"

Ed's voice shook. "That's not a light."

Howard swallowed hard. "That's a vessel."

Nadine's face went pale. "And it's low."

Jalen's eyes narrowed. "Lower than it should ever be."

Again, Mara felt the pressure change, subtle but unmistakable, as though the air was being held by a larger hand.

Then the radio rig crackled behind them. Not the same as the earlier knocks using mirrored patterns. Something different. A tone that wasn't merely heard. It was *felt*. It rolled through the basement like a low chord, a vibration that made the glass in the window well hum.

Howard swore softly. Nadine's analyzer screen flooded with lines showing dozens of frequencies at once, layered and clean.

Ed whispered, "It's broadcasting wide spectrum."

"Like it wants to be heard by everyone," Lila's voice quiet.

Then Mara's clean phone, lying untouched on the table, lit up. No buzz. No ring. It simply activated. The screen glowed pale gold.

Wren froze. "Mom… your phone—"

Mara turned slowly. Text began appearing on the screen. Not a push notification. Not a normal interface. Text formed letter by letter as if something were typing through the device itself.

Her mouth went dry. It read:

WE HEAR THE LIE. WE HEAR THE FEAR. WE HEAR THE REFUSAL.

For a moment, Mara couldn't breathe.

"It's… talking," Wren whispered.

Nadine's disbelief came out tight and strained. "That's impossible."

Jalen stared at the phone as if it were a weapon. "It's not impossible," he rasped. "It's just… beyond us."

More text appeared.

THE WOUND CAN BE BOUND. NOT WITHIN YOUR CURRENT CONTROL. WE MAY INTERVENE. CONDITION: WEIGHT LIFTED.

Lila swallowed hard. "Weight…"

Mara's hands shook. "What do you mean by weight?" she whispered, though she had no idea if it could hear her.

The screen paused. Then a new text formed.

SELECTION.

SECRECY.

SACRIFICE OF MANY FOR FEW.

Tears stung Mara's eyes. "That's ELXON," Wren said, her voice breaking.

Nadine's jaw tightened. "They're calling it out."

The text continued.

WE DO NOT REPAIR A CAGE. WE DO NOT BLESS A FLEEING FEW. WE REPAIR A HOME WHEN HOME IS CLAIMED BY HOMEKEEPERS.

Howard whispered, "Homekeepers."

Her eyes filling with tears, Lila said, "Those who stay."

"The worthy," Jalen croaked.

Mara's throat tightened. "But who decides worthy?"

After a brief pause, the final line appeared, landing like both a blade and a blessing:

YOU DECIDE.

Silence swallowed the basement. Outside, the sky held the faint outline of something vast. Inside, the phone glowed with an answer that offered no comfort. Only responsibility.

Nadine spoke first, voice low. "This changes everything."

Ed swallowed hard. "The world will demand proof."

Mara nodded slowly. "And ELXON will try to seize it."

Wren's hand found hers again. "Mom…how do we fight this?"

Mara stared at the glowing words—**YOU DECIDE**—and felt the ethical dilemma sharpen into its final form:

If humanity wanted to be saved, it could not outsource its conscience. Not to ELXON. Not to visitors. Not to anyone.

She looked up at the others: Lila, Howard, Ed, Nadine, Jalen, Wren, and felt the weight of billions of lives pressing through a single room and into her chest. Then she spoke, quiet but steady. "We make the choice visible."

Howard frowned. "How?"

Mara's eyes hardened. "We expose ELXON's final move. And we stop them from turning the future into a gated colony."

Nadine's jaw clenched. "And how do we stop them without chaos?"

She drew in a breath. "By doing the one thing they can't control. We tell the world the condition."

Wren blinked. "The condition?"

Mara nodded, throat tight. "Just the truth: the repair won't happen for a world that chooses selfish escape over a shared home."

Lila whispered, "That will divide people."

"Yes," Mara said.

Ed's voice went thin. "And it will enrage ELXON."

Her gaze didn't waver. "Then they can be enraged. They already are. The question is whether we still refuse them."

Outside, toward the wound, the ring glowed brighter, steadier, readier, waiting. As if the planet itself had become a stage. And now humanity had to perform the only act that mattered:

Not the act of escaping.

The act of staying.

CHAPTER 21 — You Decide

Mara didn't sleep.

No one did. Sleep required a future that felt dependable enough to risk unconsciousness.

In the church basement, the air had changed after the message came through the phone. It felt thicker, heavier, as if everyone were carrying the same invisible object in their chest.

YOU DECIDE.

Those two words were not comforting. They were a handoff. A burden passed from the sky to the ground.

Nadine kept the clean phone on the center table like evidence from a crime scene. No one touched it. Howard set up a camera over it, capturing continuous footage of the screen, the timestamps, the environment, and every possible layer of proof.

At another table, Ed ran signal analysis, saving the wide-spectrum broadcast signatures in multiple formats, copying them to drives until the redundancy itself began to feel absurd.

Wren sat close beside Mara, shoulders pressed together, quietly repeating the same phrase under her breath like a mantra: "Truth. Calm. Care. Refuse."

Across the room, Lila watched everyone the way she watched a congregation in grief, quietly, mercifully, without allowing hysteria to become holy.

Jalen sat with his jaw clenched, eyes flicking to the stairs every time footsteps moved overhead.

At last, Mara spoke. "Before we do anything, we decide what we're releasing."

Howard answered first. "Everything."

Nadine shook her head. "Not everything. Not raw enough to give ELXON a triangulation map and a playbook."

Howard bristled. "They already know."

Her eyes cut toward him. "They know patterns. They don't know *all* the patterns. We don't hand them our network like a gift."

Ed lifted a hand. "We can release proof without releasing the location."

Wren's fingers hovered over her keyboard. "We can redact metadata."

Mara nodded once. "We release in layers." Her eyes returned to the phone. The pale gold text still glowed faintly on the screen as if it had burned itself into the pixels.

Layer one: the words. Layer two: the signal data. Layer three: independent confirmation of the ring and the atmosphere stabilizing near the wound. Layer four: the moral framework, without turning it into religion, without turning it into a mob.

Because the mob was what ELXON wanted. If the public turned violent, the visitors would see exactly what the "weight" was made of. And if the visitors were serious about the condition, violence could fail the test faster than any rocket could.

Mara drew a breath. "We release the message," she said. "But we don't frame it as 'aliens will save us if you behave.'"

Lila nodded instantly. "Good."

"We frame this way," Mara continued. "There is evidence of an external intervention capability, and evidence they will not reinforce a system of elite abandonment."

Nadine's mouth tightened. "And then we say: *you decide* what kind of civilization you are."

Jalen's voice came rough and hoarse. "That will make ELXON desperate."

Mara nodded. "Yes."

Howard grunted. "Then we'd better be faster than desperate."

Wren looked up. "Are we…allowed to say it's not human?"

Ed shook his head gently. "We say 'unknown origin.'"

Mara nodded. "And we show our receipts."

The calm network had become a printing press. Wren drafted the release packet like a surgeon laying out instruments:

- A one-page public statement: calm, factual, actionable.

- A technical appendix: spectra, magnetometer correlations, signal traces.

- A Q&A: "What we know / what we don't."

- A community checklist: UV protection, supply coordination, neighbor check-ins.

And near the end, in bold:

DO NOT ATTACK ELXON PASSENGERS. DO NOT TARGET YOUR NEIGHBORS. PROTECT EACH OTHER.

Mara stared at that line until it felt as if it might burn. Then she nodded. "Post."

Wren swallowed once, then hit upload. The packet went out across mirrors, radios, transcript relays, and every channel not already owned by ELXON money. It didn't explode like a bomb. It spread like a seed.

Within minutes, the response began. From ordinary people and from ELXON.

The crackdown didn't arrive first like boots and guns. It arrived as language. A major network interrupted regular programming with a breaking statement. On screen, an ELXON representative stood behind a podium, face smooth, tone professional, eyes empty. The representative said, "A coordinated misinformation network has released fabricated content designed to destabilize the public and interfere with critical continuity operations."

Mara's stomach tightened.

The smile on the screen sharpened slightly. "Let me be clear: no non-human phenomenon exists. No 'ring' exists. Any alleged communications are digitally manipulated."

Howard muttered, "Sure."

Then the representative continued, more coldly than before. "Additionally, due to the clear threat posed by this misinformation campaign, the ELXON Foundation is partnering with relevant agencies to secure sensitive infrastructure temporarily. Individuals involved in spreading destabilizing content may be subject to investigation."

Wren's face drained of color. "They're criminalizing the truth."

Nadine's eyes narrowed. "They're creating legal cover for raids."

"And for fear," Lila added quietly.

Mara stared at the screen and felt the old ethical dilemma rise again, sharper this time. If truth were treated like a crime, would people still choose it? Or would they retreat into lies because it felt safer?

The answer came faster than she expected. A livestream popped up. Ruth Calder again, but this time with someone standing beside her: a young father holding a blanket-wrapped child, cheeks red from cold and worry.

"This is my daughter," the man said, voice trembling. "Her skin burned today from sunlight that shouldn't burn in December." He held up a printed UV reading from a local clinic. "I don't care what ELXON says," he continued. "I care what reality says."

Ruth looked straight into the camera, jaw set. "The calm network is not destabilizing. It's stabilizing the only thing that matters: human behavior."

Then another video surfaced.

A small town mayor, unknown nationally, standing outside a community center. "We will not allow violence," she said. "We will not allow scapegoating. We will not allow hoarding. We are opening this center for supplies and support, and anyone threatened for speaking truth will be protected here."

Then another.

A police chief, face tense, eyes tired, speaking with careful precision. "My officers have received advisories about certain individuals," he said. "I will not be participating in any private organization's bounty campaign. We are here to keep public safety, not enforce corporate secrecy."

Nadine went still. "That," she whispered, "is the crack."

Howard exhaled. "People are refusing."

And then the internet did what it always did, at its best: It turned pressure into pattern. A hashtag began to spread. Not sensational. Not violent. Just two words. **#WeDecide**

It wasn't a plea for rescue. It was a declaration of ownership. Of home. Of refusal. Mara's breath caught in her throat. Wren looked at her, eyes wet. "It's working."

Mara wanted to believe it. Then the basement lights flickered. Not the gentle breathing-wave flicker this time. A hard flicker. Once. Twice. Three times.

Nadine spun toward the stairs. "Movement."

Jalen was already on his feet, pain forgotten, grabbing a metal chair to use as a weapon.

"Not like that," Lila said quietly, stepping between him and panic with a single look.

Then came the sound. A low hum, deep enough that Mara felt it in her teeth.

"The field is changing," whispered Ed.

Howard looked at his magnetometer and went pale. "Big change."

Wren's voice shook. "Is it the ring?"

Mara didn't answer because she didn't know.

Outside, headlights swept across the church windows. Then another set. Then another.

Nadine's face tightened. "Not locals."

Howard muttered, "Too coordinated."

Lila's voice was steady but soft. "Everyone breathe."

Jalen's eyes narrowed. "They're here."

Mara's heart hammered. Not because she feared dying. Because she feared the test. If ELXON forced a confrontation here, if fear turned into violence, what would the watchers in the sky conclude about humanity?

Nadine moved quickly to a side monitor, pulling a security camera feed from the church entrance. A line of vehicles in the lot. Unmarked. Two men are stepping out wearing tactical gear with no official insignia. Private. Corporate. ELXON's shadow enforcement.

Wren went white. "They can't—"

"They can," Nadine said. "And they will."

Mara took one slow breath. Then she made a choice. Crossing to the center table, picked up the clean phone and held it like a torch. "Everyone," Mara said quietly. "We do not fight."

Jalen's jaw clenched. "Mara—"

"We don't fight," Mara repeated, voice firm. "We document. We witness. We stay calm."

Howard looked sick. "They'll take everything."

Mara nodded. "Then we make sure what matters has already left this room."

Wren's fingers flew. She announced, "Mirrors are live. Packet is everywhere."

Ed swallowed. "If they take us—"

"They won't take the truth," Lila said softly.

Heavy footsteps sounded overhead. Then the basement door at the top of the stairs rattled. A voice called down, amplified slightly, professionally calm. "Open the door. This is a security operation."

Nadine whispered, "They won't say whose."

The voice continued. "We are here to secure equipment and ensure public safety."

Mara could feel her pulse beating in her throat. She looked at Lila, who gave her one small nod. Then at Wren, who squeezed her hand and mouthed: *We decide.* Then at Jalen, who swallowed his rage like poison and nodded, barely.

Mara lifted her chin and spoke loud enough to carry. "You are being recorded," she said. "And the world is watching."

Silence answered from the top of the stairs. Then the door began to open. Mara's heart hammered, not with fear, but with the awful, fierce clarity of the moment:

This was the test. Not whether the sky could repair the wound. But whether humans, when cornered, hunted, desperate, could still choose **truth without violence**.

The footsteps started down the stairs.

And above the church, near the wound, the ring held its position—waiting to see what "you decide" meant when it cost something.

CHAPTER 22 — Don't Make Them Your Enemy

The men came down the stairs as if they belonged there.

Two in front, one behind, all in deliberately generic tactical gear with no badges, no agency patches, no accountability. Their boots thudded on the wooden steps with heavy, measured force, and with each step, the basement seemed to shrink. They moved with practiced calm. That kind of calm wasn't peace. It was control.

At the bottom step, the lead man raised a hand. His voice was professional, almost friendly. "Dr. Keene," he said, as if he were introducing himself at a fundraiser. "We're here to secure sensitive equipment and prevent destabilizing content from escalating public harm."

Mara's throat tightened, but her voice stayed steady. "What authority are you acting under?" she asked.

The man smiled faintly. "Continuity Emergency protocols."

Nadine's laugh was sharp and humorless. "That's not an authority. That's a slogan."

The second man's gaze snapped toward her, recognition sharpening it.

Mara saw it. The slightest pause. The subtle adjustment. They knew exactly who Nadine was. Which meant ELXON had briefed them.

The lead man ignored Nadine and turned his attention back to Mara. "We're not here to arrest anyone. We're here to remove equipment being used to distribute fabricated content. If you cooperate, this stays calm."

Calm as a hymn, Lila stepped forward. "This is a church," she said. "If you intend to search or seize anything, you will present a warrant."

The smile didn't leave his face. "Ma'am, we don't need a warrant for voluntary compliance."

Lila's eyes stayed steady. "Then you'll be leaving."

He inhaled slowly, as if choosing patience over annoyance. "Pastor," he said, voice smoothing further, "children are watching these false claims. Communities are on edge. People can get hurt."

Mara felt the manipulation like a hand around her throat: *We're here to protect the vulnerable... by silencing you.*

Wren rose to her feet. Her voice was tight but clear. "You put a bounty on my name. Don't pretend you're protecting children."

All three men looked at her, brief and assessing. The third man, silent until now, shifted his stance. One hand hovered near his belt, not a gun, but a device: A jammer. A cuff. Something designed to end choice cleanly.

Beside Mara, Jalen tensed. His grip tightened around the metal chair in his hands. Lila lifted a hand slightly to anchor him. "No violence," she murmured, barely audible. The muscle in his jaw jumped, but he lowered the chair an inch.

The lead man looked back at Mara. "Hand over the devices," he said. "The phone. The spectrometer. The radio equipment. You can keep your personal belongings. We will inventory everything and return it once stability is restored."

Howard let out a low growl. "You mean once the launches are over?"

The man's smile thinned. "Once stability is restored."

Mara took one slow breath. She could feel the entire world in the room now, not metaphorically, but practically. Their release packet had spread. Ruth's broadcast had gone viral. People were watching nodes like this one as symbols. If she fought, the story became violent. If she surrendered, the story became silent. But there was a third option.

Witness.

Mara lifted her hand, holding the clean phone, which was still faintly glowing pale gold. "You want this?" she asked.

The men's eyes fixed on it. "Yes," the lead man said. "That's part of it."

Mara nodded once, as if agreeing. Then she turned slightly, not toward the men, but toward the camera Howard had set up. She raised the phone so the lens could see the screen clearly. She spoke calmly." This is what they're trying to take. Not because it is dangerous, but because it is inconvenient."

The lead man's smile vanished. "Put it down."

Mara didn't move. "We have released evidence," she said, voice still steady. "We have urged calm. We have urged care. We have urged nonviolence. If you take our instruments, you will not take the truth. The truth is already in the world."

Nadine's voice was quiet yet hard edged. "And so are your faces."

The second man shifted, irritated now. "This isn't a debate."

Lila stepped closer, her presence soft but immovable. "Then it's a theft," she said. "And God sees thieves, too."

The lead man's jaw tightened. Behind him, the third man raised a small, handheld, black device with a short antenna. A jammer.

Mara's skin prickled. "They're going to kill the signal."

Howard swore and checked his recording. "Still writing to local drives."

Wren's fingers flew across her keyboard, pushing one last backup out through the mirrors.

Then the basement Wi-Fi died. The livestream froze. For one distorted moment, the room felt cut off from the world. But the ham rig still crackled softly. Good old tech, stubborn tech, immune to the clean digital kill switch.

Howard leaned toward it, voice low with grim affection. "Bless you, analog."

The lead man stepped forward, reaching for the phone. Mara raised it higher. "Stop." Not angry. Commanding.

He hesitated. Only a fraction. Because something else had changed in that fraction. The air in the basement thickened again. The subtle pressure shift. The strange hum in the teeth.

Ed whispered, "Field change."

Howard's magnetometer line jumped.

Lila's eyes widened slightly, then steadied.

"They're… here," whispered Wren, voice trembling.

Still running on battery, Nadine's analyzer spiked so hard it chirped continuously.

For the first time, unease crossed the lead man's face. "What is that?" No one answered. To answer him would speak aloud the truth he was there to steal.

Then the basement lights did something they hadn't done before. They didn't flicker. They dimmed, slowly, evenly, as if someone had turned down the power with a careful hand.

The work light Lila had used earlier glowed pale gold for a second, unplugged, then went dark. A hush settled over everything, like sound itself had been asked to be quiet.

Wren's breath hitched. "Oh my—"

The lead man's composure cracked. "What did you do?"

"We didn't do anything," Mara said steadily.

The phone in her hand warmed slightly. The screen brightened. Text appeared again. Not pale gold this time. Brighter. Clearer. As if the sender had stepped closer.

WE SEE THE GRAB. WE SEE THE CAGE-KEEPERS. WE SEE THE HOMEKEEPERS.

Howard's mouth went dry. "It's… addressing them."

Nadine whispered, "It knows who's who."

The lead man's eyes were fixed on the phone screen. His face changed, fear sliding under authority. "Give it to me," he said tightly. "Now."

Mara didn't move. Lila took a slow step forward and raised her empty hands. "You're being witnessed," she said quietly. "By more than us."

The lead man's eyes darted upward, as if he could see through the ceiling into the sky. Then, his earpiece crackled.

Mara couldn't hear the words, but she saw the effect they had on him. His face drained of color. He touched his earpiece. "Repeat." Another burst came through. His jaw tightened. He looked from the phone to Mara, and something like desperation crossed his face. He turned sharply to his team. "Change of plan."

The second man snapped, "What—"

"We're leaving," the lead man cut in.

Howard blinked. "Leaving?"

The third man lowered the jammer, eyes wide. "Why?"

The lead man's voice came out low and urgent. "Because ELXON just lost three launches in a row. Not explosions, intercepts. And they're freaking out."

Nadine's eyes widened. "Intercepts."

The lead man swallowed, eyes on the phone as if it were a verdict. "They think this—" he gestured at Mara's hand "—is connected."

"They're right,"

Backing toward the stairs, the lead man looked less like a predator and more like a messenger for a collapsing empire. But before he left, his gaze locked on Mara's. "You have no idea what you're doing," he said, voice strained. "If you interfere with continuity, if you convince the public to turn on ELXON, people will die."

Mara's voice stayed calm. "People are already dying," she said. "You just didn't count them."

He flinched as if she'd slapped him. Then he turned and rushed up the stairs, his team following. Boots thundered away. The basement door slammed. For a long moment, no one moved.

Then the lights came back on. Slowly. Evenly. As if the room were being handed back to itself.

Howard exhaled shakily. "Well. That was… something."

Nadine's shoulders dropped a fraction. "We didn't get raided."

"We got… warned," Ed said, swallowing.

Wren stared at Mara's phone. "They made them stop."

Mara's throat tightened. "Not for us," she whispered. "For the test."

Lila nodded slowly. "They prevented violence. They removed the immediate threat without making us strike."

Jalen's jaw clenched. "Selective intervention."

Mara looked back down at the phone. New text appeared, slower now:

DO NOT MAKE THEM YOUR ENEMY. THE CAGE IS THE ENEMY. THE FEW INSIDE ARE STILL OF YOU.

Wren's breath caught. "It's telling us not to attack ELXON passengers."

Ed's voice was thin. "It's telling us to stay human."

Nadine whispered, "It's telling us the test is happening right now."

Outside, distant booms rolled across the horizon. Maybe launch attempts, explosions, or something stranger still. Toward the Atlantic rim, the aurora's gold seam brightened.

Mara looked around the basement at the people who had just been threatened and had refused to become violent.

Truth. Calm. Care. Refuse.

She swallowed hard. This wasn't just a moral lesson. It was a criterion. And now, with the visitors' message on her phone, Mara understood the terrifying next stage: If communities turned on ELXON passengers, if fear hardened into a mob, the ring would not repair the atmosphere.

But if communities protected even those who had tried to flee… Then humanity would be claiming its home. And the sky might finally answer with something more than a brace.

Lila spoke softly, voice steady. "Then we tell the world."

Mara nodded, heart hammering. "Yes." Barely above a whisper, she said, "We tell them: **Don't make them your enemy.**"

CHAPTER 23 — The Human Shield

Ruth Calder didn't sleep either.

When Mara finally reached her again through a patched relay chain and a ham bounce that sounded like it had traveled through a storm, Ruth answered on the first ring.

"Tell me," Ruth said. No greeting. No softness. Just urgency.

Mara held the clean phone up to Howard's camera and kept her voice steady. "They came. ELXON's private security. No badges. No warrant."

Ruth exhaled sharply. "And?"

"The visitors intervened—minimally. They stopped the raid without provoking violence."

A silent pause. Ruth's voice became quieter. "Then the test is active."

"Yes," Mara said. "And we received another message." Mara read it aloud:

"DO NOT MAKE THEM YOUR ENEMY. THE CAGE IS THE ENEMY. THE FEW INSIDE ARE STILL OF YOU."

Silence on Ruth's end for a moment, as if she were absorbing the full weight of it. When she spoke again, her voice was tight with emotion. "That's the most human thing I've heard from the sky," she said.

Mara's throat tightened. "Exactly."

Ruth continued, "Then we do the hardest possible thing."

Mara already knew what she meant. "We protect them," she whispered.

"Yes," Ruth said, her voice hardening. "We protect ELXON passengers because if we let greed turn us into a mob, we prove the cage was right."

Mara's stomach clenched. "People will hate that."

Ruth gave a short, grim laugh. "Of course they will. Hate feels like power. Restraint feels like weakness, right up until it becomes salvation."

Mara looked around the basement. Lila listened with wet but steady eyes. Nadine's jaw was clenched so tight it looked painful. Wren hovered close as if she could physically hold her mother upright. Jalen stared at the floor, breathing through anger the way a man would try to breathe through poison. Mara steadied her breathing. "We need a message."

Ruth answered instantly. "We deliver it together. Now."

Within minutes, the calm network was assembling a global broadcast—no studio, no orchestration beyond what necessity forced. Ruth on her ranch in Texas. Mara in the church basement in Kansas. Lila in frame beside Mara. Ed and Howard visible behind them, with instruments and the whiteboard bearing the four words. Wren at the edge of the shot, fierce-eyed. Nadine half-shadowed, unwilling to be the face but equally unwilling to hide.

Eli and Mark built the mirrors like scaffolding around a burning building, redundant links, transcript feeds, radio relays, and local downloads. When the broadcast began, it didn't feel like a live stream. It felt like a hand reaching out across a frightened planet.

Ruth spoke first. "I'm going to tell you something that will make you angry," she said, face lit by a floodlight, wind tugging her hair. "And you have the right to be angry." She held the camera's gaze. "But anger is not a license to become cruel."

Emotion tightened in Mara's throat.

Ruth continued. "ELXON passengers, those boarding those vehicles, are not all monsters. Some are cowards. Some are desperate. Some are misled. Some are complicit." She paused. "They are still human."

On the mirrored feeds, the live comments began racing past:

"NO THEY AREN'T!" "THEY CAN BURN!" "WHY SHOULD WE HELP THEM?" "THEY LEFT US!"

Ruth did not flinch. "If we turn them into enemies," her voice steady, "we become what ELXON believes we are: a species that eats its own." She lifted a hand. "Don't do that."

Then Mara spoke. "You are being tested," she said quietly. "Not as prophecy. As fact. You are being tested by the same moment that is testing ELXON. Not with weapons. With choices."

She lifted the clean phone and held the message toward the camera, blurred slightly to protect trace patterns, but still readable. Beside her, Wren audibly caught her breath.

Mara read aloud: "**DO NOT MAKE THEM YOUR ENEMY. THE CAGE IS THE ENEMY.**"

The comment feed shifted. Not all at once. But enough to feel the change. Less screaming. More stillness. Mara continued. "We cannot prove with absolute certainty who sent this. But we can prove the atmospheric stabilization near the wound. We can prove the ring's presence. We can prove the signal patterns. We can prove the intervention that prevented violence tonight."

She glanced at Lila. Calm and clear, Lila stepped forward. "Some of you will be tempted to attack buses. To block roads. To pull people out and punish them. Her eyes hardened slightly. I understand the temptation. But hear me: if you do that, you will injure your neighbors, you will injure your own soul, and you will fail the only test that matters."

She lifted her chin. "Protect each other. Even those who have not protected you."

The stream's comment feed shifted again. Still not all at once. But visibly.

"I don't know if I can." "What if they're taking kids?" "What if my sister is on one of those buses?" "I hate this, but… okay." "So, how do we instruct people?"

Ed stepped forward and delivered the practical part, which he did best. "If you are near a launch site or a transfer corridor, don't gather in crowds. Do not attempt to stop vehicles. Your job is safety, not vengeance. Provide water. Provide medical help. Monitor UV exposure. Support emergency services."

Howard added, gruff and plain: "Document everything."

Then Nadine spoke, and the tension in her voice made every word feel expensive. "ELXON will attempt to provoke chaos. They will plant stories. They will use agents to incite violence. They will try to make you look like a mob so they can justify force." Her eyes were cold. "Don't give it to them."

Finally, Wren leaned forward, voice shaking but fierce. "If you see a bus, and you feel rage, remember there might be someone on it who didn't choose this. Someone who was pressured. Someone who is scared."

She swallowed. "And even if they did choose it, you don't get to become their executioner. That's not who we are."

Tears burned behind Mara's eyes.

The broadcast ended with the four words on the whiteboard behind them. Truth. Calm. Care. Refuse. The calm network pushed it everywhere. Then, as if the world had been waiting for permission to choose restraint, something extraordinary happened.

A verified feed from a transfer corridor near Cape Canaveral appeared—shaky cellphone footage, timestamped, geotagged.

A line of black buses moved slowly under heavy security. People stood along the roadside. Not a riot. Not a mob. A crowd, yes, but quiet. Many held signs reading **WE DECIDE**. Some held printed QR codes linking to the calm network packet. Almost all carried water jugs.

The buses slowed. A window cracked open. A woman's face appeared inside, pale, terrified. Then, from the roadside crowd, an older man stepped forward and raised a bottle of water like an offering. He did not shout. He did not spit. He simply lifted the bottle. The bus door opened a few inches. A gloved hand reached out. Took the water.

A small, second hand emerged. A child's hand. Mara's breath caught. Wren whispered, "There's a kid on the bus."

The crowd didn't surge. They stayed back. They let the child drink. Then the video captured a moment that hit Mara's chest like a blow: a woman in the crowd began singing, softly at first, then louder—an old hymn. Not because she expected God to fix physics. Because singing was what humans did to keep fear from growing teeth. Others joined in. The sound was shaky, imperfect. Human. But it held. The buses moved again. No violence. No chaos. Just grief and restraint braided together.

Mara stared at the screen as tears slipped down her cheeks.

Lila whispered, "That's it."

Ed nodded, voice thick. "That's the choice."

Swallowing hard, Howard said, "That's Homekeeping."

Nadine's analyzer chirped just then. She looked down, then up, face pale with something like awe. "The stabilization just increased," she whispered. "By another two percent."

Mara's heart pounded. "Now?"

Ed checked his node feed from the Atlantic rim. "Confirmed," he said, voice shaking. "The field above the wound is strengthening."

Outside, through the window well, the aurora's gold seam brightened. And then, far off toward the horizon, the ring near the wound flared, softly, steadily, like a tool engaging deeper. Not a miracle. A mechanism. A response.

Mara caught her breath. "They're answering."

Jalen's eyes shone, though he didn't let the tears fall. "They're not saving the rich," he said hoarsely. "They're saving the choice."

Ruth's voice crackled through the radio again, faint but fierce, and full of wonder, "Tell me you can see that."

Mara nervously wet her lips. "We see it."

Ruth exhaled. "Then keep them calm. Keep them human."

Mara looked around the room, taking in the basement, the people, the world beyond. ELXON was still launching. But now the public had done something ELXON could not buy: They had become a shield, not of violence, but of humanity.

And the sky had responded.

CHAPTER 24 — Worthy on Paper

ELXON didn't know how to lose.

They had never built systems to fail gracefully. They built systems to *win*. To buy time, buy silence, buy people, buy reality itself if reality refused to cooperate.

So, when the ring brightened, and the public didn't turn into a mob, ELXON did what power always did when it felt itself slipping: It tried to tighten the cage. The first move came as a broadcast, slick, calm, framed as leadership.

A new ELXON spokesperson appeared on every major network at once, face composed, voice warm. "Tonight," she said, "we witnessed destabilizing misinformation that attempted to weaponize fear. We also witnessed something extraordinary: a demonstration of atmospheric stabilization technology."

Howard snarled, shaking his head. "Still claiming it."

The spokesperson continued, smiling gently. "In moments like this, humanity must choose unity. ELXON is committed to preserving the human future. To that end, we are launching a new initiative…"

A graphic appeared behind her:

THE WORTHINESS PROTOCOL

Wren's face went pale. "Oh no."

The spokesperson spoke as if she were announcing a scholarship. "Due to unprecedented public interest in continuity operations, ELXON will expand access through a merit-based selection process. Participants will be evaluated based on psychological resilience, cooperative behavior, and potential for contribution. This ensures the best of humanity, our most stable, most capable citizens, will represent Earth in the next chapter."

Mara's stomach turned.

Nadine whispered, "They're trying to hijack the test."

Ed's voice was thin. "They're turning morality into paperwork."

The spokesperson added, softly, "We encourage citizens to demonstrate calm, refrain from violence, and report destabilizing actors. Those who support unity will be considered."

Howard's jaw clenched. "They're using 'calm' as a leash."

Lila's eyes hardened. "They're turning neighbor against neighbor."

Cold, clean anger rose in Mara. "They heard the condition," she whispered. "And they're trying to counterfeit it."

"Worthy on paper," Jalen said.

The second move followed within minutes. The #WeDecide tag suddenly flooded with new posts, thousands of them, all nearly identical in phrasing and formatting, urging people to "report calm network agitators" and "apply for Worthiness Protocol evaluation."

Bot swarms. Disinformation.

Nadine's eyes narrowed. "Synthetic amplification."

Wren's fingers flew, tracing patterns. "Same language blocks. Same timing. Same IP clusters."

Howard muttered, "They're manufacturing consent."

Then the third move, the dangerous one, arrived not as words but as logistics. Node alerts flashed:

CONFIRMED: Armed private security deployed at transfer corridors.

CONFIRMED: Passenger buses rerouted through populated areas.

UNCONFIRMED: Controlled "incidents" near launch site—provocation suspected.

Mara's throat tightened. "They're creating chaos."

Ed looked pale. "Why would they do that if calm is their message?"

Nadine's voice was cold. "Because chaos gives them a reason to use force. And force gives them control."

"And control lets them pick who is 'worthy,'" Lila whispered.

Mara stared at the three moves like a chessboard revealed:

1. Claim the ring as their tech.

2. Counterfeit the condition into a program.

3. Provoke chaos so they can punish it.

And beneath all of it, the same intention:

Keep the public from claiming the home.

At 11:18 p.m., Ruth called again, voice clipped with urgency. "Mara," she said, "they've put my face on a list."

Mara's chest tightened. "A list?"

A bitter laugh came back through the line. "Their Worthiness Protocol is a trap. And now they're calling me 'a destabilization leader.' They're instructing supporters to report my location."

Wren's face drained. "They're hunting Ruth."

Nadine's jaw clenched. "They'll use her as an example."

"Good luck to them," Ruth said, voice hard. "I'm not moving."

Mara's stomach dropped. "Ruth, you have to—"

Ruth cut her off. "Listen to me. They're staging something at Canaveral."

Mara's pulse jumped. "What?"

Her voice lowered. "They rerouted three buses, VIP passengers through an outer corridor where crowds have gathered peacefully. They're deploying private security with nonlethal weapons and... something else."

Mara pressed her lips together, then asked, "something else?"

"Live-feed drones," Ruth said tightly. "Over the corridor. They want footage. They want a clip of the public 'attacking' or 'rioting' so they can justify sweeping crackdowns."

Mara's throat tightened. "A false flag."

Ruth didn't say the words. She didn't need to. "They're going to make calm impossible," she said. "And if people break, if one person throws a rock, the story becomes 'See? Humanity is violent. Only ELXON can preserve civilization.'"

Mara saw the trap snap into focus. The visitors' message had warned them: *Do not make them your enemy.* ELXON was trying to force people to do exactly that.

"Can we warn them?" Wren asked, her voice shaking.

Nadine narrowed her eyes. "Yes. But the warning has to reach the right people, fast."

"We blast it," Howard said.

Mara's stomach clenched. "If we blast it too wide, ELXON will trace our nodes faster."

Nadine nodded grimly. "And they'll come harder."

Ed looked at Mara, voice thin. "Then what's the next move?"

The weight of **YOU DECIDE** felt heavy on Mara's shoulders. There was no perfect choice. Only choices that revealed who you were.

If they stayed quiet to protect themselves, people in that corridor could get hurt, and violence might ignite, failing the test. If they warned too openly, they risked exposing the network and losing the ability to keep the world calm.

Mara's throat tightened. Beside her, Wren squeezed her hand. "Mom… people will get hurt."

Mara nodded slowly. Lila's voice was gentle, but unyielding. "Love costs," she said.

Jalen spoke quietly. "If we lose the network, we lose the world."

"If we lose the people at the corridor, we lose the test," Nadine added.

Howard muttered, "Damn."

Mara looked at the phone on the table, still glowing faintly. She remembered the visitors' words:

WE DO NOT REPAIR A CAGE.

ELXON was building a cage out of fear. Mara took a breath. "We warn them."

Nadine's eyes sharpened. "How?"

"Targeted," Mara said, her voice steadier now. "Not to everyone. We broadcast to local leaders; pastors, mayors, community organizers, and the people already running calm. We send them one message: *Keep your distance from buses. Bring water. Bring cameras. Do not engage security. Do not throw anything. Sit down if provoked. Sing. Pray. Breathe.*"

Lila nodded immediately. "Yes."

Ed added, "And we tell them ELXON wants a clip. Deny them the clip."

Howard grunted. "Deny them the narrative."

Nadine's fingers moved fast, pulling a list of local calm contacts from the network.

Wren drafted the message with brutal simplicity:

ELXON MAY PROVOKE INCIDENTS. THEY WANT FOOTAGE OF VIOLENCE. DO NOT GIVE IT. KEEP DISTANCE. SIT IF PROVOKED. SING. DOCUMENT. HELP PASSENGERS AS HUMANS. THE CAGE IS THE ENEMY.

Mara stared at the words, throat tight.

Ruth's voice came through again, urgently. "Mara, I can go live and warn them."

"No," Mara warned gently. "If you go live, they'll use your warning as 'proof' you orchestrated it."

Ruth was silent for a beat, then exhaled. "You're right."

Mara's chest ached. "We'll do it through local channels."

Nadine nodded. "Sending." Messages went out, dozens, then hundreds, riding the calm network's human web faster than any algorithm.

In Florida, in Texas, in Ohio, in California, people received the warning not from faceless feeds, but from someone they recognized: A pastor. A teacher. A neighbor who had been calm all day. And because the warning came from trust, it landed.

At 11:47 p.m., a live feed from the corridor popped up. One of the calm leaders had placed a camera behind a line of people holding water and blankets. Buses approached slowly, headlights bright. Private security formed a line. The crowd was quiet. Someone started singing again, softly, shaky, but steady.

Security moved forward with megaphones. "You must disperse," a voice blared. "This is a restricted corridor." The crowd didn't rush. They didn't throw anything. They didn't scream. They sat down. Right there on the roadside, in winter air, people sat as if they were in a peaceful protest from another century.

Mara's breath caught. "They listened," Wren whispered.

Security advanced, confused now, their body language tense. A few raised weapons that looked like non-lethal launchers. The crowd remained seated. A woman held up a sign: **WE SEE THE CAGE.**

Then just at the edge of the camera frame, a man darted forward. Fast. Unsteady. He lifted his arm as if to throw something.

Mara's heart seized. Wren gasped.

Before the man could release anything, two people in the seated crowd grabbed his legs and pulled him down gently, not violently, more like they were protecting a friend from stepping into traffic.

The man shouted and flailed. The seated crowd did not hit him. They didn't pile on. They held him, murmuring, "No. No. Let's be calm."

Mara's throat tightened with tears.

Lila whispered, "That's the test."

On-screen, security hesitated. Because what do you do with a crowd that refuses to become your justification?

Mara watched the corridor hold its calm under pressure. And then, far above the Atlantic rim, caught in a separate feed from an amateur astronomer, the ring brightened again, steady as a heartbeat.

Ed's node reports updated: **STABILIZATION UP 6%.**

Howard's magnetometer line smoothed slightly, less jagged, more coherent, like the planet's field was being gently combed.

Awe and terror braided together in Mara's chest. They were doing it. But only because humans were doing their part.

"ELXON's last play is failing," Nadine said softly.

Jalen stared at the screen, eyes wet. "So, they'll escalate."

Mara nodded slowly, throat tight. "Yes. And next time they won't aim for nonlethal."

Outside the church, the aurora glowed pale gold along its seam. Above the world, rockets still climbed and died and vanished.

And somewhere beyond it all, something vast waited, ready to bind the wound, ready to repair the home if humans could keep choosing the hardest thing.

Restraint. Care. Refusal. Not against people.

Against the cage.

CHAPTER 25 — Proof of Worth

ELXON stopped pretending any of it was voluntary.

It happened in pieces, at first with small clips, scattered reports, blurred videos that people argued about until the metadata and the pattern made denial impossible.

A woman in Los Angeles filmed a convoy of buses under police escort and whispered into her phone, "They're taking people."

A man in Johannesburg posted a shaky clip of a line outside a continuity center. Guards checking IDs, turning away families, letting through only those with a certain band on their wrist.

A nurse in London shared a message from a friend: *They told us it's 'community relocation.' They won't let us leave the building.*

And then a document leaked, an internal ELXON directive labeled **WORTHINESS PROTOCOL: COMPLIANCE MEASURES**.

Wren read it aloud in the basement, her voice shaking with disgust. "Participants who demonstrate destabilizing behavior, resistance, refusal of relocation directives, or dissemination of misinformation will be classified as…" She swallowed. "…non-cooperative and ineligible for continuity operations."

Howard spat the words like they were poison. "Eligibility."

Nadine's face was stone. "They're turning morality into obedience."

Lila's hands trembled slightly around her mug. "They're trying to define 'worthy' as 'compliant.'"

Cold fury settles into Mara's bones. "They're trying to lift the weight by… pretending."

Ed's voice was thin. "If people see forced boarding—"

"They'll panic," Wren finished, eyes wide. "And then everything we've built—"

Lila stepped forward, calm but tight. "Then we don't let panic be the headline."

Mara stared at the screens. Her spectrometer chimed softly, incessantly, like it couldn't stop reminding her that physics didn't pause while humans debated ethics.

Ed's model updated again. The stabilization near the wound had increased overnight, slowly, steadily. But inland proxies were still worsening. Not catastrophic yet. But it's edging closer. A fragile hinge in the world.

At 6:41 a.m., Ruth went live again. Her face looked tired now. Not exhausted, Ruth did not seem built for exhaustion but etched by the pressure of being the voice that could not crack. "I need you to hear me," she said. "ELXON is no longer offering seats."

Her eyes sharpened. "They are taking control." She didn't show graphic footage. She showed **verified documentation**:

the directive, the convoy routes, the "continuity centers," the wristbands.

Then she did something Mara hadn't expected. She played a clip of herself speaking to a man in a security uniform outside a corridor. The man's face was blurred, but his voice was raw.

"They told us we were protecting people," the man said. "They told us we were preventing chaos. But I saw a mother begging for her kid to come with her, and they—" His voice broke. "They shut the door."

Ruth looked into the camera with jaw clenched. "If you are a soldier, a police officer, a guard," she said, "hear me: you are not a tool for corporate selection. You are not a lever for the cage."

Her voice softened, not with pity but with invitation. "If you have to disobey an immoral order to remain human," Ruth said, "disobey."

Mara felt Lila's hand touch her shoulder, a silent understanding: this was civil courage spreading. Within minutes, reports poured in. Small refusals.

A police chief in Ohio declining to escort an ELXON convoy.

A bus driver in Texas walked away from a scheduled route and left the keys on the seat.

A security worker in Florida was handing bottled water to a passenger who appeared to be about to faint.

They weren't revolution. They were cracks. But cracks were how cages failed.

Then the panic threatened to enter through a side door: supplies. Not because the calm network told people to hoard, Mara had been relentless about that, but because humans were human.

When people feel uncertainty, they reach for what they can carry. Grocery shelves thinned in hours. Pharmacies developed lines. Gas stations filled. The calm network's feeds began to fill with the same question again and again: **"Should I stock up?"**

Wren read it, eyes wide. "This is where it breaks."

Lila shook her head. "Not if we give them a better way to feel safe."

Mara's mind snapped into action. "Community stock," Mara said. "Not personal stock."

Ed nodded in agreement. "Supply pooling. Rotation. Distribution to vulnerable first."

"And a no-price-gouging watch," grunted Howard.

Nadine's eyes sharpened. "And a rumor watch."

"We can push a new packet. Quick," Wren added.

Mara nodded. "Do it."

They drafted it fast, simple, practical, almost boring:

- Buy **two days** extra, not two months.

- Pool supplies at community centers.

- Make lists of elderly, disabled, infants.

- Share refrigeration.

- Set up neighborhood "UV buddy" checks.

- Do **not** fight over gasoline. Carpool. Combine trips.

Then, in bold:

HOARDING IS THE CAGE TRAINING YOU TO LIVE ALONE.

Lila added another line, quiet but firm:

CARE IS A FORM OF SURVIVAL.

The packet went out.

It didn't stop the initial surge entirely, but it slowed it. Redirected it. People began filming themselves dropping supplies at churches, schools, recreation and community centers.

Not perfect. But better.

Then ELXON struck Ruth directly. A new video surfaced, slick and polished, claiming Ruth Calder had been "financially compensated by foreign adversaries." The clip spliced old footage of her smiling at an unrelated event with ominous music and captions like:

TRAITOR?
WHO BENEFITS FROM PANIC?

Nadine watched it with her jaw clenched. "Classic smear."

Ed's face tightened. "People will believe it."

Shaking her head slowly, Mara said, "Some will. But not all."

"It's so unfair," cried Wren. Her eyes burning with anger and despair.

Mara reached for her daughter's hand. "Unfair is a weapon. Don't let it control you."

But the smear wasn't ELXON's real attack. The real attack came that afternoon, when a report hit the calm network from a node near a continuity center in Arizona:

CONFIRMED: Forced boarding attempt. Crowd gathering. High tension. Then, another message, seconds later:

SECURITY USING SMOKE. PEOPLE RUNNING.

Then:

UNCONFIRMED: GUNSHOTS.

Mara's stomach dropped. Lila's face went pale. Howard's hands tightened on the table edge.

Nadine's voice was tight. "This is what they wanted."

"Chaos," Wren whispered, terrified.

Mara's heart hammered. "We need clarity fast."

Ed pulled up the feed. It was shaky and chaotic. People are yelling. Smoke drifting. Security personnel shouting through megaphones. A bus door slammed. A woman screamed.

Then the camera swung upward by accident and caught the ring. Far away toward the wound. Dimmer. Not by much. But enough that the air left Mara's lungs.

Howard saw it too. "It dimmed."

Ed refreshed the readings, voice shaking. "The stabilization…" He stopped. The numbers had stalled. Not reversing or collapsing. But stalled. As if the tool above the wound had paused. Like a hand had stopped mid-motion.

Mara's chest tightened with terror. "They're stopping."

Lila's voice was barely audible. "Because of violence."

"The test is failing," Nadine said in horror.

Jalen stared at the screen, jaw clenched. "Or being manipulated."

If this was truly conditional, ELXON had found the cruelest lever: provoke violence to halt repair, then claim, *See? Only we can save you.*

Mara's clean phone, still on the table, lit up again. Without being touched. The screen glowed pale gold. Text formed:

WE FEEL THE SURGE. WE FEEL THE STRIKE. WE FEEL THE TURNING.

Mara's hands shook. Wren whispered, "Ask them. Ask what we do."

Gripping the table edge for support, Mara whispered, "What do we do?" her voice cracking despite herself.

The screen paused. Then the next line appeared, and it landed like a hammer on the heart:

CALM IS NOT PASSIVE. CARE IS NOT SOFT. REFUSE THE CAGE WITHOUT BECOMING IT.

Tears stung Mara's eyes.

Nadine stared, whispering, "They're telling us the only path."

More text appeared, clear, direct:

SHOW THEM THE HUMAN SHIELD. REMOVE THE FIREMAKERS. PROTECT THE TRAPPED.

"Firemakers?" Howard questioned.

Ed swallowed and said, "Inciters."

"Agents," added Nadine through a clenched jaw.

Suddenly, it became clear to Mara. "Nonviolent intervention," she said. "We stop violence without violence. We isolate agitators. We protect passengers and bystanders. We document. We keep crowds seated."

Lila nodded, voice steady. "We mobilize the calm leaders."

Wren's fingers flew, sending targeted instructions to nodes near hot spots:

SIT. SING. DOCUMENT. KEEP DISTANCE. IDENTIFY AGITATORS. DO NOT STRIKE. PROTECT CHILDREN. MAKE SPACE FOR MEDICS.

Nadine added a second message, colder and more tactical:

WATCH FOR UNMARKED INCITERS.

WATCH FOR PEOPLE PUSHING CROWDS FORWARD.

ISOLATE WITH HANDS-ON-ARMS ONLY. DO NOT HIT. DO NOT CHASE.

Mara stared at the dimmed ring on the feed and felt the terrible truth: The visitors weren't punishing humanity. They were responding to what humanity *chose to become* under stress.

The question wasn't whether you felt rage. The question was what you did with it. And the only way through was to build something like a shield made of restraint, not weapons.

The screen on the clean phone held one final line, appearing slowly, as if the sender wanted Mara to feel every letter:

THE REPAIR IS FAST IF THE HOME IS CLAIMED FAST.

She swallowed hard. Fast. That meant there was still time. But not much. Mara looked at the basement crew, voice firm. "We have to scale the human shield," she said. "Tonight."

Howard stared. "How?"

She didn't flinch. "By making it the story. Not the rockets. Not the ring. Not ELXON. The story is this: we protect each other, even when provoked."

Wren nodded fiercely. "We decide."

"We keep choosing," Lila whispered.

Outside, the aurora's gold seam flickered faintly but held. The ring had not vanished. It had paused. Waiting to see what humans would do next.

And Mara understood: the repair wouldn't be handed down like grace.

It would be invited by a planet full of people refusing to become a cage.

CHAPTER 26 — The Wave

The next twelve hours became the longest day in human history.

Time didn't move like it used to. It stuttered instead—leaping from alert to alert, feed to feed, one fragile decision to the next. The world was no longer running on clocks. It was running on **choices**.

At 4:18 a.m. Central, the first message hit the calm network:

CONFIRMED: ELXON initiating "Wave Launch." Multiple sites.

Nadine read it and went still. "That's their biggest push."

Howard's jaw clenched. "Trying to outrun the repair."

Ed's voice was thin. "Trying to outrun their own fear."

Mara kept her eyes on the ring feed. It stayed dimmer than before, paused like a hand held back. "We keep the home claimed," she said quietly. "We keep the human shield."

Outside, dawn arrived under aurora, green and pale gold smeared across a sky that should have been ordinary. Instead, it looked bruised and stitched at the same time.

In Florida, crowds gathered again, not to riot, but to sit.

In Arizona, calm leaders formed lines between security and passengers, holding water, signs, and printed QR codes like shields.

In Germany, South Korea, Brazil, and Nigeria, similar scenes unfolded—different languages, same posture: people standing or sitting in deliberate restraint, refusing to be provoked into violence.

The calm network wasn't one organization anymore. It was a reflex spreading through humanity. **The human shield.**

Then ELXON launched the wave. It began with a synchronized set of ascents; bright columns rising from ocean platforms, desert bases, remote airstrips. On screens across the globe, the night turned into a web of fire. For a moment, the spectacle was almost beautiful.

Then the failures began. Not just one or two. A pattern. A rocket lifted cleanly from an offshore platform, its guidance wobbled, corrected, wobbled again, and the craft burst into white light over the ocean. Debris rained down. The livestream cut to an ELXON logo.

Another launch rose from a desert site, then vanished, no explosion, no debris, only absence, as if it had slipped behind an invisible curtain.

A third rose and… bent. Not like a plane. Not like physics. Its path curved sharply away from its intended trajectory, as though the sky itself had become a river current, and the craft had been caught in it.

Howard's mouth went dry. "Interdiction."

"Selective," Ed observed, hands trembling.

Mara's chest tightened, trying to understand. "Not all of them."

Some still got through. Some streaked into the dark and disappeared beyond Earth's curvature, leaving only a fading glow and the hollow ache of abandonment.

ELXON had planned losses, but not for *uncertainty*. Explosions could be explained. Explosions still fit inside a story of risk. What they could not explain was being *stopped by something they could not control*.

At 6:02 a.m., a leak appeared on the calm network: an audio clip from inside an ELXON command channel, panicked voices, the kind that never made it into official statements.

"We're losing corridor stability—" "—we can't lock the transit window—" "—it's like they're closing the gate—" "—we need to accelerate—"

Then a voice cut through, colder and steadier than the rest: "Make the public the problem. If they riot, we regain justification."

Cold anger settled into Mara's bones. "They're still trying to provoke violence."

Wren's eyes flashed. "Then we don't give it."

An hour later, the world tested that promise. Outside a continuity center in Phoenix, a crowd surged, not forward, but sideways, away from a sharp bang.

Someone had thrown a smoke canister into the seated group. People coughed. Someone screamed. A ripple of fear traveled through bodies like an electric current. The camera shook.

Mara's heart seized.

This was the moment when fear could become fists. Instead, a calm leader, an older woman in a neon safety vest, stood up and raised both hands. "DOWN," she shouted. "SIT DOWN."

And to Mara's astonishment, the crowd obeyed. Not instantly. Not perfectly. But enough. People sat again, coughing, eyes watering, hands shaking.

Then the woman did something else: she pointed at the man who had thrown the canister. He was trying to disappear into the crowd. Three people moved toward him carefully, not to strike or attack. They hooked their arms through his and guided him out the way you might escort a drunk man out of a wedding before he ruined it.

He shouted. He resisted. They didn't hit him. They held him. A medic approached. Police approached. Cameras filmed the whole thing. The inciter was removed. The crowd stayed seated.

Mara's throat tightened. "Remove the firemakers," she whispered.

Across the globe, similar scenes repeated. Calm leaders began posting a new phrase:

"WE SIT. WE SING. WE WITNESS."

Then something shifted. At 7:14 a.m., the ring brightened again. Steadily, like a machine powering up.

Ed's node feeds updated: **STABILIZATION RESUMED. UP 3%. UP 5%.**

Howard's magnetometer line smoothed further, now less jagged.

The spectrometer chimed a softer tone, still warning, but no longer frantic.

Wren stared at the screen, breath caught. "It's back."

"Because we held," Lila whispered.

Nadine's face had gone pale with something close to awe. "Because we refused the cage without becoming it."

Then the visitors did something new. They made their work visible. A live feed from an amateur astronomer on a sailboat in the Atlantic captured it first: the ring, huge, pale gold, hovering near the wound. Around it, faint arcs of light began to form, like threads being drawn through the air.

Not lightning. Not Aurora. Something more precise. Geometric and deliberate. The arcs connected to the ring, then extended across the thinning region like stitches.

Mara's breath caught.

"They're binding it," Howard whispered.

"They're building a lattice," Ed said, voice shaking with awe.

The footage spread instantly. This time, ELXON couldn't cut every stream fast enough. The ring's work was too visible, too widespread, too undeniable.

Networks still tried to reframe it as ELXON stabilization tech, but the public wasn't asleep anymore. People could recognized the difference between a corporate press release and a sky behaving like a surgeon.

At 8:03 a.m., another message appeared on Mara's phone, brief, precise:

WE BEGIN BINDING. KEEP THE HOME CLAIMED. DO NOT HUNT THE FEW.

She gulped while looking at the message. "They're still watching behavior."

Jalen's voice was hoarse. "They're still insisting on the human part."

Then ELXON made its last, most desperate move. Not a program or a smear. A command. The Worthiness Protocol shifted from 'apply' to 'comply'. New alerts came in:

CONFIRMED: ELXON security ordering communities to disperse at gunpoint.

UNCONFIRMED: Shots fired near Los Angeles corridor.

CONFIRMED: Forced boarding at Nevada base.

Cold crept through Mara's chest. "They're going to create blood,"

Nadine's eyes went hard. "Blood makes fear. Fear makes mobs. Mobs make proof that humanity is unworthy."

Lila's voice was calm but fierce. "Then we refuse again, louder."

Mara looked at the footage of the ring stitching the wound and felt the truth of it settle in. They were close. So close to full repair. But the condition had never been simply *be calm*. It was **claim home**. And claiming home meant refusing ELXON's cage logic everywhere, at scale.

Mara turned to Wren, voice steady. "We need a global refusal," Mara said.

Wren blinked. "Like… what?"

"Not violence," Mara said quickly. "Never violence."

Ed leaned in. "Then what?"

Her mind sparked with the simplest, most powerful thing people could do: Stop cooperating. "Work stoppage," Mara said. "A coordinated pause. A refusal to provide services to ELXON operations. Bus drivers. Fuel handlers. Air traffic techs. Contractors. Quiet refusal."

Nadine's eyes widened. "A nonviolent strike."

Howard nodded and grunted. "That'll shake them."

"And it doesn't harm passengers, just the machinery," Lila added.

Jalen's jaw tightened. "Can we coordinate that fast?"

Wren's fingers hovered over the keys. "With the calm network… yes."

Mara nodded. "We push a call: **Refuse to build the cage. If you work in logistics, security, transportation, comms, fuel, pause. Document. Step away."

Nadine added, "And we tell them: protect passengers as humans. Refuse the cage systems."

Lila whispered, "Homekeepers."

Wren began typing, and within minutes the call went out across the calm network with astonishing speed:

GLOBAL HOMEKEEPER REFUSAL—

NONVIOLENT PAUSE

DO NOT TRANSPORT FOR ELXON.

DO NOT FUEL ELXON.

DO NOT ESCORT ELXON.

DO NOT ENFORCE CORPORATE SELECTION.

STEP BACK. DOCUMENT.

PROTECT PEOPLE.

REFUSE THE CAGE.

It wasn't universal. Nothing ever was. But it didn't need to be universal. It needed to be contagious. Within an hour, the videos began appearing: A bus driver filming the keys on his seat. "I'm not doing it." A fuel handler in Nevada walking away from a depot. "Not for them." A security contractor removing his vest. "I won't be the cage." A low-level engineer crying openly into the camera. "They told me it was the only way. It's not."

A huge lump filled Mara's throat.

Ed's model updated again. Stabilization near the wound increased sharply. **UP 10%. UP 12%.**

Howard stared at his screen. "That jump—"

"It responded." Nadine was stunned.

Outside, the aurora's gold seam brightened into a clear band. And over the Atlantic, the ring's lattice thickened, threads locking into place like a net designed not to trap, but to heal.

On feeds worldwide, the sight was unmistakable: The sky was being stitched.

For the first time since ELXON began, the people were no longer watching rockets. They were watching the **repair**.

And with fierce clarity, Mara understood: The visitors were not selecting who would escape.

They were deciding whether Earth would remain a home.

And humanity, through millions of quiet refusals, was finally claiming it.

CHAPTER 27 — When the Gate Closed

ELXON's final carriers were not rockets.

They were cities with engines.

That was what the leaked schematics had hinted at all along: the "mainline vehicles" were never meant to be launched from a single pad. They were assembled in pieces, orbital segments, sky ship hulls, engines built through hidden contracts. Then they were to be mated above the atmosphere where laws and cameras thinned.

Now, in the last gamble, ELXON tried to lift them anyway.

The calm network knew before the public did. Nadine saw it first in the logistics chatter, in the sudden shift in coded language: *heavy transfer, priority hull, window lock.* Jalen heard it on the ham relays, voices that sounded like men praying to machines. Ed's models revealed the timing: they were trying to launch before the lattice fully bound the wound, before the "brace" became a barrier.

Howard put it bluntly, eyes on the screen. "They're making a run for it."

Mara was sick to her stomach; a run for it with people inside. Because ELXON didn't just have billionaires and leaders aboard. Now it has *passengers.* Some willing. Some coerced. The Worthiness Protocol trapped many by threatening the loss of everything and the suffering their families would face. They were told compliance was morality. And now those passengers were about to become bargaining chips in ELXON's final play.

At 9:22 p.m. Central, a live feed from a coastal platform appeared, mirrored too widely now to cut. It showed the impossible. A massive structure rising slowly from the ocean, not on a flame pillar like a rocket, but on a deep, resonant thrust that made the water tremble.

The craft's underside glowed a harsh blue-white. The silhouette looked wrong for human engineering. It looked too smooth, too heavy, too ambitious.

Howard whispered, "That's their ark."

Wren's voice cracked. "How many people are in it?"

Nadine's jaw tightened. "Thousands."

Mara stared at the screen and felt the ethical dilemma sharpen into a blade: If the ark launched and escaped, ELXON would keep the cage alive somewhere else. If it failed catastrophically, thousands would die. If it were intercepted and turned back, stranded under a failing sky, then those people would face the rage of the world below.

The gate, Mara realized, wasn't just a corridor through space. It was a moral corridor. And it was about to close.

Above the Atlantic wound, the ring's lattice burned brighter than ever, threads locked, arcs steady, like a surgeon's hands finally confident enough to stitch deeper. For a moment, the ring looked less like a tool and more like a boundary. A line you did not cross without permission.

The ark climbed.

The crowd noise on the feed swelled. People were screaming, cheering, and sobbing, all at once. Then a second camera angle caught something that made Mara's breath stop:

Between the ark and the sky, space… folded. Not like a cloud. Like reality itself had been bent into a thin membrane. A corridor. A passage. ELXON's gate.

The ark angled toward it.

Howard swallowed hard. "That's the transit window."

Nadine's eyes were wide, her face pale. "They're trying to ride the corridor before it closes."

Mara's clean phone lit up. No vibration. Just light. Text appeared quickly, as if the sender no longer had patience for gradual revelation.

THE CAGE RUNS. THE HOME HOLDS. THE GATE CLOSES.

Wren's breath hitched. "They're closing it."

Mara's hands shook. "Wait, what about the people inside?" The phone screen paused. Then:

THE FEW CANNOT FLEE WITH THE MANY IN CHAINS

WE WILL NOT CARRY THE CAGE FOR YOU.

Lila whispered, "They won't let the ark through."

Ed's voice was thin. "But if it fails—"

Jalen's eyes were haunted. "They'll force a choice on us."

On the screen, the ark reached the corridor. The air around it warped. Its lights flickered. Then, impossibly, it slowed, as though it were trying to push through heavy water. Its engines flared. It strained forward. And the corridor refused. Like a door being held shut. The ark shuddered. People on the feed screamed.

The craft lurched sideways, trying a different angle. Ahead, the corridor tightened, visible now as a faint ringed boundary. Then, in one clean, terrifying moment, the corridor snapped closed. Not with an explosion. With absence.

The distortion vanished like a blink. The ark's nose, already angled into where the passage had been, struck nothing, and yet the whole craft rocked violently, as if it had slammed into an invisible wall.

Its engines screamed. The ship pitched. For a breathless second, it looked like it would fall into the ocean and kill everyone inside. Then it steadied, barely, hovering low over the water, trembling like a stunned animal.

Howard exhaled a shaky breath. "They stopped it."

"They refused the escape," said Nadine shakily.

Wren's eyes shone with tears. "They saved the people from dying in space."

"But now the ark is stuck," Jalen said, jaw clenched. Stuck above an ocean. Stuck with passengers inside. Stuck in a world that knew exactly what ELXON had tried to do.

And then came the part Mara dreaded most. The public reaction. Feeds lit up with rage.

"MAKE THEM GET OFF!" "LOCK THEM UP!" "THEY TRIED TO LEAVE US!"

Wren's face went pale. "It's starting."

Lila stepped forward, voice firm. "Then we stop it."

The clean phone buzzed with a new ELXON statement, an emergency broadcast. On screen, the spokesperson looked strained now, the polished mask beginning to crack. "Due to an unexpected atmospheric anomaly," she said, "continuity vessels are experiencing a temporary transit disruption. ELXON is coordinating with partners to restore safe passage."

Howard muttered, "Partners. Sure."

The spokesperson's eyes hardened. "We urge citizens to avoid launch corridors," she continued. "Any interference with continuity operations will be considered an act of sabotage against humanity's survival."

Cold anger rose in Mara. "They're blaming the public again."

"Additionally," the spokesperson said, "due to escalating destabilization, ELXON is authorizing immediate relocation compliance measures. Non-cooperative individuals may be detained for public safety."

Wren whispered, "Detained."

Nadine's face went white. "They're doubling down."

Mara's phone lit again.

NOW IS THE FINAL WEIGHT. DO NOT TURN. HOMEKEEPERS PROTECT ALL OF YOU.

She caught her breath. The visitors weren't asking for worship. They were asking for one final, brutal human act: Protect the trapped passengers. Yes, even now. Because if the world became a mob, then the cage would simply return wearing a new costume.

Mara turned to the basement crew. "We need to shift the public narrative immediately."

Howard frowned. "What then? Not they tried to leave?"

Her eyes hardened. "No. They're here now. All of them. And the only future that exists is the one we build together."

Ed nodded slowly. "We frame it as reintegration."

Nadine swallowed. "And we warn people: ELXON will try to use the trapped passengers as human shields."

"Then we become a human shield again," Lila said, calm and clear.

Wren's jaw clenched. "How do we stop people from attacking the ark?"

"We tell the truth," Mara said. "We tell them the gate is closed. There is no escape. And if we kill each other now, we prove we don't deserve the repair."

Howard muttered, "Harsh."

Mara nodded. "True."

Then Jalen spoke quietly, voice raw. "And we tell the passengers: you're not our enemy. Get off the bus. Get out of the ark. Come home."

Nadine looked at him, surprised.

His eyes were haunted. "I was almost them," he said. "I felt the temptation."

The calm network moved. Ruth went live again at once, her voice hard as iron. "The gate is closed," Ruth said. "There is no ark to a new world." She stared into the camera. "Every passenger on that vessel is now part of this world again. They are not targets. They are not trophies. They are people trapped in a bad plan."

Then Mara spoke, showing the ring and lattice feeds. "The repair is ongoing," she said. "But it is conditional on behavior. Our behavior. We have seen it pause when violence surges." She held the camera's gaze. "This is your final choice:

Become a mob or become a home."

Across the feeds, calm leaders echoed the message in their own languages, cadences, and moral vocabularies.

Don't attack. Don't hunt. Protect. Document. Help.

And then something beautiful and terrifying happened.

In Florida, near a corridor, a crowd that could have turned violent instead gathered with blankets, water, and first aid kits.

They formed a line, a buffer between angry outsiders and the trapped passengers being ferried off the ark to shore in small boats. Passengers stumbled onto land, People were crying; some were furious, some were ashamed.

A woman in a designer coat sobbed, "They told us—"

A man shouted, "We're being kidnapped!"

A teenager clutched a stuffed animal with huge, stunned eyes.

And the crowd, ordinary people, did not strike them. They handed them water. They guided the elderly, wrapping blankets around their shoulders.

They filmed ELXON security again, trying to corral passengers into vehicles and keep them under control so they could be used.

And when one passenger fell to her knees and whispered, "I'm sorry," an older man in the crowd, with a sunburned face and rough hands, bent down and said quietly: "Then stay."

Mara watched that clip and felt her throat tighten. Stay. Not as punishment. As belonging.

Above the Atlantic, the ring's lattice brightened again, stronger, steadier. Ed's feed updated:

BINDING STRENGTH INCREASED. REPAIR SEQUENCE IMMINENT.

Mara's chest ached. They were doing it. The final weight was lifting, not because the rich were punished, but because the world refused to become a cage.

Through the window well, Mara stared up at the sky and whispered to herself: "This is what worthy looks like."

Not purity. Not wealth. Not escape. Just the stubborn, trembling decision to keep each other human.

CHAPTER 28 — The Home Claimed

The sky did not split open with trumpets.

It did not roar. It did not announce itself with the kind of spectacle humans usually demanded before they believed anything mattered.

It simply… **worked.**

Over the Atlantic wound, the ring brightened until it no longer looked like light sat all. It looked like a structure—**a** geometry that holding the air in place, the way bones hold a body together. Around it, the lattice thickened, threads tightening and locking with a precision that made every human-made system seem suddenly crude.

Across the world, people watched the atmosphere being treated like an injured living thing. And they watched themselves, too. Quiet, seated, holding water bottles and blankets, refusing to turn into predators.

That mattered most. Because the repair didn't accelerate when ELXON begged or threatened. It accelerated when the human shield held.

At 11:03 p.m. Central, Ed's models updated and then updated again, faster than his fingers could keep up. His voice shook. "It's happening."

Mara leaned in, heart hammering. The ozone proxy near the wound rose, not by fractions now. By steps. **Up 18%. Up 24%. Up 31%.**

Howard stared at the magnetometer line smoothing into something he'd never seen before: a stable pattern, coherent and strong, as if the planet's own field had been combed back into order.

Nadine whispered, stunned, "They're rethreading the shield."

Hands pressed to her mouth, tears slipping down her cheeks, Wren whispered, "They're fixing it."

Mara didn't answer at once. Her scientist brain wanted to resist the word *fixing*. Fixing implied finished.

This was not finished. It was a beginning.

Outside, the aurora, green threaded with pale gold, spread like a quilt across half the sky, visible in places never seen before. People stood in driveways, parking lots, and fields, wrapped in coats and staring upward in disbelief.

And in that upward gaze, something shifted in human posture. For days, people had looked at the sky as if it were an enemy. Now they looked at it as if it were a mirror.

At the Atlantic shoreline, the last ELXON ark hovered low over the water, engines trembling, its dream of escape dead. Small boats continued ferrying passengers to land. They brought a mixture of the wealthy, the coerced, the confused, and the newly aware of the cage they'd been invited to live inside.

The crowd waiting for them was not gentle, exactly. But it was human. Blankets. Water. Medics. Calm leaders directing people away from confrontation, guiding the frightened into warmth.

Not forgiveness as a performance. Just a refusal to become monsters.

Ruth Calder went live one final time. Her face was tired in a way that felt earned, not broken. "The gate is closed," she said simply. "So, we stop acting like escape is an option. We stop building cages. We stop trading truth for comfort."

Her gaze did not waver. "We claim the only home we've got." Then she stepped back and let the cameras show the shoreline: passengers stepping onto sand and being met not with fists, but with blankets and hard-eyed truth.

Some of the passengers cried when they realized no one was going to kill them. Some cried because shame felt like an ocean, and they didn't know how to swim it.

A man in an ELXON-branded jacket tried to bark orders. The crowd ignored him like he was a loud radio in an empty room.

A teenage girl with a diamond bracelet stood shivering, staring at the aurora as if she were seeing the planet for the first time. A woman near her with sunburned hands and a rough coat wrapped a blanket around the girl's shoulders and said, not unkindly: "Welcome back."

That clip traveled around the world faster than any rocket had. Because it carried something ELXON had never been able to build: a story that made people want to be better.

ELXON tried to fight back. They issued statements that contradicted each other, frantic and increasingly absurd. They claimed control of the ring. They insisted the repair was coordinated through their stabilization initiative. They promised new selection windows, new procedures, new authority.

But the world had already watched the gate close. The world had already watched the ring brighten when humans chose restraint.

The world had already watched ELXON panic. And the most dangerous thing for ELXON was no longer outrage. It was laughter. Not mocking laughter. Disbelieving laughter, the kind that stripped power of its mystique.

Nadine watched one spokesperson on-screen attempt to smile through visible fear, and she exhaled softly. "Their machine is collapsing."

Mara stared up through the window as the aurora pulsed, green and gold. It seemed as if Earth were breathing again.

On the center table, the clean phone began to glow. Then it lit up one last time. Text appeared, slower now, less urgent, as if the sender had stepped back.

THE WOUND IS BOUND. THE HOME IS CLAIMED. THE WEIGHT HAS LIFTED ENOUGH.

Mara's throat tightened.

"Enough?" Wren whispered.

Mara swallowed hard. "Enough… to start."

The text continued.

WE WILL STAY NEARBY. WE WILL NOT RULE YOU. WE WILL NOT CARRY YOUR CAGE. YOU WILL CARRY YOUR CHOICE.

Her hands trembled. She reached out, fingers hovering over the screen without touching it. "Who are you?" Mara whispered.

The phone paused, as if translating the question into something it could answer without giving humans a name to worship. Then:

WE ARE THOSE WHO LEARNED TOO LATE. WE RETURN WHEN OTHERS MAY LEARN IN TIME.

Mara's breath caught. Not saviors. Not gods. Witnesses of their own regret. A civilization that had lost something and refused to watch another world lose it the same way.

The final line appeared, and it felt like a hand placed gently on a shoulder, meant to steady.

KEEP YOUR HOME. KEEP EACH OTHER.

Then the screen dimmed. The phone went dark.

Outside, the aurora softened slightly, the gold seam thinning into the background like a thread pulled tight and then tucked away. Over the Atlantic, the ring remained faint, less visible, but still present. Like scaffolding left in place while the work set up.

Ed's models stabilized. Not perfect or back to normal. But no longer hanging on the cliff-edge.

Howard's instruments calmed into lines that didn't scream.

For the first time in hours, Nadine sat down and stared at her hands like she didn't entirely recognize them.

Jalen lay back on the cot and let his eyes close for ten seconds of earned darkness.

Lila bowed her head, not in celebration, but in gratitude without victory.

And Wren leaned into Mara's side, quietly shaking with the release of adrenaline and grief and wonder.

Mara wrapped an arm around her daughter and stared at the sky through the window well.

She thought of the people who had died in failed launches. The people who had been coerced. The people who had hoarded. The people who had shared. The people who had attacked. The people who had restrained the attackers without striking back.

The planet was still scarred. The atmosphere was still vulnerable. The world was still full of humans; messy, complicated, and capable of terrible things.

But it was also full of something that had spread faster than fear: a refusal to let the future be built on abandonment.

In the days that followed, there were trials. Not just legal trials, though those came too, but moral ones. Governments convened in public, not behind closed doors. Several world leaders resigned. Some were arrested. Many fled and were brought back. The ELXON brand shattered; its assets were seized; its private security networks were exposed; its contracts were dragged into public court hearings streamed to billions.

A new term entered the global vocabulary:

Homekeepers.

It was not a party. It was not a religion. It was a **practice**.

Local councils formed in communities everywhere: transparent, practical, and gloriously boring in the best possible way. Supply pooling became normal. UV safety became routine. Truth audits became common: data shared publicly, assumptions challenged openly, and secrecy treated as a risk rather than a privilege.

Even some former ELXON passengers, humiliated and now grounded, joined the work. Not as heroes. As laborers. As people learning what it means to stay.

Ruth Calder refused any official position offered to her. When reporters asked why, she smiled tiredly. "I've had enough titles," she said. "I'm interested in behavior now."

Mara returned to her instruments. To data. To measurement. To building systems that did not depend on secrecy. And at night, sometimes, when the aurora faintly shimmered in places it never had before, Mara would stand outside with Wren and look up.

Not begging. Not worshiping. Just watching. Remembering.

Because she understood the last truth the visitors had given them: Repair was not an ending. It was a chance. And chances were fragile.

They required care. They required refusal. They required truth and calm held together like a thread in torn fabric.

Wren slipped her hand into Mara's and whispered, "Do you think they'll come back?"

Mara stared at the faint gold seam, now soft as a memory. "I think they never left."

And Wren smiled, not because everything was okay…

…but because they had lived through something vast enough to break the world, and watched it hold.

She had seen the sky open. She had felt the presence of something beyond them. And she had watched millions of people choose all at once, not fear…but each other.

And somehow, impossibly, each individual choice had mattered. Because they had all chosen the one thing worth carrying forward.

Together.

Across the world, the signal did not disappear. It fractured and multiplied. In living rooms, in hospital break rooms, in truck cabs and midnight kitchens, people watched the same image and came to the same quiet understanding.

The sky was not as safe as they had believed. But neither were they as helpless as they had believed. Phones lit up. Messages spread. Not panic, but coordination. Not chaos, but a desire to question and learn.

And in places ELXON had not accounted for, people began to choose each other. Not because they had been told to. But because they understood, finally, that survival had never been meant to be purchased.

In a glass-walled room far from Kansas, the stream replayed on a silent loop. No one spoke while it ran.

When it ended, a man at the head of the table leaned forward, fingers steepled, eyes unreadable. "How far did it spread?"

"Everywhere," someone answered.

A pause. The man's gaze shifted, not to the screen, but beyond and inward. "Then we're already late." He stood. "Move Phase Gate forward." No one objected.

Outside the sky remained unchanged.

The timeline did not.

A Note to the Reader

Thank you for reading *Homekeepers at the Last Gate*, Book One of the Homekeepers series.

If you enjoyed the story or found meaning in its themes; if it left you thinking about purpose, stewardship, or the unseen threads that guide our lives, I would truly appreciate you sharing your thoughts in an honest review on Amazon. Your voice helps carry the story forward and connect it with other readers.

Thank you for walking this path with me. The gate is only the beginning.

The story continues.

.

With a grateful heart,

Dave Barnabas

About the Author

Dave Barnabas is the pen name behind the *Homekeepers* series, chosen to reflect its themes of guardianship, faith, and unseen responsibility.

The author writes under this name to allow the story to stand on its own, apart from personal biography.

Bonita Hicks
Kaku Publishing

Coming Next in The Homekeepers Series

The sky was repaired, but the world did not return to what it was.

As governments reckon with the truth and survivors come home, quiet questions begin to surface. Not every launch failed. Not every ship was lost.

Wren and the Homekeepers are pulled back into the spotlight as a new investigation uncovers a secret buried beneath the miracle—a contingency meant to save humanity if restraint failed.

And somewhere beyond the repaired sky, the visitors wait.

They helped once. They will not do it again without a cost.

The Homekeepers return in Book Two: *The Vanished Sky*

www.ingramcontent.com/pod-product-compliance
Lightning Source LLC
Chambersburg PA
CBHW071403300726
48976CB00006B/1973